Rigged

The Michael Quiel Story

MICHAEL QUIEL

PAGE PUBLISHING, INC.
Conneaut Lake, PA

First originally published by Page Publishing 2020

Cover design and editing by Ron Lee—US-Observer

ISBN 978-1-64334-875-9 (pbk)
ISBN 978-1-6624-0754-3 (hc)
ISBN 978-1-64334-876-6 (digital)

Printed in the United States of America

AUTHOR'S NOTE

All conversations in the book are reconstructed from memory. They should not be viewed as verbatim records. They capture the gist of the conversations as I recall them. All the reconstructed conversations are factually accurate to the best of my recollection.

Although this book includes my observations and comments about tax and financial legal issues, I am not providing information or advice on which the reader should rely.

It is important to me that all of the profits generated from this book will go to benefit innocent victims of false charges and prosecution.

DEDICATION

My father-in-law USAF Colonel John Lee gave his life for this great country. He not only entrusted me with his daughter, he is still the driving force behind my pursuit of justice.

Colonel Lee believed with his whole heart in our great nation and the rule of law, and he believed in me. His principles and guidance helped shape who I am in every aspect of my life. His final words of advice regarding the federal tax charges levied against me were his most poignant.

In March of 2011, Colonel Lee lay on his death bed—Agent Orange confirmed to have caused his brain cancer. He had been incoherent for days. In what would be his last lucid moment, Colonel Lee looked me right in the eye and said, "I believe in you. Fight the government for yourself and your family."

You see, he respected the government but also understood the destruction they were capable of inflicting. I had the last five minutes of his attention before the cancer and pain meds took his conscious mind away. Colonel John Lee died several days later.

This book is for, and because of him.

I'm still fighting, John...

This Could Happen to You

Do you believe in the American system of justice? If so, I'm happy for you. You're one of the lucky ones. I no longer have the luxury of belief. That may sound like a cynical statement coming from a third-generation navy man who, in many ways, has been fortunate enough to live the American Dream. But I have seen our justice system from the inside out. I have been convicted of tax fraud, gone to prison, lost a rewarding career, and watched my family endure relentless stress simply because I followed the legal rules of business.

How could such a thing happen in America? And why?

Because we have a prosecutorial system that emphasizes conviction rates rather than the carriage of justice. Because we have a political system that allows the government to break its own rules, without consequence, in order to gain legal advantage over private citizens. Because we permit high-level corporate executives to escape prosecution by making backroom deals with the government that turn civilians into sacrificial lambs. And because when you attain a certain level of success in the field of "high finance," you're presumed guilty rather than innocent.

These are sad truths I have learned the hard way.

I am not a hero, and I have no intention of painting myself as such in this book. I reserve the word *hero* for people like my father-in-law, John W. Lee, who served in combat and died from cancer caused by Agent Orange. He was the real deal. All I did was try to live the right way, treat people fairly, and never knowingly break the law. After being honorably discharged from a distinguished career in the US Navy, I married my high school sweetheart, had three amazing daughters, and started two successful stock brokerage firms, which I operated ethically and conscientiously. Yes, I bought some nice homes and toys and enjoyed many of the perks of success. Nothing illegal about that.

On the heels of the dot-com bubble burst in the early 2000s, I retired from being a stockbroker and decided to try my hand at investing. I wanted to build something more substantial for myself and my family. Turned out I had a knack for investing in startups, and using my knowledge from the stock brokerage business, within a few years, I had reached my goal of making $20 million, exceeding even the success I'd attained as a stockbroker. As with my brokerage firms, I ran this new business in a way that was legal and above board, while helping a lot of people and charities along the way. That's my "boring" story.

Again, I'm not saying I'm a hero, but I am hardly the sleazy, tax-evading white-collar criminal that US prosecutors have attempted to paint me as. And I refuse to quietly accept that characterization. That's one of the main reasons I wrote this book—I promised my family and my late father-in-law that I would fight this thing to the end.

In many ways, my real crime was success. In America, we have a strange double standard when it comes to financial prosperity. Almost everyone wants it. Some of us pursue it with single-minded dedication. Nearly all of us dream about it. We say we love America because it is the land of opportunity. We celebrate the belief that in America, anyone, regardless of economic class, ethnicity, education, gender, or religion, can achieve the American Dream. And yet, when someone actually does that—works the system and attains wealth—we become jealous and suspicious of that person. Rather than cheer their success and draw inspiration from it, we assume they must have done something wrong.

I know; I used to think that way myself.

Our suspiciousness runs especially deep toward people who earn their wealth in the fields of stock trading, investing, and financing. These activities seem mystical and unknowable to many who choose to make their living as professional service people or by earning an hourly wage. And we all have a tendency to distrust what we don't understand. Unfortunately, this distrust filters down to law enforcement agencies as well. Contempt for the "investor class" is common. There is an unspoken suspicion that anyone who makes a living by moving money around is cheating somehow—at least by avoiding paying their fair share of taxes—and that if you just dig deeply enough into their affairs, their guilt will be uncovered.

My financial success was what got me in trouble. It was my ability to generate money that attracted the interest of the attorney who ended up forming the offshore business structure that got flagged for tax fraud. It was my busy and successful investment business that kept my attention away from micromanaging this attorney, who, it turned out, wasn't doing what I paid him to do—namely, to ensure that my international interests, minor though they were, remained legal and tax compliant. It was also my success as an investor that allowed prosecutors to create a "fraud" case against me where none existed and paint an illusory picture of me as a wealthy tax evader hiding my assets in Switzerland. They didn't understand my business model, and neither did the jury.

But here's where the story becomes bigger than my individual case. My conviction on tax crime charges was set in motion by a corporate bailout deal made at the top levels of national government. As part of the Big Bailout of 2008, UBS, a large Swiss bank with divisions in the United States, was given an infusion of tens of billions of dollars, courtesy of the government, in order to keep itself solvent. At the same time, UBS was also involved in a multimillion-dollar tax evasion investigation. "Coincidentally," shortly after the bailout funds were received by the bank, UBS agreed to pay a fine of $780 million and give up the names of about three hundred US citizens it alleged to be hiding money from the IRS in UBS accounts. In return for coughing up these names, UBS's executives were allowed to cut a "deferred prosecution" deal for themselves and skate free.

Long story short, "Michael Quiel" popped up on the short list of UBS names. As a result, instead of getting the benefit of a standard IRS examination, my case went directly to the DOJ (Department of Justice), where it was treated from the start as a criminal case, even though no criminality had been established. I call that presumption of guilt. A deal was then cut with my *attorney*—yes, the person I paid to legally protect myself and my businesses—who made it appear as if I had willfully engineered a tax evasion scheme that in fact I knew nothing about. Attorney-client privilege was thrown out the window, and a cascade of mind-boggling decisions were made, resulting in dire consequences for me and my family.

Here's the insane bottom line: Even though the court determined that *I didn't owe the government a penny in tax money*, I still went to prison for avoiding taxes!

This is a story about a broken legal system in which innocent people are thrown under the bus for the advancement of government employees' careers, in which corrupt banking executives are allowed to avoid prosecution by turning in their own clients, and in which guilt is assumed because no one can understand the complexities of the truth.

There are no murdered bodies or smoking guns here, just a man and his family who were put through the wringer for no good reason. My wife suffered a debilitating case of PTSD. I lost out on a potential multi-billion-dollar business deal. My daughter had her identity stolen. These are just a few of the issues we've dealt with, as a result of this case of false prosecution and conviction. Perhaps you won't find any sympathy in your heart for an investor and hedge fund manager who has made millions of dollars and owns a home on a lake. Perhaps you'll assume I was guilty, as many others have. That's okay. I'm not looking for sympathy or moral support. But do remember this: if I can go to prison for making perfectly legal and routine business decisions, the same thing can happen to you. Shoot, you don't even have to own a business to be caught up in a false prosecution.

CHAPTER ONE

Busted

I love golf. In fact, I'm kind of obsessed with it. I built a home right on the fairway at Firerock in Fountain Hills, Arizona. I find the game mentally refreshing. For me, it's the intensity and concentration that is relaxing. Because in order to play the game well, you need to shut out all other thoughts and distractions. So, for the four hours or so it takes to play eighteen holes, your mind is focused only on knocking a white ball into a round hole. You are fully in the present moment. You don't have room for other worries.

And on January 29, 2012, I had a lot of things to worry about. For the previous year and a half, I had been under investigation by the Department of Justice and the criminal division of the IRS. My records had long ago been subpoenaed, and my attorneys and I were waiting anxiously to learn whether the government would indict me. Word was out that something was going to come down soon.

An hour didn't pass that the questions didn't swirl through my mind: *How did I get in such deep shit just by following the rules? Why did my own lawyer give up sensitive information that could be used against me? Why hadn't I been given the due process of a regular IRS review? What if—God forbid—I actually got charged? What if I got convicted? How would my wife and daughters handle it? What would happen to my reputation? What would happen to all the business deals I had in the works?*

9

And the most immediate fear of all: *What if they actually arrest me and throw me in jail?*

Fortunately, I had a defense attorney, Michael Minns, who was one of the best criminal tax lawyers in the country. He seemed to have the case well in hand, and he had told me repeatedly that—while nothing was impossible—it was highly unlikely that I would be physically arrested on the charges I faced. I wasn't a flight risk. I had a good reputation in the community. No violence had been committed. It was purely a paperwork case. And Minns had been assured by Monica Edelstein of the federal prosecutors' office that I would be allowed to turn myself in peacefully, should any indictments come down.

Still, that didn't stop me from sleeping with one eye open or breaking into a cold sweat every time I spotted a Crown Victoria with tinted glass.

Not today, though. Today was a Sunday, a glorious Sunday—sunny, temperature in the seventies, like most late January days in Phoenix—and I was on the ninth hole at Firerock Country Club, one of my favorite spots in the world, enjoying a round of golf with my friend Nick. It was one of the rare moments since the investigation had heated up that my mind felt almost completely at ease. After all, the feds weren't going to bust me in the middle of a golf game on a Sunday afternoon.

Right?

That's why I didn't even look up when Nick's phone rang. I kept my eyes on the ball and—*thwack*—made a short wedge shot onto the green.

"Rory McIlroy won't be losing any sleep over that one," I said to Nick, "but I'll take it."

Then I looked at Nick's face. It was turning as green as the Bermuda grass that surrounded us on all sides. He hung up his phone and stared at me, stunned, for a moment before speaking.

"That was Ted from the clubhouse," he said. "There are five guys with guns up there looking for you. They told the staff not to warn you, but I guess Ted didn't want you being blindsided."

It took me a moment to digest what Nick was telling me. Shit. Monica Edelstein, the prosecutor, had changed her mind, I guess. They weren't going to let me turn myself in.

I nodded gently at Nick and picked up my ball, feeling oddly calm, the way you sometimes do when the other shoe drops and a worst-case scenario you've been dreading for ages finally comes to pass.

"Sorry I can't finish our game today, Nick," I said, packing my pitching wedge into my golf bag with surprisingly steady hands. "I'll see you later, okay?" And with that I walked away. My feet seemed to be moving on their own.

* * *

The ninth hole at Firerock runs adjacent to the parking lot, so the first thing I did was head for my car and retrieve my briefcase from the trunk. I'm not sure why I did that, but it seemed like a logical move at that time.

When I turned from the car and started toward the clubhouse, I saw a man standing by the golf club drop, wearing a polo shirt, a side arm, and a padded dark-blue vest with white lettering on it.

"Michael Quiel?" he asked, stopping me in my tracks.

I nodded.

"I'm with the Internal Revenue Service Criminal Investigation Division," he said.

If you've never heard the words *criminal investigation* spoken to you by an IRS police officer with a gun, I can't explain the effect they have on your digestive system, even when you're fully prepared for them.

"You need to stay right here, sir," he informed me.

At that point, four more IRS agents filed out of the clubhouse. All armed.

Yes, five men armed with guns to arrest one hedge fund manager armed with a briefcase. Your tax dollars at work.

I was instructed to put the briefcase back in my car. Then an agent snapped a pair of handcuffs on me. "Mr. Quiel, you have been charged with conspiracy to defraud, two counts of making and subscribing a false tax return, and two counts of willful failure to file an FBAR report of foreign bank and financial accounts." I heard the words, but I couldn't wrap my mind around them.

As all this was occurring, my friend Chuck happened by, about to climb into his golf cart.

"Do you need anything, Mike?" he asked, seeing my obvious distress.

"Yes," I told him, "please call Vicki and ask her to call Michael Minns, my attorney."

I wanted to get the name Michael Minns out there in the hopes that it might discourage any funny business on the part of the agents. Minns had a reputation as an IRS killer.

At this point, Chuck, God bless him, approached the most alpha looking of the agents and said, "I need to see your warrant and your badge."

"I don't need to show you that," replied the agent.

"Yes, you do," said Chuck without blinking. "You're on private property."

The agent looked to his supervisor, who nodded and confirmed, "Yeah, you have to show him."

After a belligerent pause, the agent handed his badge and paperwork to Chuck, who took his sweet time examining it. When Chuck returned the materials, the agent asked him, "Do you represent Mr. Quiel?"

Chuck didn't say a word, just turned and walked away, leaving the agents staring after him in confused silence. I'll always love Chuck for that moment.

A couple of the agents pressed my head down and shoved me into the backseat of one of the waiting squad cars, where they let me sit and stew in my thoughts for a few minutes. And that's when reality started to sink in. I was under arrest; I was really under arrest. My mind and heart began to race. My biggest fear was that Vicki, my wife, had also been arrested. There was no good reason to arrest her, but her name was on some of my corporate paperwork, and I'd been reading some nightmare stories about spouses getting indicted alongside their husbands.

I knew that loose lips around federal agents was not a good idea, so I restricted my conversation to two simple questions.

The first was, "Did you arrest my wife?" They said no.

The second was, "Did you go to my house?" I wanted to know if my kids had been treated to the IRS Armed Traveling Circus. The agents said no to that, as well. That was a relief. I wondered how they had found me at the golf course then. I didn't ask.

Off we drove.

Our destination? The Maricopa County 4th Avenue Jail.

* * *

The 4th Avenue jail is a state-of-the-art brick fortress in lovely downtown Phoenix that was built by Joe Arpaio—a.k.a. America's Toughest Sheriff—as part of the largest county jail expansion in US history. At first I couldn't figure out why the feds had arrested me on a Sunday. After all, for charges like mine, you are usually processed through the US Marshals Service office, and the Marshals' office is closed on Sundays. Then it hit me: that was exactly *why* they had done it on a Sunday. They *wanted* me to experience the fine accommodations of the 4th Avenue jail. They wanted me to spend some time with the weekend crowd of crackheads, drunks, and wife beaters. And arresting me on a Sunday was a way to ensure that happened.

I was soon to learn that much of what federal enforcers and prosecutors do is pure theatrics, designed to intimidate and frighten everyday citizens.

The first place you're taken at Hotel Arpaio is the processing room. This is a large central area where new inmates are stripped and forced to stand in line naked with all the other "guests." It's a very effective way of reminding you that you are nothing but a generic criminal. You may have been "special" on the outside, but you're not special in here. They issue you a black-and-white-striped convict's uniform, just like the ones you see in Bugs Bunny cartoons, a pair of prison flip-flops, and believe it or not, a set of pink underwear (Arpaio, who lost his seat in the November election of 2016, apparently found this little touch hilarious). None of the stuff fits, of course, and it's designed to be as humiliating as possible. They also take your mug shot, your fingerprints, and your medical information, as well as all your clothing, money, and personal items.

After the initial processing, you play this bizarre game of musical jail cells. Throughout the course of the evening, they move you from cell to cell for no apparent reason. It's all part of the intake process, I guess. But I'm sure it's also designed to convey the message, "Yours is not to reason why. Yours is but to jump when we say jump."

At one point, I and a group of other "guests" were issued pillows and blankets and marched to a different section of the jail. There we were allowed to sleep in a cell for exactly one hour. Then our blankets were taken back, and we were marched back to our former area. I guess there must be a legal requirement that prisoners who are held for a certain length of time be permitted to sleep, so the good sheriff does exactly the minimum required to meet that regulation, nothing more.

Sleep deprivation, of course, also makes you confused and compliant.

The food situation was similar. Inmates are fed only twice a day. This is a problem for someone like me. I'm an all-day nibbler, not a big-meal guy. So by the time I actually ate a meal, my head was swimming from low blood sugar, and I was ready to confess to murder.

These were just minor inconveniences though. No big deal. After all, I'd been through navy boot camp, and that made Joe Arpaio's accommodations seem like a country club. The real hardship was the anxiety of not knowing what was going on in my world outside. What did my wife Vicki know? What did my kids know, and how were they handling it? Had the feds arrested Steve Kerr, my business partner? Had they arrested my business and tax attorney, Chris Rusch? I had no answers. These questions burned in my mind and gnawed at the lining of my stomach.

There are phones throughout the 4th Avenue jail, where you can make collect calls, outgoing only. So throughout the course of the evening, I did manage to call home several times. Vicki, of course, was in a panic, so it was difficult to have a calm conversation with her. I was able to get my kids on the phone and explain to them what had happened. Up until then, I hadn't told them much about the trouble I was in with the government. I hadn't wanted them worrying. But now they needed to know everything.

Needless to say, they too went into a panic. Their dad going to jail had never been even a remote possibility on the radar screen of their lives.

One of my biggest concerns was what was going on with Steve Kerr, my partner. By making some phone calls, Vicki learned that he was in Colorado and was able to give him a heads-up about my arrest. This was lucky for him, because if the feds had found him first, they would have bused him all the way back to Arizona—a treatment fondly known as diesel therapy. But because Vicki got to him first, he was able to call his attorney, who contacted the US Marshal's office and informed them that Steve wished to report voluntarily. (However, I later learned that prosecutor Monica Edelstein—a person I would come to dislike immensely—told Steve this was not acceptable; they needed to physically arrest him. Steve was told to *drive* back to Arizona, not fly. Had he tried to fly, he would have been arrested and bused back to the Grand Canyon State. They actually told him to go to his attorney's office, where they handcuffed him in the parking lot before he could go inside.)

I was also extremely worried about the status of Chris Rusch, the attorney who had done the bad work for Steve and me that got us in this trouble. Was he in custody? And if so, what was he saying, and to whom was he saying it? Being completely in the dark about what was happening with the other key parties in the case was far more stressful than anything that was happening to me in the jail.

At some point in the evening, Joy Bertrand, a local attorney who was part of my defense team, came to the jail. She assured me that my lead attorney Michael Minns was on his way from Texas for my arraignment and together they were doing everything in their power to make sure I'd be out on bail within twenty-four hours.

The next morning—a Monday—my street clothes were returned to me, and I was shackled and taken to the US Marshals Service office in the federal district court building in Phoenix. Again I was strip-searched and rectally examined (after all, I might have become a drug mule during my sixteen-hour stay in county custody). Then I was placed in a holding cell, along with another white-collar guy.

As in the Hotel Arpaio, the marshals come and get you out of your cell several times to do various tasks, such as fingerprinting and paperwork, much of it an exact repeat of what I'd just had done at the county jail. One time the marshals brought me back to my cell and "accidentally" put me in the wrong cell—one that housed a group of Mexican gang members. There I stood like an idiot in my shorts, yellow golf shirt, and sixty-dollar haircut, in the middle of a pack of tattoos and sleeveless shirts. The gang guys immediately started talking among themselves about me. I knew enough not to show any fear, but it didn't take long before they started physically menacing me, walking around me in circles, giving me the eye. The marshals came and removed me before things got ugly, and as they did, one of the gang guys whispered to me, "You're lucky." Again, the message my hosts were sending me was, "You're in *our* house now, and we can make your life miserable anytime we choose."

Hours passed and I started to get worried. What if I didn't get arraigned today? Mondays are notoriously busy days in courtrooms because the judges, clerks, and lawyers have to sort through the hundreds of arrests that come in over the weekend. I knew that the US Marshal's office didn't house prisoners overnight, so I couldn't go back to my previous cell. That meant if I didn't get before a judge today, I'd be taken to the Central Arizona Detention Center in Florence until my arraignment. Florence was where all the really scary inmates were housed. I could just imagine the fun I was going to have there, in my shorts and yellow golf shirt, among the who's who of the federal Most Wanted list.

The more I thought about going to Florence, the sicker I felt.

Minutes dragged by like hours. I never thought I could want to stand before a judge so badly. All I wanted was to get my processing over with, go home, get some sleep, regroup, and start figuring out what the hell my next step was. But as each hour passed, I became more and more convinced that I'd be spending the night in a bunk bed in Florence with a meth cook named Tito.

Luckily, around midday a pair of armed marshals came for me. They yanked me from my cell, still shackled, and ushered me to a federal courtroom in the same building. There I was told I would be seen by a federal magistrate judge.

When we arrived at the smallish courtroom—one of many within the federal district court building—it was bustling with Monday activity, both inside and out. Bailiffs hurried back and forth, while attorneys held urgent conversations with one another and confused family members spoke tearfully to loved ones. As soon as I entered the crowded courtroom, I started scanning the crowd for Vicki. I spotted her on a pew, looking pale, but before I could even make eye contact with her, the marshal snapped at me, "You can't look at her," and gave my shackles a hard yank.

I guess I didn't really believe that looking could be regulated by law enforcement, so I started scanning for her again. I just wanted to see her face, get a read on how she was doing. After thirty years of marriage, I knew that one glance would tell me how she and the kids were holding up—and how worried I should be about them.

No sooner did my eyes flick in Vicki's direction than the marshal barked at me, "I *said*, don't look at her! One more try and you'll have to leave the room for the proceeding." Whoa, easy there, Sparky.

I snapped my eyes front and center, but not before catching a glimpse of Minns, my lawyer. Thank God he was here. He looked calm and assured; that was good. I was eager for the proceeding to be over so that I could grab a meal with him and start discussing our next steps.

I guess I was expecting the process to drag on for hours, so I allowed my mind to drift. That was why it took me by surprise when I heard Monica Edelstein, the federal prosecutor, say something to the tune of, "Your Honor, the people request that the defendant, Michael Quiel, be remanded into federal custody pending trial."

Excuse me, what was that again? I felt the full weight of fear descend on my chest like a dropped barbell. They were talking about holding me in federal prison until the trial. And that trial might be twelve or eighteen months away! My God, could they actually do that to me? I hadn't been given due process yet. How could they put me in jail without a conviction? Eighteen months in jail would destroy my business, not to mention what it would do to my family and my sanity.

But Edelstein looked deadly serious, and the judge seemed to be carefully weighing her words.

Up till that moment, I hadn't seriously considered the possibility that I'd be incarcerated while awaiting trial. It just didn't seem possible. But then, I realized, none of this had seemed possible a few days ago—that I would be charged with a list of federal crimes, that I would be arrested by armed federal agents on a golf course in the middle of a Sunday afternoon, that I'd be stripped naked, probed, shackled, and thrown in a cell with drug dealers and gang members.

So maybe all my previous assumptions about how this was going to play out were dead wrong. Maybe the government powers that be were planning to make an example of me.

I stole a forbidden glance at Vicki. The expression I saw on her face made my heart feel sick. The US Marshal, on the other hand, was wearing the self-assured smile of a school bully about to collect his milk money.

Oh my god, the realization hit me like a slap in the face, *I might not be walking out of here today. I might be going to jail, directly to jail. Do not pass Go. Do not collect $200...*

I might be spending the next eighteen months of my life in federal prison...

CHAPTER TWO

Credit Card Blues

My problems all started with a credit card.

I guess I'm not the first person in history to utter those words. My issue wasn't buying expensive items I couldn't afford, though, or paying my bills too late. Rather, it was a simple failure to report some relatively minor charges on an old offshore credit card. This triggered my first unpleasant run-in with the IRS, which, in turn, led me to seek the services of Chris Rusch, the attorney/conman who ended up getting me sent to prison and costing me about $8 million, a lucrative investment career, and many years of peace of mind.

To set the stage for how all that happened, we need to go back a few years, to when the credit card in question was first issued.

In the '90s and early 2000s, I worked as a stockbroker. It was during this period—from about 2000 to 2003—that I acquired and used a Visa card issued by a bank in Belize. The card itself was perfectly legal and legit. I received it as a payment vehicle for some consulting work I was doing for a gentleman who lived in my town and who also ran several businesses in Belize, Earl Gilbrech. Over a period of about four years, I ran up a total of about $221,000 in charges on this card. Most of these were business expenses, such as travel and office equipment. I made the charges; Earl paid the bill.

The expenses were approved by Earl as part of my compensation arrangement with him, so all my charges were above board from a business perspective. The problem was that these charges *should* have been reported on my tax return as income, but they weren't. My bad. Although the vast majority of the expenses would have been deductible if I *had* put them on my tax return, not all the charges fell into this category, and they all should have been reported. I freely admit this. It was my own mess-up that caused my grief.

Now, you may be tempted to form some judgments about me right away. *Hmm, this guy rang up over two hundred thousand dollars' worth of expenses on a Visa card and then "conveniently forgot" about them. He's obviously a tax dodger.* But here's what you need to understand—and it's a critical point for appreciating my whole story: The amount I purchased on that card, though it may sound like a lot, was actually a tiny percentage of what I was earning at that time. You see, when I was using the credit card, I was making a million or so a year as a stockbroker. Not boasting, just stating the facts. There is no way I would have deliberately put my business, my reputation, or my family at risk by trying to skip taxes on an additional $55,000 income (on average) a year, most of which was tax deductible anyway.

During the early 2000s, my tax returns were prepared *very* carefully—the securities business attracts a high level of IRS scrutiny—and I paid a small fortune to the IRS every April 15. I was happy to do so and always paid my fair share. The amount of tax that would have been due on that *additional* annual $55K in charges, after deducting the business expenses, would have been a drop in the bucket. Certainly not an amount worth risking the ire of the IRS for.

Again, I get that failure to report over $200,000 in "income" might seem like a big deal, but it's important to put this thing in perspective. Why? Because it was a lack of perspective that strongly contributed to the larger IRS problem I went to trial over. In the latter case, the amount of money I was allegedly hiding in a Swiss bank account—though it seemed like a huge sum to the investigators, the jury, and even, to some extent, my own attorneys—was only a small fraction of what I was earning through my business during those years. It makes no sense, in either of these two cases, that I would risk losing everything I had built in order to gain what amounted to nickel-and-dime savings in taxes. I'm a risk taker by nature, but I only take risks that make calculated business sense. I'm not reckless, and I like to sleep at night. That's why I prefer to pay my taxes fully, legally, and even overgenerously. In fact, I always bent over backward to do everything right, tax-wise, because I knew I was in a business that gets a lot of unfavorable scrutiny.

That's what I want you to see about the charges on that Belize-issued credit card. It was not an amount for which I would have risked getting into trouble. I valued my business, my family, and my reputation much too highly to take that kind of chance. My accountant never told me to report a business credit card on my personal return, I never received a 1099 form for the "income," and most of it would not have been considered income anyway. That's why I didn't report it. I was technically incorrect in my slip-up, but there was no nefarious intent on my part.

So maybe the bigger question you're wondering about is, how was it that I came to earn enough income that I *could* lose sight of $220,000 worth of credit card charges? How did I become a successful stockbroker who often earned that amount in a month? Let's turn the page back a few *more* years…

* * *

My father, Robert Quiel, was a huge influence on my early life. Following in his footsteps, and those of many other men in the Quiel family, I served in the US Navy after finishing high school then took up his career path as well.

My stint in the navy ran from 1981 to 1985. I entered the service as an enlisted man. I didn't have a college degree—still don't—so I wasn't eligible for the commissioned officer track. I started out washing airplanes for a squadron in Virginia Beach, Virginia. Not the most auspicious career launch, I'll admit. But after about six months, I was selected to go to navy "A" school. This is a technical training program where you learn advanced job skills. Navy A school was a tough program to get into when you were already serving in a squadron. In fact, only two people in my entire squadron of about three hundred were selected to attend.

It was about halfway through my service period when I returned to my hometown of Spokane, Washington, to marry Victoria Lee, my high school sweetheart. She was the daughter of USAF Colonel John Lee, a man I admired tremendously and whose approval I always sought and valued—both as Vicki's father and as the distinguished military man he was. I never wanted to let John Lee down, in anything I did, either in business or in life.

Vicki moved to Tennessee with me while I attended A school in Memphis. She and I lived in housing that was condemned by the military and then reopened up by a private party. I remember when we turned the lights on in the kitchen, the entire countertop would seem to move as dozens of cockroaches ran for cover.

My special training was as an aircraft electrician. And that's what I did for the remainder of my navy stint.

In the four years I was in the US Navy, I rose from the rank of E1 seaman recruit, to E5 petty officer, second class, which is the biggest advancement you can make in four years on the enlisted-person track. I also received some special awards and commendations, such as a Swordsman of the Month title. I believe I served my country conscientiously and at a level "above and beyond the call of duty."

I was honorably discharged from the navy in 1985. At that time, Vicki and I returned to Spokane to live, and still following in my dad's footsteps, I joined up with him in his business. He owned a small stock brokerage firm there.

My dad took me under his wing and trained me as a broker. At that time, he traded on the Spokane Stock Exchange, a tiny regional stock exchange that had opened in the 1800s. The Spokane exchange traded in a lot of mining equities that were issued as penny stocks— that is, stocks that sell for under a dollar a share. It was here I learned the ins and outs of the industry. The exchange eventually closed down in 1991 due to a decline in silver and gold prices and a drop-off in investor interest. It was the last of the country's regional stock exchanges.

I got my securities license in January of 1987, after several unsuccessful attempts. I took to the work pretty quickly and enjoyed it. It was exciting and challenging, and hey, I could do it in a clean shirt. It sure beat working as an aircraft repairman, at least in my mind at that time, and it seemed to offer a brighter future.

I had been working the business with my dad for only about nine months when Black Monday happened and the bottom dropped out of the market. My dad lost almost his entire net worth overnight. This was my first taste of the truly scary side of the securities game. When it's going well, you can make great money. But when it turns sour on you, there's no worse business to be in. If you're over forty-five, I don't have to tell you how bad Black Monday was. It was the single largest one-day drop in market history. I saw people lose their minds, as well as their portfolios, that day.

My dad was knocked down, but not out. He decided to move to Scottsdale, Arizona, and start the business afresh. In the '90s, Scottsdale was a rapidly expanding suburb of Phoenix that offered a comfortable lifestyle and had a growing population of mature and wealthy individuals. Many well-off retirees lived there. Dad thought it would be a great place to run a successful brokerage firm. As for Vicki and me, we had also heard good things about Scottsdale. It had reputation as a "Miami of the desert"—lots of exciting nightlife, along with good restaurants, golf, and arts culture, as well as lots of natural Southwestern beauty. It also seemed like a safe and comfortable place to raise a family. We were game for a new adventure. So we packed up and relocated to Scottsdale.

In Scottsdale—where I still reside most of the time—I opened a couple of brokerage firms with my father. We did well for ourselves and made pretty good business partners for a while. I can't swear I always got paid at a level commensurate with the contributions I made to the business (ahem, Dad), but I definitely learned a great deal. The knowledge I gained while working with my father gave me the foundation to start my own business and to go on to make a great living for several years in a lucrative business that I enjoyed.

In 1994 Dad and I sold the firm to a large brokerage outfit, and that was when I went out on my own for the first time. Well, not exactly on my own; I brokered for a small regional firm out of Minneapolis. I opened a one-man satellite office out of my home and functioned essentially as my own company while also serving as part of the larger organization. It was a pretty scary proposition at first, after working only with my dad for the previous six-plus years. I didn't know how I stacked up competitively against others in the business.

Turned out, I was good at this thing—legitimately good, better than I'd realized I was. Not only had I acquired a good knowledge base from working with my father, but now, out from under his shadow, I was free to do things my way. To let my own strengths and talents blossom. So with that combination of trained experience and the ability to operate as "my own man," I started making real money for the first time in my life. Vicki and I bought a house in nearby Fountain Hills, and I started building some financial security for my growing young family. The house had a complete home office built in, equipped with a soundproof door to keep out the sounds of squealing young children. It was my place of business for years.

As a stockbroker, I had a targeted approach. I didn't spend a lot of time making cold calls or sending out marketing brochures. My angle was more efficient: I went after people who were making business deals. My thinking was that people who were buying and selling businesses were often getting their hands on large amounts of stock, windfall-style. Simply put, I wanted to get that stock in my hands so that I could start managing it and investing it. My approach worked. I became the largest-producing office for this brokerage house. That was a significant accomplishment, given the fact that the firm had some branch offices with twenty-five or thirty people in them. I don't know what those people were doing all day, but I was a solo operation and I was outproducing every other office in terms of gross commissions. My monthly commissions ranged from $125,000 to $250,000. Yes, I hustled like crazy to earn that money, but I tried to work smart too.

During this time—in part because of the kinds of clients I was working with—I learned a lot about start-up businesses. I became more and more interested in how companies got off the ground. I was fascinated by the early stages of building a business—the idea pitching, the short-term funding, the long-term investing, the process of becoming a public company. I became something of an expert on how start-up companies do things, like build a workable management team, create successful business plans, attract investors, go public, and strategically achieve high market valuations.

Around the year 2000, I was introduced by a mutual friend to Earl Gilbrech. Earl was a pretty interesting guy, a businessman and consultant who had his fingers in a lot of different pies—real estate, financial services, public/private partnerships. He was heavily involved in international business deals, particularly in Belize, where he owned a second home and was well-known by the government and business elite. He opened the first life insurance company in Belize and also had a shipwreck recovery company there. I liked Earl right off the bat, and we became friendly with each other. It happened that he needed some consulting from me in the area where I'd been gaining some expertise. Earl wanted to move some private companies into a position where they could become public entities. There were several steps and stages to this process, and I helped Earl navigate the whole thing.

As a way to handle my compensation and cover expenses I incurred, Earl gave me a Visa card issued by a bank in Belize. I was hesitant to accept it at first—I would have preferred a simple cash arrangement—but because Earl was so insistent, I reluctantly took the card. I used it from the year 2000 through part of 2003 for a variety of purposes: to submit consulting charges, to pay for business expenses, and occasionally, to purchase items for myself and my family in lieu of cash payments. Again, most of it was tax-deductible business expenses, but I admit the card was kind of a mess, a commingling of personal and business charges. If I had it to do over, I would handle it differently. At that time, though, it was a very minor blip on my overall radar screen; I was busy building a successful brokerage business and didn't pay the card much mind.

Earl passed away from cancer in 2003. I stopped using the card, called the issuing bank, and told them to cancel the account. End of story.

I wish.

* * *

Fast-forward to 2006. One day I get a call from Mike Stuck, my accountant. "Hey, Mike," he says, "we've got a situation here. A Cheryl Bradley from the IRS showed up at my office today. She wants to audit you for the years 2000 to 2003."

I had met Mike Stuck through Earl—the two of them shared an office, in fact—and began using Mike as my own accountant, starting with my 1999 tax returns. Mike is a good person and a terrific accountant, and I still work with him today.

But I can't say I welcomed his news that day.

Getting audited by the IRS is a spooky proposition, even if you don't think you've done anything wrong. It's kind of like having the police show up at your door—as far as you know, you haven't broken the law, but then again, anything is possible. Your fear of the unknown is triggered. Fortunately, I had had one previous "inquiry" by the IRS, and it had turned out fine. It involved some stock I received as compensation for work I did for a public company. There was a misunderstanding about when I received the stock, and Mike gave the IRS a detailed explanation and a bunch of papers. The IRS accepted his explanation, and the issue went away. So I had confidence in Mike, and I wasn't *too* worried, but still…An IRS audit is not a recreational activity one seeks out with open arms.

And this new one was a *general* audit, not an issue-specific one. In case you've never had the pleasure of an IRS audit, Uncle Sam can audit you in two basic ways. Sometimes a question comes up regarding a specific issue from a past tax year. The IRS asks you for more documentation about that particular item. You then provide it to them, and if they are satisfied, the issue is resolved. That was what happened with my first IRS go-round.

The other type of audit is a more general one, where they ask to see a pile of records for a given tax year or years. This is the scarier type of audit, because you have to send the IRS a lot of material. No one—not even the most law-abiding citizen on the planet—wants the IRS sifting through their financial records with a fine-tooth comb. There are a lot of gray areas when it comes to tax law, and you just don't know what the IRS is going to find or *think* they've found.

So Mike Stuck sent in everything, including the kitchen sink, and we waited. I threw myself into my work and tried to forget about it, but when you have an IRS audit in process, it is never far from your mind. Again, I had nothing specific to worry about, but you hear stories of people being blindsided by unexpected issues.

Weeks went by and I finally received a call from Stuck as I sliced my way down the fairway on a cool February day in 2006.

"Mike, we've got some good news and some bad news," he said.

"I'm having a bad game, so start with the good."

"The IRS is happy with the bulk of the records we sent them."

"Great. And the bad?"

He paused in a disturbing way. "They're *very* interested in some charges you made on a Belize-issued credit card."

My heart sank.

Damn.

Damn, damn, damn.

That stupid card, I had forgotten about it. I'd never had a good feeling about it in the first place, and now I knew why. It was a potential hornet's nest. Most of the charges on it were legitimate business expenses and therefore tax deductible. But that might be hard to prove, especially now that Earl was three years dead.

This was when the fear kicked in. I wasn't afraid of what this problem might cost me in cash. The entire amount of the charges, over a four-year period, was, as I said earlier, about $221,000. By this time—in 2006—I was earning many times what I had made even as a stockbroker. Even if I'd had to cut a check for the entire amount of the credit card charges (not just the *tax* on those charges), it wouldn't have hurt me to do so. My *real* concern was over what other hidden doors this audit might open and how it might affect my current business and my reputation. As someone who dealt professionally with other people's money, it was crucial that my name remain untarnished.

I needed this problem to go away. Fast. And Mike Stuck couldn't really help me.

I needed a lawyer.

CHAPTER THREE

Enter the Dragon

I did not want this problem lingering on my doorstep. You see, by the time the IRS issue with the Belize credit card surfaced—in 2006—I was no longer a stockbroker. I was into a whole new business, one that was turning out to be extremely lucrative for me, but which was also highly reputation sensitive. I was now running my own investment company. I could not afford to have it tainted by any kind of IRS difficulties, and I could not afford to be threatened with legal actions. The potential cost to me would be staggering.

A bit more background here. My career change came about in the early 2000s. As you know, after my dad and I sold our brokerage firms, I began working as a solo operation for a Minneapolis brokerage. By the time 2000 rolled around, I was doing very well. I had two full-time traders working for me in Minneapolis and was making up to a quarter of a million a month in commissions.

So why would I even consider quitting that kind of gig? Well, this was the period when dot-com valuations were blowing up like an overinflated wad of Bazooka Joe. Everyone wanted to get into Internet stocks. If a company had a "dot-com" in its name—I don't care if it was WatchingPaintDry.com—people wanted in. It was a crazily lucrative time for stockbrokers, but it was also a stressful time—if you had a brain and a conscience. You knew the bubble was going to burst at some point, and you hated seeing your clients abandoning the tried-and-true principles of good investing in order to chase stocks that you knew were overvalued. You knew a day of reckoning was coming, probably soon, and you dutifully tried to warn your clients about it.

But at the same time, hell, you made your money on stock transactions, and who were you to stand in the way of your clients' dreams of getting rich on the next Amazon or eBay? So I was making incredible money in the late '90s, but I was also losing a lot of sleep. I'd been through Black Monday as a young stockbroker, and I had no desire to repeat that experience. I didn't want to see clients I cared about going broke overnight.

I can remember sitting at my desk in Fountain Hills, turning on my computer, and watching with a weirdly detached feeling as the dot-coms rolled over, just as I'd known they eventually would. I suddenly realized I didn't have the stomach for this anymore. I picked up the phone and called one of my partners at the Minneapolis firm.

"Kevin," I said to him, "I'm getting out."

"What do you mean, getting out?" he said with a voice approaching panic. "Who gave you a better offer?"

"No one." I laughed. "I'm getting out, as in out of the business."

"Mike, you can't be serious."

"Yes, I can," I replied. "I've made enough money in this game. I'm in pretty good shape financially right now. I can't stand the smoke and mirrors anymore. I want to try my hand at something more substantial."

"You're just freaked out because the Nasdaq took a swan dive into an empty pool. We all are. But you know the way the game works—what goes down must come up. Take a few days to think about it and—"

"I *have* thought about it, Kevin. I'm getting out. You can have all my accounts."

"What?"

"You heard me. My accounts, they're all yours. Good luck, my friend."

And with that, I was no longer a stockbroker.

To be honest, I had been thinking about a career change before the bubble burst. I knew I wanted to be on the deal side of the business. Instead of just buying and selling stocks in companies, I wanted to get involved with the companies themselves. As an investor. I knew that the *real* money, in any business deal, was on the investment side, not in providing services for fees. Over the years, as I've mentioned already, I had learned a lot about how companies get started, attract investment money, go public, and increase their valuations. I had a good eye for what made businesses succeed and fail. I knew how to package a business idea to money people. I thought I had the potential to build some substantial wealth by investing, short-term, in start-up companies.

My idea, in very simple terms, was to create a business model like this: provide short-term funds for start-up companies, acquire stock in those companies in return, strengthen the companies, introduce them to longer-term money, help them get their market value increased, then sell the stock once its higher value was realized. It was not a business model that most people could capitalize on—there was a huge amount of risk and patience involved—but I thought I had the right skills and resources to pull it off.

So that was what I started doing. I started looking for people with promising young companies and/or business ideas that needed funding. My entire involvement with a company was during that short-term investment period. Of course, I wanted my companies to succeed in the long term, but whether that happened or not was irrelevant to the success of *my* business. For me to make money in a business deal, what I needed to do was to find the right business team with the right idea, help groom the company into an attractive investment opportunity for long-term investors, and ensure that its market valuation would increase when it went public. If all those pieces came together, my short-term investment could pay off in multiples. Again, it was a risky model, but with big risks come big paydays.

My goal at the outset was to make $20 million. I thought this was both an ambitious and a realistically attainable goal. The goal wasn't a make-or-break factor for me—if I didn't reach, it I wasn't going to die or hang my head in shame—but I believed, and still do, that it's important to have a target to aim for. Otherwise, you're just flopping around like a goldfish on a rug.

Slowly, my new company got rolling. The company was just me, really, backed by some of the money I had made as a stockbroker. I helped start a few companies, just as I'd planned, by providing short-term funding for them. I knew it was going to take a while, maybe years, before some of these companies started making *me* money. I knew I was in the "deposit" phase of my new career, not the "withdrawal" phase. Luckily, I had enough resources, for the time being, to weather a few lean years.

Of course, if I had *more* money to play with, I could make bigger and better deals.

That's when a partner came into the picture. As some of my companies started to gain momentum, I reconnected with a guy I'd met a few years earlier named Steve Kerr. He was also an investor. Back in 1989, Steve had walked into the brokerage I ran with my dad. I remember being impressed by his smarts and his ability to make deals. I had kept him in the back of my mind as someone I might want to work with someday, but for many years, our business goals did not really align.

Now, though, it seemed we might be able to help each other.

Steve, I learned, was in the process of putting together various business deals, as was I. Some of his deals sounded interesting to me; some of mine sounded interesting to him. We started talking. It seemed our interests overlapped to a large degree. Better still, we had skill sets that complemented each other's. Steve was more of a "front man." He was talented on the investment side, finding investors for projects. He had a lot of contacts and experience in that area. I was more of a "back office" guy. I was good at making sure all the groundwork was done correctly within the companies. I knew how to coordinate the lawyers and accountants and also how to help young companies with business challenges. If there were problems, I could jump in and solve them.

Steve and I were different but compatible. We realized that by going in together on business deals, we could not only double our financial wallop but also play better to our individual strengths. Long story short, we became partners. We weren't legal partners, and we never owned anything together. *Coinvestors*, I suppose, would be a more correct term. Even though we went in together on many deals, we operated as separate legal entities. This suited both of our personalities and also kept us out of regulatory headaches. Had we acted in concert all the time, we would have been considered a single unit by the SEC. That could be cumbersome in terms of valuing and reporting issues. It was more advantageous for us to remain officially separate. So we struck up an informal partnership and started doing deals together.

And so, by the time 2006 rolled around—the year Cheryl Bradley from the IRS came knocking on Mike Stuck's door—things were really turning around for me, business-wise. Some of the companies I'd invested in were starting to pay off, and in a big way. In the year 2006, in fact, I reported about $6.5 million in income. I don't say that to brag, but just to point out that from a strictly financial point of view, the tax on that $220,000 in credit card charges was a *very* minor issue for me, a nuisance really. But from another angle, it was worrisome. I was now making "real money" and developing some serious credentials as an investor. I absolutely could not afford to have an IRS issue getting me or my business into trouble. So while the cost of *solving* the problem would be minor for me—I was ready to write a check at the drop of a hat—the cost of *not* solving the problem was potentially huge. Because I now had a tremendous amount to lose.

This made me extremely eager to find someone who could solve my tax problem quickly and cleanly. Maybe too eager.

* * *

I started looking for a tax attorney online. That might sound strange. After all, couldn't someone in my position—who worked with well-connected businesspeople all the time—find a lawyer through personal referrals? Well, here's the thing: I really didn't want my colleagues to know I had a potential legal issue. That could have affected some of my deals in progress. Steve Kerr, of course, knew about the situation and didn't have any concerns, but this was not the kind of thing I wanted to broadcast. I needed to handle it delicately.

In retrospect, I wish I had found a lawyer in a different way. But when I found Chris Rusch via a Google search, he seemed like just the guy I was looking for. His website was tastefully designed, and his home page listed among his specialty areas delinquent tax returns, criminal tax, and international business tax. The "About" text stated,

> My tax law firm is focused [on] solving state and IRS tax problems on behalf of entrepreneurs, individuals, closely held corporations, and businesses, as well as individuals with international issues.

> I have extensive experience representing clients before the Internal Revenue Service, the California Franchise Tax Board and taxing authorities from other states. I handle complex audits, appeals of IRS and California FTB tax assessments, removal of state and IRS tax liens, tax levies and wage garnishments, filing of late and delinquent tax returns, and can reduce your tax bill with an Offer in Compromise.

Evidently, Rusch had also written a book called *The Expatriate's Tax Bible: The Complete Guide to U.S. and Foreign Taxes for the American Abroad*.

In short, I couldn't have written a better job description for what I was seeking in a lawyer. So I picked up the phone, called his number, and left a message with his service. A short while later, Rusch called me back.

He talked as good a game as his website advertised. He asked me to describe my tax issue to him, and he listened carefully, without interrupting—always a good sign in my book. He asked the right questions. I don't recall the conversation verbatim, but I believe it went something like this:

"I understand your situation, Mr. Quiel. It's extremely easy to get in trouble with foreign-based credit cards. The IRS takes the position that everyone who uses these cards as a financial tool is a tax dodger, but the fact is, most people aren't even aware they need to report this stuff."

"Right," I agreed. "To be honest, it completely slipped my mind."

"I hear you. Did you know that fewer than one in ten US citizens who have foreign-issued cards actually report income gains from those cards on their 1040s?"

"Wow. So…can you help me with this?"

"I'd have to review your records in detail, but I believe I can. I understand these types of issues, and I've dealt with them many, many times. I was a tax specialist before I became an attorney. The good news, Mike—may I call you Mike?—is that the IRS wants its money. It doesn't want to send people to prison." Then he paused briefly and added, "For the most part."

Prison? Why was he even bringing that up?

"Let me ask," he said, "are you in a position to pay what you owe, including any possible fines and interest penalties?"

I told him I was.

"Then you should have nothing to worry about here. I'm confident we can get this problem behind us quickly and with no blowback on you or your business. You are not the only one facing this issue, believe me. Thousands upon thousands of US citizens are dealing with the exact same thing."

Somehow it made me feel better to know I was not alone in this.

"In fact," he continued, "a substantial percent of my business revolves around helping people who have credit card issues just like yours."

"Why is that, do you suppose?" I asked.

"Oh, there's no *supposing* about it. The IRS has been cracking down, big time, on people who fail to report foreign accounts.

They've been able to put pressure on the credit card companies, forcing them to open their books in a way they've never done before. So a *lot* of names are surfacing. That audit you went through? Well, let's put it this way; the IRS didn't stumble on your name by chance."

"Are you saying the credit card company *gave* them my name?"

"You didn't hear it from me, but of course, they did. The audit was a song-and-dance number by the IRS. They knew what they were looking for right from the start. They just wanted to get at your records."

"Holy crap. So what do you recommend?"

"Tell you what. Why don't you do a little research online, think about it for a day or two, and call me back if you think I can help you."

No pressure, no sales ploys. I liked that.

After I hung up, I did what Rusch suggested. I started looking into the IRS story and quickly learned that he was right. I found numerous articles, going back a few years, that described the IRS's major crackdown on foreign accounts. One in the *LA Times* (August 16, 2002) stated,

> The federal government Thursday widened its probe into offshore tax cheating, asking a federal court in Miami to grant it access to MasterCard International Inc. records on credit cards issued by banks in 30 countries used as tax havens by Americans.

It went on to say that hundreds of thousands of Americans who were holding assets in undisclosed offshore accounts had already been identified and that if the federal court granted the request, MasterCard would have to turn over records for many US clients for the years 1999, 2000, and 2001. The article, and others like it, described how American citizens, for years, had used foreign-issued credits cards as a ploy to access offshore cash. The laws of the issuing countries forbade the credit card companies from turning over records to the United States, so until recently, there was little the

IRS could do about it. As a result, the United States was losing an estimated twenty to forty billion dollars a year in taxes. No wonder Uncle Samuel was pissed. In my case, though, I hadn't wanted a foreign card to begin with! The only reason I ever used a card issued in Belize was because that was where Earl Gilbrech did business. I wasn't trying to hide anything. Good luck explaining that to the IRS, though. This was starting to really worry me.

The articles further explained that the IRS was no longer taking the situation lying down. The agency had sought—and attained—greater legal authority to go after the foreign credit card companies. According to the *NY Times* (March 30, 2002),

> SAN FRANCISCO, March 29—Visa International will receive a summons from the Internal Revenue Service to turn over records of offshore accounts held by Americans suspected of evading taxes.
>
> ...MasterCard, the second-largest brand, has turned over 1.7 million records involving 230,000 accounts. The American Express Company agreed this week to turn over similar records.

So there it was in black and white. There was no doubt in my mind now that my name had popped up on a list that had been turned over to the IRS (the same thing would happen later in the big case that went to trial). It had taken them a while to track me down, but now I was squarely within their gun sights. Fine. I wanted to pay what I owed. Let's just get it over with. The part that worried me, though, was reading stuff like this (from the *LA Times*):

> "Criminal prosecutions are going to skyrocket," said Ian Comisky, partner in the Philadelphia law firm of Blank, Rome, Comisky & McCauley... The numbers are so massive that the question

36

is going to be whether they'll have sufficient
resources to handle all the prosecutions.

Holy crap. Well, Rusch was right about one thing: I was hardly alone in this. But it seemed that the IRS wanted more than just to recoup its losses; it wanted to punish people. I was terrified about the possible consequences for my business, not to mention my personal reputation. Prosecution? In federal court? No way. Nope. Couldn't allow that to happen.

My eagerness to resolve the situation shifted into overdrive. I called Rusch back and made hasty arrangements to meet with him in person.

On March 13, 2006, I flew out to his office in San Diego—a short flight from Phoenix—and took my papers with me. Rusch skimmed through the documents.

"As far as I can see, yours is a pretty straightforward case," he said. "You made the charges on the account, you don't plan to refute them, you want to pay up, and you're not looking for a reduced settlement. Of course, with the IRS, nothing's a sure thing, but I think we can resolve this pretty fast."

Just what I wanted to hear. I wanted it to go away. Period. I didn't really care how much it cost. And I made that clear to Rusch.

I have since learned that this is not a good posture to adopt when dealing with the IRS. The IRS's chief weapon is fear. It knows that anytime you see "Internal Revenue Service" on a piece of mail, your blood pressure shoots into the red zone. It knows that if it even *hints* that you're in tax trouble, you will cheerfully surrender your firstborn child to the US Treasury, just to make the situation go away. And that's the way the IRS likes it.

In truth, I have learned, you are better off relaxing and taking your time. The IRS actually moves very slowly and inefficiently. Its employees have job security and are in no big hurry to resolve cases. They don't personally care whether the government gets its money or not, and they're not personally upset with you for being tax delinquent. It's all in a day's work to them. I have found that if you allow a case to drag out, the IRS often becomes much more flexible over time. Compromises are struck. Sometimes key people at the IRS even die or retire, and problems literally disappear. I have seen this happen.

But I didn't know this at that time.

"Do whatever it takes, Chris," I said. And I proceeded to write him a check for the entire amount of his services; I believe it was $17,000.

"Okay, Mike," he said. "I'll let you know how it goes."

And the waiting game started.

CHAPTER FOUR

Let's Become a Swiss Bank

It was a sunny day in June when I got the call at my home outside of Spokane.

"Mike, this is Chris Rusch. Great news. The IRS accepted our offer."

"Wow, Chris, that's music to my ears." The IRS issue had been hovering over my head like a storm cloud for months now.

"All we have to do is sign the Closing Agreement," he said. "Oh, and pay Uncle Sam a little cash."

"Great job, Chris. You've made my day."

I let out a massive sigh of relief and wandered out onto our long, sloping lawn that winds down to the Spokane River. I just stood there for a long while, breathing in the river-freshened air. Our summer home in Nine Mile Falls, Washington, is a tranquil sanctuary that sits on two and a half wooded acres, with no neighbors on either side. It has a boathouse, a guesthouse, a manmade pond with a waterfall, and all the boats and toys to make it a welcoming destination for family and friends. That spring I had been unable to really enjoy it, though, as I waited for the "verdict" to come in.

After Rusch's phone call, it felt like a vise had been loosened from my chest. I hadn't realized how much this IRS case had been eating at me. It wasn't the money part that troubled me; it was the fear of further complications. As a stockbroker, I had always taken care to go the extra mile for my clients and to conduct all my legal and tax business in the most transparent, by-the-books way possible so the idea of being labeled a "cheater" had really blindsided me. I knew some people to whom the cheater label could be applied, but I wasn't one of them. I'd always tried to play it clean.

Oh well, at least it was over. All I had to do now was cut the US Treasury a check for about $232,000. I decided to celebrate by taking one of the jet skis for a spin.

Celebrate paying the IRS $232,000? You bet. I was so relieved to have the matter behind me I was actually physically happy to write the check. It didn't matter to me that I'd be paying a lot more than I technically owed. Rusch had gotten the deal done quickly and efficiently, which was what I had asked him to do. I had hired him in mid-March of 2006, and now the matter would be resolved by mid-June. That's *lightning* fast for the IRS, where cases can often drag on for years.

So I was feeling good about Attorney Chris Rusch. In truth, he hadn't done anything extraordinary. He had simply filed amended tax returns for the years 2000 through 2003, along with all the necessary supporting documents. He had not even consulted with Mike Stuck, my accountant, to recalculate all my business deductions. Doing so would have saved me a boatload of money, but it also would have taken extra time to prepare and would have delayed the IRS's review and approval process. So Chris simply submitted the amended returns in the least complicated way possible. Yes, I ended up paying far more than I probably could have negotiated for, but it was a price worth paying to get the burden off my back.

What Chris *didn't* file—and this becomes very important later—was FBAR forms. FBAR is the reporting of foreign bank and financial accounts, which the government requires you to file when you own offshore accounts with over $10,000 in them. *Should* he have filed these forms? No, actually. He was correct in *not* filing them. If my Belize card had been a debit card, he would have had to file an FBAR, but because it was a straight credit card, no FBAR was required. The reason this is important is that later both he and Cheryl Bradley of the IRS testified in court—falsely—that I *did* file these FBAR forms. Why would they do this? To allow the prosecution to make it appear to the court that I *was* familiar with FBAR filings, so that some of my criminal charges would stick. In fact, though, I knew nothing about FBARs in the year 2006. I did not know whether I was required to file them (I wasn't), and I did not know whether Rusch had, in fact, filed them (he hadn't). It just never came up in my awareness at all. The term FBAR had no meaning to me whatsoever; it might as well have been BARF.

Anyway, I was delighted to have this credit card nuisance behind me and to write a check for the entire amount I owed—an amount painfully inflated by interest and penalties. On June 16, 2006, I signed a Closing Agreement with the federal government. This is a legally binding agreement that basically says your liability to the IRS has now been permanently settled.

Amen and good riddance.

* * *

The ink had barely dried on the agreement when Steve and I started receiving e-mail solicitations from Chris Rusch about business ideas and tax-saving strategies. These ideas generally revolved around using offshore financial structures, which Rusch offered to help set up for us.

One of Rusch's suggestions involved an offshore life insurance policy, where we could somehow take a tax deduction for the premium. Neither Steve nor I was interested in pursuing this. Another solicitation involved protecting our business assets by moving them offshore. If you move your assets offshore, Rusch explained to us, creditors can't come after you for them. We had no interest in this idea either. Frankly, it reeked of sketchiness, and I was a little surprised Rusch would even suggest it to us.

What Rusch did not understand was that any business involving securities—such as mine—must be *very* scrupulous and transparent. You can get in a lot of trouble for taking shady actions and not disclosing them. You can't just go moving your assets to Switzerland in some half-baked attempt to hide them. You have to tell your clients, coinvestors, banks, and government regulators everything you're doing, all the time. If you don't, you can be sued, sanctioned, or indicted.

Steve and I, in fact, were constantly angling for ways to be *more* transparent, not less so. I, personally, have always gone overboard with disclosure. When I was a stockbroker, I would turn cartwheels to explain to clients the risks involved in any stock transaction. Same thing later with my coinvestors. Even though the latter weren't paying me a fee—so I didn't technically "owe" them full disclosure—I would always go out of my way to explain to them that their investment was not guaranteed and there was a good chance they could lose all their money. My feeling is that if I tell you there's a 70 percent chance you will lose money on a deal, and you decide to do the deal anyway, then we're both on the same page and no one is being duped or manipulated. I'm sure I've lost a lot of potential business by being so forthright, but I have *never* want to be accused of "tricking" anyone by failing to disclose key facts. Disclosure is baked into my DNA.

I explained this to Chris in no uncertain terms early in our relationship (which is why I found some of his later claims about me so mind-boggling).

Frankly, I was surprised he was approaching us about business deals at all. After all, he was my attorney, not my financial advisor or business partner. Steve and I hadn't asked for his "help" in this way. But at the same time, I did appreciate that he was looking out for our business interests, and I was building some trust in his know-how.

Because of that, he was the person I went to when Steve and I needed some help doing a charitable donation. We both wanted to give some money to the Rypien Foundation, a nonprofit organization headed by former NFL quarterback Mark Rypien. Mark, as you may recall, was the MVP of Super Bowl XXVI. He also lost a three-year-old son to cancer. I went to high school with Mark, and he and I had remained friends, so his foundation was always at the top of my charity list.

Steve and I had been enjoying a nice run of financial success, and we wanted to give back by making a substantial donation to

Mark's cause. We wanted to do it in the form of stock, though, rather than cash, so we asked for Chris's help. This required Chris to write opinion letters about the value of the stock, which ended up coming in at around two and a half million dollars. This was more than a "routine" legal task. In order to get his valuation accepted, the charity had to run it past their team of lawyers. I also needed Mike Stuck to approve it. Chris did the work, and it held up under scrutiny. The charity accepted the donation, and Steve and I were able to claim substantial tax deductions. Everybody won. Score points for Rusch.

As an offshoot of this, Chris suggested that Steve and I set up our own family charitable foundations, through which we could donate stock, liquidate it, and donate the cash to various charities. Chris did all the work setting the foundations up and, again, did a good job. More points for Rusch.

Rusch's mental wheels were always turning. I think it took him a while to understand how Steve and I made our money. When he began to get a better sense of how we operated, he finally proposed a business idea we were willing to listen to.

Chris Rusch wanted to start a Swiss bank. Yes, you read that right, a Swiss bank. That's not as crazy as it probably sounds. The idea was that if we could set up a credible banking structure in Switzerland, it would give us access to European investment money. Europe was the logical next place for Steve and me to look for investors. We had already been able to put together about $200 million worth of financing deals in the United States. Securing a place at the table in the banking capital of the world—Switzerland—seemed like just the right next step for us.

To be clear: that was the *only* interest Steve and I had in Rusch's idea. It represented *access*. Period. If we could tell a young company that was considering working with us, "Listen, we can walk you in the door of a Swiss bank that can finance you out," this could add immeasurably to our lending appeal.

Again, you have to understand our business model. We were not fee-based consultants; we were investors only. The way we made money was by providing young companies with short-term money and then helping them secure a longer-term financing arrangement.

Essentially, we would walk in the door of a young company and say, "We'll write you a check for a million dollars. We'll introduce you to people who can raise you twenty million more, and we'll also introduce you to people who can help you prepare for that step. We'll take you public, and here's the public company you'll be able to create. You don't have to pay us anything unless and until the long-term money comes through."

Why would we provide such a service for free?

Because it worked for us. And because it wasn't free.

You see, when a long-term finance offer did come through for one of our companies—let's say it was for $20 million—we would get paid back with interest. We would also have bought a great deal of stock in the company at a relatively minuscule price. Then what would happen is this: The long-term lending institution would have to justify why it spent $20 million. That meant it would have to put an official valuation on the company. Essentially, that involves making a five-year projection of what the company will earn and cutting it in half.

Presto, the company suddenly has a value that's a hundred times what we bought it for. And hey, guess who owns a big pile of its stock?

When a deal like that goes nicely, who needs to be paid a fee?

I'll give you one example of a company we actually worked with, to help you understand our business model. One of my former brokers contacted me about an inventor who was supposedly a pretty brilliant guy. So I called the guy and set up a meeting with him. He waltzed into the meeting room with a glass of saltwater, a piece of magnesium, and an electric fan. He dropped the magnesium in the saltwater and flipped the On switch. The fan spun, with no other energy source.

Steve and I were intrigued, naturally. But we were even more intrigued by the byproduct of the process, which was hydrogen. Hydrogen, as you probably know, can be used as vehicle fuel. Now, this was at a time when the whole country was going green. The president was talking about green energy and about using hydrogen as an alternative to gasoline. This technology looked smoking-hot.

So Steve and I—along with a few other people, including a world-famous golfer whose name you would recognize, and his agent—did a bridge loan of $1.5 million for this inventor's company, which was called Ecotality.

It happened that the inventor had contacts at the NASA Jet Propulsion Lab. The NASA folks believed they could get his hydrogen-producing technology lightweight enough to put on vehicles. If this could be accomplished, then buses and trucks, and maybe someday cars, could generate their own hydrogen on the fly and wouldn't have to go to a fueling station. Also, they wouldn't need to have a hydrogen bomb strapped to their backs in the form of a hydrogen fuel tank.

No sooner had we done the bridge loan than we walked into Brookstreet Capital in southern California. We already had a relationship with these people because we'd done a bridge loan for them once before. Brookstreet was immediately interested in Ecotality's technology and in the company itself. They wanted in. During the sixty days it took to put the paperwork together, Ecotality signed a deal with the Jet Propulsion Lab to start developing the product to put on vehicles. The company was then able to raise $17 million very quickly. Steve and I (and our other partners) got paid back in short order, and I also now owned a bunch of stock in the company. When we'd originally gotten involved, the stock was trading at a quarter a share. It went up to $2 a share due to all the excitement from NASA's involvement. Show me another investment that can give you a 700 percent return in a few months' time. We were able to make millions on the stock we sold.

About a year later, the Jet Propulsion Lab concluded it couldn't get the technology lightweight enough. So the product ultimately failed, and the company went into a slump. But this didn't really affect Steve and me anymore, except in the value of the stock we still held. That's because we had already made our money.

The point is, Steve and I made our money primarily in the deal-making stage. First and foremost, that involved providing bridge loans and working to connect the borrowing company to longer-term financing. Secondarily, we made money on any stock we acquired, if we could get the company's valuation increased.

Having an "in" at a Swiss bank could help us in two ways. First of all, it would give us great negotiating power with any new company that was considering accepting a bridge loan from us. Not only would our ability to connect them to Swiss investors make us stronger as a lender, but we could also command better loan terms. For example, if we asked for a certain interest rate for a certain loan period and the borrowing company said, "No, we can't do that," we could say, "Yes, you can, because we're going to take you to a Swiss bank that will lend you $20 million."

Secondly, it would put us at the table with European investment bankers. That was what most interested us about Rusch's proposal. We knew that if we could get in the room with these people, we—especially Steve—could figure out a way to interest them in some of the deals we were working on. Then, once we'd done a deal or two with them, we'd have built some relationships for the future. Because that's the way the investing business works. It's all about relationships.

So those were the reasons—and the *sole* reasons—we were receptive to Chris Rusch's proposal about starting a Swiss venture. He knew overseas money people, and we didn't. He knew how to set up a foreign corporation. He knew about international tax law. He might be able to actually help us. It seemed worth our risking a relatively small amount of money—in the form of stock we couldn't really sell in the United States at the moment anyway—to see if he could pull something off. We weren't pinning a lot of hope on his venture, and we didn't have the bandwidth to direct it or manage it—we were too busy putting together deals in the States—but if Rusch thought he could make something happen in Europe, maybe it wasn't the worst idea in the world.

CHAPTER FIVE

The Setup

When I spoke with Chris Rusch by phone about his Swiss idea, I remember being very specific about my concerns.

"I have no interest in running a bank," I told him. "I don't want that kind of responsibility. The way I work is I make deals and walk away from them when I'm done. I prefer to stay light on my feet. Steve and I don't control any of the companies we get involved with; that's not the way we operate. We're investors only."

"Understood," said Rusch.

"And besides, there's no way I'm moving to Switzerland. I like cheese and Toblerone, but not *that* much."

"I'd be willing to move there and handle the day-to-day stuff," offered Chris. "I've been thinking about making a change in my life anyway, so I was already considering moving to Europe. This would be a good excuse."

"Okay, just so we're clear about that. You would need to personally set up, manage, and operate the fund. You would also need to make sure it's 100 percent kosher from a tax angle and take complete responsibility for all reporting requirements. Steve and I want nothing to do with running or controlling this thing."

"You won't have to, I promise."

"Five percent is the maximum percentage we want to own, as investors. There are too many SEC restrictions when you own more, and we don't want to go down that road." SEC reporting requirements become much more onerous when you cross the 5 percent ownership threshold.

"That's fine," replied Rusch. "We can set it up so that you own whatever percentage you want. Once I'm over there, I can get to work bringing other shareholders on board."

I was running out of objections.

"There's another thing," I said to him. "We're not giving you cash. We're willing to put some stock into this venture, because frankly, we can't move it very fast over here anyway. So if you can figure out how to sell it over there—"

"I work with stock in Europe all the time," said Rusch confidently.

"Then you have our blessings. Go ahead and fund your bank."

We gave Rusch the green light to set up the Swiss Venture fund. In December of 2006, Steve and I each contributed $2.6 million worth of shares of Ecotality and a handful of other companies. One of these was Intelligentias, a security software company whose software helped catch the Madrid bomber. Another was Nascent Wines, a food and beverage distribution company for which we had provided a bridge loan and which later became an $80 million company. There were a couple of others too.

What's important to understand—sadly, the jury never did—was that the stock we gave Rusch was fully owned and paid for by us. This was not stock we were receiving as fees for doing any kind of ongoing service. We weren't trying to hide *income* in Switzerland. This stock was a fully owned asset, just like a house or a boat. When we moved it to Switzerland, it was never our attempt to gain any kind of tax benefit. No one involved in our case seemed to understand this—either because they didn't understand how securities work or because they simply assumed *moving money to Switzerland equals tax dodging*. Or both. No one seemed to realize that if we had kept the stock in the United States, we would only have had to pay the 15 percent long-term capital gains tax on any earnings the stock gained. But by moving it to Switzerland, we now had to pay regular income tax of about 35 percent on anything the stock earned. Clever move, eh?

In fact, if we had just given Rusch a house or a boat to sell, instead of stock, there never would have been an issue. But what we did was exactly the same thing in principle. We gave him a wholly owned asset. What he did with it from that point forward should have been on him, not on us. But because it was *stock*, everyone's brains misfired. They didn't understand how stocks work.

What's also important to understand is that this stock was not a huge risk for either of us, because the stock wasn't doing much for us anyway. Ecotality wasn't like some big stock trading on the New York Stock Exchange that you can instantly liquidate into cash. The stock was a "sleeper" asset. If we could make it work for us by helping our business, great. But if we lost it all, it wasn't going to cost either of us a moment of sleep. In fact, the moment we gave it to Chris, we "wrote it off" as a loss in our minds. That's the way investors have to think; you don't invest money you can't afford to lose. Steve and I were used to "losing" on as many deals as we won on.

Even if the gamble did work, the payoff was not going to come in the form of hard cash, but only in an expanded ability to do business in Europe.

I can't emphasize this enough: We weren't using the Swiss structure as a clever way to hide cash. In fact, we didn't even have *access* to the money over there, and the way the accounts were set up, we couldn't have taken money back out of Switzerland even if we'd wanted to. A pair of Swiss bankers would later verify this in court. The reason we were funding this venture was strictly so that we could have an inroad to Swiss investment money. Nothing more, nothing less.

Our main marching orders for Rusch were for him to keep us 100 percent tax compliant. That was the most important point. After my fiasco with the Belize credit card, I was gun shy about doing an offshore endeavor, and the last thing I wanted was to even create the *appearance* of tax shenanigans. To ease our minds about that, we formally hired Chris Rusch to serve as our tax attorney. His Job One was to keep us legal, above board, and IRS compliant. To ensure this,

Steve and I each paid him a fee of $45,000. We did this in September of 2006, *before* he took any official steps to launch the Swiss venture. And his fee was paid in cash, not stock.

In a letter, signed on September 18, Rusch specifically agreed to serve as our "tax and business counsel." His letter also states, "We have agreed to advise and represent you as counsel in the following respects: International business planning, to include international joint ventures in Europe and general corporate services."

Rusch was our tax attorney, first and foremost. Anything else he was able to do for us business-wise would be gravy.

* * *

Rusch got things rolling in late 2006.

From a business point of view, we trusted his international experience to set up the corporate structures correctly. From a tax point of view, we trusted that the $90,000 we paid him as a tax attorney would keep us safe and compliant. Steve and I stayed in the background and let him do his thing. Again, we weren't interested in micromanaging this venture; it was Rusch's baby. All we wanted from him was to move things forward at a decent pace and to give us occasional status reports.

In retrospect, maybe it should have occurred to me that Rusch was putting himself in a position that created a potential conflict of interest. Serving as both our business planner and our attorney was probably not a great idea, but it didn't bother me at that time. To me it actually seemed convenient to have him playing both roles. If there was any conflict, it was *Rusch's* responsibility, as an attorney, to point that out. That is the duty of a lawyer. If there were legal/ethical issues with his wearing both hats, he should not have accepted the attorney fee.

Rusch's *potential* conflict of interest would later turn into an *actual* conflict and would be the reason he eventually had to stop serving as our lawyer.

But at that time, in 2006, we didn't have any qualms about the arrangement, and everything seemed to be going according to plan.

Rusch did all the initial corporate paperwork in a way that looked completely legal and standard. He set things up so that Steve and I would each own 4 percent of two separate banking entities. I don't remember how we came up with that specific percentage; I think Rusch proposed it and we went along with it. Steve and I truthfully didn't care what percentage we owned, as long as it didn't cross the 5 percent threshold. This thing *wasn't about ownership* to us; it was just an entry ticket to the Swiss investment banking community. But a hugely critical point to remember is this: As 4 percent owners, we were *not required to file FBAR reports or report the ownership to the IRS.*

Rusch proceeded to open holding accounts, two for each of us, in Switzerland. *He* directed all the money and assets, and he decided which banks to use. So the accounts were set up at UBS and Banque Pictet & Cie, respectively. The purpose of these accounts was to facilitate the sale of the stock. Rusch needed a place to hold the money, temporarily, until he could use it to set up his own bank. That was how Steve and I passively became account holders at UBS—a fateful occurrence, as it would turn out.

Chris initially had some trouble moving the stock we gave him—the people in Europe preferred cash—but then the Ecotality stock started heating up. Eventually he was able to sell the stock we gave him for several million dollars.

We knew he had done this, and after a while, we started wondering why things weren't moving a little faster in Switzerland. It wasn't a major concern for us by any means, and we weren't micromanagers, but we did make a couple of trips to Switzerland just to see how things were going. I think on one of those occasions we were in London anyway, so we just hopped over to Switzerland to see him.

On these trips, we met with some of the other key players involved. We were reassured to see that these people actually existed. Up till then, we'd had only Rusch's word for it. We were able to meet with an investor or two, as well, whom Chris introduced to us.

One of Rusch's strategies, which Steve and I agreed with, was to purchase two aged Swiss corporations to convert into our banks. The reason behind this was simple. We felt our banks would have more cachet in the banking community if they had a pedigree and some history behind them. So Rusch went shopping for some seasoned corporate entities that we could purchase. He found a couple of good ones. One of these was Swiss International Trust, which was established in 1959. Rusch paid $181,000 of our stock-sale money to acquire this company. Steve Kerr became a 4 percent owner in that one. The other was Swiss Fidelity International, established in 1981. For that one we paid $131,000, and I became the 4 percent owner. Both of these companies had the advantage of respectable-sounding names and existing corporate structures. Neither of the companies had any assets—there was nothing in them but their names and their historic existence—but that was all we were looking for. On one of our visits to Switzerland, we met with the people selling these companies, and everything seemed on the up and up. We were glad to see that Chris was spending some of the money from the sale of our stock and that the Swiss Venture seemed to be moving forward.

Seemed is the keyword here. The Swiss operation never ended up getting any real traction. But Rusch did end up accessing (read: stealing) a lot of our money.

I'll never know, I suppose, whether Rusch was planning to hoodwink us right from the beginning or not. Personally, I don't think so. I still like to believe that he had good intentions at first. I think he genuinely wanted the Swiss bank venture to fly. I also think he wanted to form a profitable, long-term relationship with Steve and me, not to screw us over. But then he just got in over his head. I think his failure to get things going in Switzerland probably stemmed from a combination of two things: a basic weakness of character—he couldn't resist the temptation to "appropriate" our money—and a lack of business competence. I mean, if he had been consciously angling to rip us off, he wouldn't have invested the money in buying those corporations, right? He would have found a way to keep it in his pocket.

Of course, a more cynical (perhaps realistic) person might say that this was all part of the con. A conman has to make some sacrifices to keep a con going, after all. That's how he builds your confidence. My later attorney Michael Minns believes Rusch was probably playing us all along or was at least setting things up so that if every-thing fell apart, we would be left holding the bag.

Maybe the truth is that I just don't like to believe I'm capable of being conned as badly as Rusch seems to have conned us.

But anyway, whenever we visited him or talked with him in 2006 and 2007, he seemed to be doing what he promised, and we had no reason to suspect he was not acting in good faith. And I can't emphasize this point enough: At that time, Steve and I were each making six or seven million a year, putting business deals together. That was where virtually all our attention was focused. That was one of the reasons we cut Rusch so much slack. We had neither the time, the bandwidth, the know-how, nor the interest to become more involved in Switzerland.

What I want to make clear, at the risk of repetition, is that it simply wasn't our role to manage the companies we invested in, once they had their hands on our money. All we did was make sure there were competent professionals in place to handle the early-stage management issues and the reporting requirements for the SEC. We never did *any* internal management with any of our investments, unless a problem came up. We were too busy setting up our next deal to worry about what was going on with the last one. We had bigger fish to fry. That was, in fact, *why we did* smaller deals. To get to bigger ones. With a firm like Brookstreet, for example, we might do a half-million-dollar bridge loan, and we wouldn't really care if the money got paid back. Why not? Because our *main* intent was to get in their door so we could bring bigger deals to them. That's how the Ecotality thing happened. On that one deal alone, we made enough money to dwarf our initial bridge loan investment. Nascent Wines was a similar situation. We ended up getting funding of about $100 million worth of investments through Brookstreet. The Swiss Venture was in the same category: a relatively small deal, made with stock that we had in surplus, in the hopes that we could walk larger deals through that door.

Were there red flags I should have noticed? Hard to say. It's true that after an initial flurry of activity, Chris was slow to get things done. Not slow enough to create major concerns, but slow enough to indicate that maybe he wasn't super-motivated to get this venture off the ground. Perhaps, in retrospect, I should have seen that he was enjoying access to our funds and was stalling on moving the business to a stage where oversight would certainly be tightened. Maybe I should have asked for more accounting of stock certificates, bank statements, etc. Perhaps I should have suspected that he was taking advantage of the fact that our minds were on other things. I don't know. But in 2006 and 2007, I had no reason to suspect any sort of nefarious intent. I had hoped he would move things along faster, yes, but his operation wasn't really on my radar screen.

As I've said more than once already—and will probably say again—a major factor working against me in my criminal case was that most people have a hard time believing that $2 or $3 million could fall off someone's radar. They assume I *must* have been scheming with the money. That's because the vast majority of Americans never deal in large amounts of cash or stock. At the risk of sounding elitist, most people (our eventual jury members included) go through their whole lifetime dealing only with the income they earn from their jobs. When they hear you say you've given someone millions of dollars' worth of stock to "play" with and don't really care what happens to it, they don't believe you. For Steve and me, though, the money we put into Switzerland was just a business write-off, like paying an electric bill. It was money already spent, and there was *much* more coming in.

The years 2007 and 2008 were especially prosperous for me. It was sometime in 2007, I believe, when I was out on the golf course, reviewing some of my accounts on my brand-new iPhone, when I realized I had reached the twenty-million-dollar goal I had set for myself when I began my investing career.

My reaction to this? I just said to myself, "Oh well, so I guess *that* happened," and headed on to the next hole. Twenty million no longer felt like a big deal.

So I was hardly losing sleep worrying about what Rusch was doing in 2007 and early 2008.

CHAPTER SIX

Zero Bandwidth

Perception is everything. I believe the main reason I was subjected to a criminal investigation, indictment, and trial was because the perception existed that I was a wheeler dealer who was defrauding the US government of tax money. Certain people within the government were so determined to see their perception validated that they were willing to stack the deck to ensure that outcome. And I believe the main reason I was assumed *guilty* in the case, by some members of the jury, is that the perception exists that the federal government only pursues cases against defendants who are guilty as sin. So if we were charged, we must be guilty. Of *something*.

Perception beats the crap out of reality, every time.

The *reality* is that I received no tax or monetary benefits whatsoever from the Swiss venture—in fact, it cost me money that will never be recovered—and that I had far too much going on in my life and my business for Chris Rusch's activities to warrant my attention.

The years 2006 and 2007, when Rusch was setting up the Swiss business, were among the busiest and craziest times in my life. First of all, there was the investment business I was involved in, with Steve Kerr as my some-time partner. Those were the years when everything was coming together for us. Our business model was working beautifully, and we were signing some of the biggest deals of our careers. We had eight or ten deals in development at once. We did Ecotality and

Nascent Wines during that period and were making more income *per year* than most people—even well-paid professionals—make in *an entire lifetime*. Try to wrap your mind around that. And we were doing it all completely legally and ethically, while happily paying the US Treasury all the tax money it was due. To put this incredible income stream at risk by doing a bush-league tax scam to save a few bucks would be like a top-paid NFL quarterback taking a $1,000 bribe from a bookie to throw a championship game—it makes no sense from a risk/reward perspective.

I sometimes think the only reason we did not make *even more* during that period was that there simply weren't more hours in the day. Both Steve and I were working our tails off. The opportunities were arising, and we were pursuing them. You see, once we had a couple of successful deals under our belts, companies started crawling out of the woodwork to work with us. As you'll recall, we offered a great value proposition to nascent (no pun intended) companies. Not only did we give them free business coaching, great contacts, and access to big-money brokerages and hedge funds, but we were also able to write them a seven-figure check on the spot, with no risk to them. So needless to say, we had a lot of suitors. Also, the brokerages, hedge funds, and investment bankers we worked with began bringing deals to us. We had to do due diligence on all these prospective deals in addition to managing all the deals we had in progress. And there were only two of us. So we were superbusy.

Steve was constantly on airplanes. He liked being on the road and enjoyed getting in front of new groups of investors, as well as pitching new deals to existing partners. He would sometimes get on a plane on a Monday and have no idea what state or country he'd end up in by Friday. I was the "hold down the fort" guy. I didn't travel extensively for work, but I probably spent nine or ten hours a day on the phone. Most of what I did was problem-solving and pulling pieces together—things like finding the right attorney for a particular offering, making sure everyone was following the securities laws, and making sure Steve and I were going to get our money paid back. There were tons of moving pieces in these deals. There were ownership issues around stock, shareholder disagreements on both sides of the deal, documents that constantly needed signing, and endless legal issues.

Getting the right attorneys involved was crucial. You could have all the parts lined up and then hire a lawyer who didn't know how to do his piece—or was too lazy or busy to get it done—and the whole deal could fall through. Much of my work revolved around "motivating" attorneys and accountants to get their jobs done promptly. Two companies could be ready to move on a merger, but if the paperwork wasn't done, the whole deal could evaporate in the blink of an eye. And if the deal didn't get done, Steve and I might never get paid back. So my job was lighting fires under people's butts and putting fires out.

What I'm trying to emphasize is that I had zero bandwidth, zero *need*, and zero motivation to be plotting an overseas scheme to save taxes on a minor cache of stock. I was too busy putting together twenty-million-dollar deals and making sure our existing deals didn't fall apart. The success or failure of any of these deals could make the difference of several million dollars in profits.

At the same time, I had a personal project going on that was sucking up what little "spare" bandwidth I had: I was building a new house. Vicki and I had decided to build our dream home along the fairway at Firerock Country Club. This was a 6,400-square-foot, $2.2 million home that we had custom designed to our specifications.

If you've ever been involved in building a custom-designed house, then you know it can be a full-time job, even if you have a building company managing many of the day-to-day details. And when you're building a house that's three times larger and more complicated than the average American home, then your workload and your aggravations triple.

I know what you're probably thinking, "Boo-hoo, break out the violins. Poor guy had problems while building his two-million-dollar mansion." And I totally agree with you. I was fortunate to be in a position where I could build a dream house for my wife and family—and I know that. But that didn't change the fact that it was a massive time and energy drain. The project was supposed to take eighteen months but ended up taking three and a half years. This wasn't the fault of Rusty, my good friend who built the house and did an amazing job. I would hire Rusty to build another house for me in a heartbeat.

But the fact is that at any given moment during a house construction, there are zillions of details that have to come together and dozens of people whose work needs to be coordinated—plumbers, pavers, decorators, roofers, landscapers, masons, tilers, drywallers, carpenters. And their work proceeds in dependency chains. The electrical work can't be done until the walls are in. The walls can't be done till the framing is complete. The frame can't be built till the foundation is in. You know the drill. If one thing is delayed, everything else has to be rescheduled. Murphy's law is in full effect. Whatever *can* go wrong does go wrong. People fail to show up, wrong parts are delivered, materials get stolen, workers show up drunk, and bad weather strikes at the most inopportune times.

Add to that the fact that in 2006/2007 you couldn't hire a contractor in the Scottsdale, Arizona, area. The housing boom was in full swing, and everyone in the construction trades had long waiting lists of customers. So you couldn't get anyone to *do* the work, and when you did, you'd have to wait for them to fit you in. And if *you* had to reschedule *them* for some reason, you might never see them again. It was a seller's market in the trades. We had to hire four different teams of framers just to get that job done, I remember. There was also a concrete shortage in Arizona, which meant we had to wait six weeks to get concrete delivered. The cabinet-making company (which I actually took public) had problems with its installation contractor, and I lost $40,000 on cabinets I'd ordered. And on and on.

I'm certainly not complaining. I was lucky to have the Firerock house—while it lasted (I was forced to sell it later when my business bit the dust)—and my construction problems weren't as bad as many of the nightmare stories I've heard. But between my superbusy investing business and building a new home, I was *occupied* nearly every second I wasn't sleeping or taking a break on the golf course. Even if I'd had the inclination to be running a criminal enterprise, I didn't have the damn *time*.

But there was something far more stressful going on in my life at that time. I was dealing with a health scare that threw me for a loop. It lasted for a few months, and it created a major distraction for me and my family. This happened in the fall of 2006, at the same time Rusch was putting the Swiss thing together—the time when I was supposedly masterminding a plot to defraud the government of tax money.

In the late summer of 2006, I began experiencing some bladder pain. I ignored it for a while, as guys will do, then finally went to see my doctor. After some poking and prodding, he recommended I schedule an ultrasound. So I did.

It was a routine procedure, and I wasn't too worried. I remember the sonographer chatting casually with me about the Cardinals as she prepped me and started the ultrasound process, and then seeing her face go pale as something on the video screen snagged her attention. Our small talk ended abruptly as she moved the transducer repeatedly over the same spot on my abdomen, studying the video screen intently.

"Something wrong?" I ventured.

"Well…I'm not permitted to discuss imagery with the patient," she said, forcing a smile that was not the least bit confidence inspiring. "You'll have to speak with your doctor. I wouldn't worry about it, though."

Right.

It was a long afternoon as I waited for the call. I couldn't concentrate on my work, so I ran some errands, did a workout at the gym, and paced the floor.

The call finally came when I was at home.

"We've found an abnormality," the doc explained. "It's a mass on your pancreas. Let's get you into the office and talk about it. For now, don't worry about it; I'm sure it's something we can deal with."

When I saw the doctor the next day, he looked about as cheerful as the sonographer had. He showed me some still pictures taken from the ultrasound session. There was a growth on my pancreas the size of a softball.

"It appears to be a cyst."

It sure did. "Is it…"

"Cancerous?" he filled in. "Hard to say, but you should talk to a gastro person, or maybe an oncologist. ASAP."

He made a referral for me with a gastroenterologist in my Blue Cross / Blue Shield network. While I waited for my appointment, I did the worst thing possible: went on the Internet. Want to convince yourself you have terminal cancer? Google whatever symptom you're experiencing. You'll find a gold mine of worst-case scenarios that inevitably lead to cancer. After a couple of hours of online research, I was terrified.

My appointment couldn't come soon enough.

"It's hard to tell with certainty from the images," the doctor explained. "But I'd put the odds that it's malignant somewhere around 40 percent." *Forty percent?* Holy crap. "We need to schedule surgery right away, Michael."

What *I* needed to schedule was a second opinion.

The second in-network doctor I saw, an oncologist, was even less optimistic. He put the odds of cancer at 50 percent. He also recommended immediate surgery and told me I would lose half my pancreas and my gall bladder in the process. My research had told me—and the doctor did not disagree—that the prognosis for patients with pancreatic cancer is around six to nine months.

Suddenly I was looking at fifty-fifty odds that I wouldn't be around in a year's time. This is a body blow to your emotions, as you can imagine. I was in the process of building my "dream house," my business was taking off, I had a wife I loved and was in the middle of raising three incredible daughters, and suddenly everything in my life was up for grabs. I realized I might not even be around to see the Firerock house *completed*, never mind live in it. The money I was making suddenly meant nothing to me at all. The idea of saying good-bye to my family was devastating beyond belief.

Vicki and I discussed the situation. She was calm and focused—at least she acted that way for me—and said, "You have to go to the Mayo."

Living near Phoenix, we are fortunate to have a main campus of the Mayo Clinic, one of the top diagnostic and treatment centers in the world, in our backyard. Vicki made an appointment for me at their organ transplant center. This was going to fall outside of our insurance network, but we agreed it didn't matter. We would pay cash if we had to. We decided to hold off on telling the girls there was anything seriously wrong until after I'd met with the Mayo staff.

There was about a two-week period where I lived with the fifty-fifty prognosis. When you're faced with the real possibility of your own demise, let me tell you, you go through some pretty intense self-examination. You evaluate your life with a new sense of urgency. Have you lived the way you wanted to live? Have you been true to your core values? What *are* your core values? What legacy do you plan you leave behind? How do you want your loved ones to remember you? If it turns out you do, in fact, have only months to live, how will you spend your remaining days?

I can tell you one thing you're *not* thinking about: How can I defraud the government of taxes by setting up a sham bank in Switzerland?

When I finally got to the Mayo—those two weeks felt like two years—they had some good news. They looked at the scans and concluded that the growth on my pancreas was only a pseudocyst, with mostly liquid inside. They told me they could take it off laparoscopically and that I wouldn't lose any organs. Best of all, they thought there was a less than 2 percent chance it was cancerous. What a relief.

Long story short, I checked into Mayo and had the surgery. The cyst was removed successfully, but unfortunately, that was not the end of the story. The pancreas, as you may know, is sponge-like in texture. It doesn't have a "skinned" surface that you can cleanly stitch up after surgery. So after pancreatic surgery, the big thing they worry about is a buildup of pancreatic fluid, as this indicates the organ isn't healing. At the Mayo, they were doing CAT scans every other day and were seeing a lot of pancreatic fluid, which wasn't good.

They wanted to admit me for an inpatient treatment. The basic idea was to starve me for ten days, in the hopes that the pancreas would shut down.

I checked myself in. They tried it; it didn't work. So they put a drain in my side and told me, "We're going to discharge you, and you can start eating again. But you're going to have to measure the fluid that comes out. It should slow down and stop. If it doesn't, we're going to have to operate again." This would mean getting the kind of surgery I was originally facing, which would entail losing my gall bladder and half my pancreas.

So I wore a drain bag on my side and tried to resume life as normal. I went golfing and did my usual things. Day after day, fluid continued to drain, and the volume didn't seem to be decreasing much. This wasn't looking good. Then, two days before I was due to have the aggressive surgery, the discharge finally stopped on its own. The drain was removed, and I kept my pancreas and gall bladder.

The bill from Mayo was around a hundred grand, but it was a price well worth paying to keep all my organs.

The bottom line, though, was that I spent about four months not knowing whether I was going to live or die. And remember, this was happening at the exact same time Chris Rusch was laying all the groundwork in Switzerland.

Let's just say my attention was…elsewhere.

Rusch stumbled through 2007, not gaining much momentum with the Swiss project. And then, of course, in late 2008, the bottom fell out of the world. The big crash of 2008 occurred.

The whole financial world went into a tailspin. It was a scary damn time, as I'm sure you recall. After months of trouble in the housing and credit markets, there was a *huge* drop in stock values. Over an eight-day period, the Dow tumbled almost 2,400 points; there was an 18 percent drop in a week. Everyone was comparing it to Black Monday in 1987 and the to 1929 crash that led to the Great Depression.

Everything in the financial world changed instantly. No one knew what the landscape would look like in the wake of the crash. Would investors be running scared, and if so, for how long? Would companies be stockpiling cash rather than taking new business risks? What would the new growth areas of the economy be?

No one knew. Certainly not I.

But one thing was for sure: I was no longer giving even a *wisp* of attention to what was going on over in Switzerland.

CHAPTER SEVEN

Crash

The major markets ended up going down by more than 30 percent that fall. To everyone in the financial sector, it seemed the world was coming to an end.

How did this affect me personally? To say it negatively affected my business would be like saying the tsunami of 2004 "negatively affected" the coast of Indonesia.

Like many people, I had much of my financial worth tied up in stocks, and suddenly the value of all that stock fell through the floor. Luckily, I had been through the crash of '87 and the "correction" of 2001 when the dot-com bubble burst, so I was mentally and emotionally—and financially—better prepared than most to face the crisis. But still, when you're watching your net worth circle the drain, and there's nothing you can do about it, you feel utterly powerless. Suddenly the entire banking and securities industries were in a shambles, and there was no way to make money in the investing business anymore. My work came to a standstill.

Unfortunately for me, I had also begun dabbling in real estate. As you know, the 2008 crash was caused by a collapse in the housing market (brought on by the explosion of subprime mortgages). So real estate was the last place you wanted to be when the crisis happened. I'd bought an office building in 2007, for which I had paid $2 million in cash. Over the course of the next two years, I watched its value plummet to $800,000. Like many others, I had borrowed against the building so that I could go out and buy more real estate. The way it worked during the housing bubble was that you could keep borrowing against the ever-increasing value of your property. You could actually *make* money by borrowing money. I did this for a while and bought some other properties. So that was good.

But then my building lost 60 percent of its value, and I had to pay back the loans. So that was bad.

But it turned out that my foray into the world of real estate— I'm not really a real estate guy—would lead to my next "big business idea." This was a venture that was initially quite successful, but then, thanks to my trust in Chris Rusch, it blew up in my face in a way that was more dramatic and devastating than I could have imagined.

The story gets a little complicated here, but it's important to understand what happened next so you can see how intimately Rusch was tied up in my finances, why I trusted and relied on the man as I did, and why it became such a huge problem for me when he turned out to be deceitful and incompetent.

I'll try to explain this next part in simple terms, and I promise it won't take too long.

Let's call this next phase of my career the real estate / hedge fund venture. The way it got started was that while the housing boom was still going on, friends of mine started bringing real estate deals to me because they found out I was funding them. So I started getting involved in financing real estate almost by accident.

It was going fine for a while, but then the bottom fell out of the housing market.

This was a crisis, obviously, but also an opportunity. Being a long-time investor, I was accustomed to looking for a silver lining in every market disaster. The heart of investing, I knew, was buy low, sell high. And whenever things went sour, as they obviously did in 2008, there were always plenty of opportunities to buy low. I was seeing $200,000 homes in Arizona selling at auction for $50,000. Though the real estate market had never really crashed like this before, it seemed inevitable that property values would eventually go up again. I knew this was a long-term investment opportunity, so I thought, "Why don't I raise some money locally and start a fund to buy some of these properties?" My previous investment business was going nowhere at the moment so this seemed to be a way to turn a bad situation into a good one.

But I didn't want to just flip houses; that was yesterday's news. As you may have surmised, I am not a conventional thinker. I saw an opportunity here to do more than just buy property and wait for its value to go up. I thought there was a way to start realizing some value immediately.

The plan was this: We would buy houses for $50,000 and spend $20,000–$30,000 to fix them up, turning each property we bought into the nicest house on the street. We'd put in new lawns and land-scaping, new carpets and tiles, new amenities, the whole works, then offer the homes for $110K. But here's where we differed from house flippers. We knew that in the wake of the real estate crash, many people could no longer get financed to buy a home. So our plan was to sell the houses to people who couldn't get normal financing. Our company would do the financing itself and would hold the paper until the homebuyer could get refinanced through an agency like the FHA. We were willing to work with buyers with credit scores as low as 500. We'd even hire a credit counselor at closing to hold their hand. Mike Stuck would do their tax returns, free, so they would be sure to get the $8,000 Obama first-time homebuyer's tax credit— and this credit would come in the form of a check from the govern-ment. The whole thing was a brilliant—if I do say so myself—setup in which everybody won. The client won by owning their own home with only 1 or 2 percent down. We, the short-term lender, won by fixing homebuyers' credit ratings and shoring them up financially with the tax credit. Mike Stuck won by getting a raft of new clients. And the whole community won by having neighborhoods improved and opening up home ownership to more people.

Vicki and I put in about $2.5 million dollars of our own money. I also approached some of my friends and business associates who had invested with me in the past and who trusted me (because I had always treated them fairly and honestly). Based on the strength of the business idea and my reputation, we were able to raise about another $3 million locally.

I realized this would be a perfect situation to call on some of that European investment money we had been trying to access. Remember, that had been the whole reason we'd given Rusch the green light to do the banking venture in Switzerland. With some European investment behind me, I thought I could take this enterprise to whole new heights.

So I gave Rusch a call. We didn't have our Swiss banking structure set up yet—that was dragging out indefinitely, especially since the crash—but I still figured he could put me in touch with some investors who might be interested in capitalizing on US housing opportunities. Rusch and I had several conversations, which boiled down to this:

"Chris, how are things going in Switzerland?"

"Well, as you know, everyone over there took a bath after the crash. So things have been stalled. No one wants to put up money for anything; they're all running scared. I'm *trying* to drum up interest, but it's going to be a while before—"

"Okay, okay, listen," I said, "I'm not calling to jump on your case about the Swiss bank situation. I've got a new venture I'm putting together." I explained the real estate idea to him. "I'm hoping you can put me in touch with some individual investors over there who might be interested."

"It sounds like a great idea, Mike. I think I might be able to generate some interest, but you've got a problem."

"Oh?"

"People in Europe won't go for it if you sell it to them as a direct real estate investment."

"Why's that?"

"Well, if a non-US resident buys property in the States, they get hit with a big penalty when they go to sell. That's why people don't like to do it. It ends up being a complicated and not-very-attractive investment for Europeans. But..." he paused and said, "there is a way to attract investors *in*directly."

"I'm listening."

"Here's what you do: You set up a hedge fund in the Cayman Islands. The *fund* then becomes the buyer of the properties. Investors in Europe become *shareholders in the fund*, not the actual purchasers of the real estate. Meanwhile, you're the manager of the fund, and you run all the operations from Arizona just as you normally would. For all practical purposes, it's a US company."

"Send me some info on it; I'll have to think about it."

The more I thought about the hedge fund idea, the more I liked it. As I said, I'm not a real estate person by nature. The businesses I understood were the hedge fund business and the securities business. I knew that my real money was not going to be made in the housing venture itself but rather in the hedge fund that supported it. If I could buy assets (houses) and increase their value, the total value of my assets would go up. Therefore, the value of my hedge fund would go up, and I would be able to attract more and larger investors to the fund. That's how all the big hedge funds get started; they bring in attractive returns for a few years, then the big money climbs aboard. I knew if I could show a 20 or 30 percent return for two or three years in a row, I could attract a *lot* of investment money. Even if could sustain at 12 or 15 percent, that would put me on the map, and I'd be off to the races.

I could easily envision building this fund into a $200 million venture, if I played my cards right and if I got European money involved. So my ultimate goal was not to succeed in real estate, but rather to *build the hedge fund*. If we set up the fund to handle any kind of assets, it could eventually invest in anything, once the real estate business cooled off.

But, of course, to build an attractive fund, you have to be able to create early returns, and that's far from easy. For me it meant that I needed to make sure the real estate venture was successful right out of the starting gate.

I called Rusch back, and we agreed that I would pay him $100,000 to set up a hedge fund for me in the Cayman Islands. Now, once again, I can guess what you're probably thinking: "This Quiel guy establishes a fund in the *Cayman Islands*; obviously he's planning another tax dodge." Nope, not at all.

Of course, everyone knows that the Caymans *are* used to avoid paying taxes. This typically occurs with securities. A US-run firm registers itself in the Caymans. It invests in US companies but keeps its stock certificates in the Caymans. Then it deposits the stock into a US brokerage account, sells it, and moves the cash back offshore, thus avoiding paying US taxes. It's fishy, I agree, but legal.

That is most assuredly *not* what I was doing. The only reason I set up my fund in the Caymans was because Rusch told me I had to do so in order to attract European investment. I had no intention of dodging any taxes, nor did I ever do so.

In fact, I made it clear from day 1, and Chris Rusch agreed with me, that I would pay both federal and Arizona state taxes on the real estate venture. And after 2009, our first year in business, I did, in fact, file both Arizona and US returns.

The great news, on the tax front, was that Chris Rusch—who helped me set up my business structure—told me that we would not have to pay tax on the *gains* our real estate enjoyed while we held it and improved it. That's because when you own an asset that gains value, you typically do not pay taxes on that gain until you do something that creates a *taxable event*, such as selling the asset. Rusch also told me we would not have to pay tax on our gains even when we sold the house *to the client*—because as the financers, we would still be holding the paper. Only when the *client* refinanced with another company, and the deal was completely out of our hands, would the gain count as profit for us and create a taxable event. Up till that point, all gains would be considered "phantom gains."

This was major for us. It meant that even though we would pay *some* taxes in our first year, a lot of our taxes would be deferred and paid later. This would allow us to post nice returns the first year we were in business, which would give the hedge fund an immediate boost. A great way to start.

So we got the business rolling. Naturally, homebuyers came crawling out of the woodwork to get the deal we were offering. Not only could previously unqualified buyers walk away with their own home, but they could also, thanks to Mike Stuck, walk away with an $8,000 check in their hands, courtesy of the first-time homebuyer tax credit. And they could do all this with little or no money down. Phoenix TV stations did news stories on us, and business-wise, we were kicking ass and taking names. The business was called Smart Safe Homes.

I still wanted to get European money involved, and that was never far from my mind. Now that we had the hedge fund structure in place that Rusch had recommended, and now that we'd raised about $5.5 to $6 million locally as a base for our fund, we seemed to be in a good position to go to Switzerland and raise more.

But everywhere we tried, we got shut down; everyone over there was still running scared because of the financial crisis.

I jumped all over Chris Rusch about this. The whole reason we'd funded his Swiss enterprise, I reminded him, was to get access to European investors. I'd set up the hedge fund the way he recommended, and I'd funded it very credibly, so where were the investors, damn it?

I asked Rusch if I could meet again with some of the bankers we'd met while we over in Switzerland. He hemmed and hawed and finally put me in touch with a couple of people, but they quickly turned out to be dead ends. I began to get very frustrated and let Rusch know it.

Finally, after further pestering, he was able to come up with a potential investor. "He read your materials," said Rusch, "and I think he wants in."

"How much does he want to invest?"

"One million, US"

"Not bad. What's this guy's name?"

"Jerome Perucchi."

The name sounded familiar. I seemed to recall him as one of the Swiss nationals who'd been involved with Rusch in the initial stages of the banking deal. "Great," I said. "Put him in touch with me, and we can have a conversation."

"Will do," said Rusch, then after a pause, he added, "Actually, why don't you let me handle Perucchi?" He explained that it might help his own credibility if he acted as the "face" of the deal in

Switzerland. I got the sense he wanted to prove to me that he could hold up his end.

"Really? You don't think I should talk to this guy or meet him?" I asked.

"You can meet him the next time you're in Europe, or when he's in the States. But I'll handle him for now. If all goes well, the funds should be in your account within a week or so."

I thought it a little strange that Chris didn't even want me to talk to the guy, but I was glad to see him taking the initiative and even gladder that he had finally delivered a "live" investor to me from across the pond. A million-dollar investment wasn't going to make or break us, but then again, it was nothing to sneeze at.

Not long afterward, the million dollars did indeed appear in our account. Rusch had delivered. It had taken some prodding, but he was *finally* getting actual European money on board. I hoped there would be more where that came from.

* * *

Before 2009 was over, I could tell it was going to be a banner year for Smart Safe Homes and the hedge fund. It was looking like we were going to post returns of 37 percent. A lot of that gain, again, was due to the fact that we hadn't had to pay taxes on our real estate's appreciation (except on the few properties that had been refinanced).

Toward the end of that year, 2009, I ran into some contacts of mine who, after hearing what I was up to, referred me to some money people in Luxembourg. This had nothing to do with Rusch; it was a totally separate thing. Based on how well my fund was doing, and on my reputation as a manager and investor, these Luxembourg folks told me they wanted to do a $3 billion offering with me, where I would manage a new fund they were setting up.

Just so you understand the magnitude of a $3 billion fund, this could represent a *$100 million* management fee for me, for the first year alone. Over twenty years, it could add up to $2 billion in fees. Yes, you read that right; billion with a *b*. So I think you understand now what I mean when I say the real estate venture was a means to an end, not an end in itself. There were far bigger fish to fry in the hedge fund world.

Here's how the Luxembourg fund was going to work: It planned to raise its money based on life insurance policies. These policies were already in existence, were 100 percent valid and vetted, and were in a category called life settlements. If you're not familiar with the concept, it's a situation where a financial entity, such as a hedge fund, purchases a person's life insurance policy for more than its cash value, but less than the death benefit. Buying people's life insurance policies sounds a little creepy, but there are many good reasons people decide to sell a policy—they want to replace it with a better one, the beneficiary dies, they can't afford the premiums anymore, or they just want the cash.

Once a life settlement is made, the buyer—the fund—becomes both the owner and the beneficiary of the policy. Then, when the person dies, the fund receives the death benefit. But…the buyer must also continue paying all the premiums until that happens. Life settlements are one of the more reliable investments out there—the payout is guaranteed, and the insured person is definitely going to expire at some point (usually sooner rather than later; settlements aren't offered to the young and healthy).

In the early part of this century, hedge funds were buying a lot of these life settlements. Often they would bundle these policies and trade them like stock certificates. So the policies would bounce from one hedge fund to another. There were billions and billions of dollars' worth of these policies floating around.

Then, what happened after the financial crisis was that everyone took their money out of hedge funds, so the funds were left holding all these life insurance policies, but they no longer had the cash on hand to continue paying the premiums. Suddenly the bottom fell out of the secondary market for life policies, and you could buy these policies for pennies on the dollar.

This was the basis of the offering in Luxembourg—the policies were already identified, vetted, and ready to go into fund, and they were available cheap. I registered in Luxembourg to do this $3 billion offering, and at the end of 2009/beginning of 2010, I was in serious talks with people over there about getting the thing funded.

So at the end of 2009, I was riding high. Not only had I survived the financial crisis, but I had found a way to turn it around. Television shows were doing stories about our company; we were buying, selling, and financing lots of houses. European money was starting to roll in, the hedge fund was doing great, and I was on the brink of putting together a deal in Luxembourg that would put me at a level of financial success I never could have dreamed of.

And Chris Rusch had played an integral role in the whole thing.

CHAPTER EIGHT

The Coming Storm

Little did I know, in fall of 2006, when Chris Rusch was setting up holding accounts for Steve Kerr and me at UBS in Switzerland, that events were already unfolding at UBS that would put me on a collision course with a major international incident. The consequences of that incident would land a mortal blow to Swiss banking secrecy and would also lead directly to my criminal indictment. Looking back now, it's as if I was driving a car that was destined to collide with a train I didn't see coming.

That train pulled out of its station on a June day in 2005, long before I even got behind the wheel of my car.

On that day in June, over a year before Rusch set up UBS bank accounts for Steve Kerr and me, a UBS banker in Switzerland by the name of Bradley Birkenfeld logged into his company's intranet and saw an internal document there that froze his blood. After reading that document, he began taking actions that would lead to his becoming the biggest financial whistleblower in US history and the first banker ever to lift the veil on secret Swiss banking practices. And as a direct result of his actions, my life was forever altered.

So how was it that Bradley Birkenfeld—a man I never met but whom I actually admire—managed to land *me* behind prison bars? It's a tangled tale, but indulge me.

* * *

Bradley Birkenfeld chanced into a banking career by way of a summer internship at State Street Bank, where his whistleblowing colors revealed themselves early. While working at State Street, he discovered some errors he believed the bank was attempting to cover up in a way that he believed amounted to fraud. He notified management, which failed to acknowledge any wrongdoing, and then eventually went to the FBI. But the feds apparently didn't understand the fine points of banking, and his employers didn't appreciate his meddling. He was put on probation and fired from that job.

Welcome to the wonderful world of whistleblowing.

Birkenfeld relocated to Switzerland, where he got his MBA and began working in the Swiss banking industry. He eventually made his way to UBS, where he became part of a wealth management team whose focus was on developing business in the United States. UBS wanted to reel in wealthy Americans who might be interested in the "advantages" (ahem) of banking in Switzerland.

So, to create mingling opportunities for its bankers among the elite, UBS would sponsor upscale events such as yacht races, concerts, and art shows. It would then fly its Swiss bankers to these events to rub shoulders with the wealthy attendees and drum up business. One technique used—according to a CNBC article published in 2015[1]— was to approach the oldest woman at the event and ask her to identify all the billionaires in the room; another was to stack parties with "two women to one man." The idea was for the UBS bankers to try to develop long-term relationships with these wealthy Americans. The ultimate goal was to market products that included investment vehicles and Swiss bank accounts that allowed account holders to

---

[1]   http://www.cnbc.com/2015/04/30/why-did-the-us-pay-this-former-swiss-banker-104m.html.

disguise their ownership through the use of shell corporations. The UBS bankers would "educate" US clients on tax strategies and help them set up these accounts.

Records show that in 2004 alone, UBS bankers made nearly 4,000 trips to the United States to meet with existing clients and develop new ones. Birkenfeld, in a *60 Minutes* interview, says it was common for the bankers to perform extracurricular services for their clients, such as buying them cars and shopping for them "at a concierge level." Birkenfeld himself once smuggled diamonds to a US client in a toothpaste tube. Large amounts of cash were often carried in and out of the United States for clients.

There was one little problem with UBS's international "marketing" practices. They were illegal as all hell. The law expressly forbids bankers not licensed in the United States to solicit business in the United States. UBS executives apparently knew about this but did nothing to inform their front-line employees about it.

In fact, management gave its bankers elaborate tips on how to avoid getting caught. Bankers were told to lie to US immigration officials and to say that they were in the country "on vacation" rather than on business trips. At training sessions, they were given role-playing exercises on how to navigate tricky situations. They were encouraged to do things like mail documents ahead of time rather than carry them through US customs and avoid using client names on electronic devices.

Bankers were even given encrypted laptops containing hidden client portfolios and product offerings. These laptops were often loaded with fake presentations and set up with self-destruct sequences, just like in a spy movie.

In fact, many of the bankers started to *feel* like undercover agents and became increasingly uncomfortable with what they were being asked to do.

One day, one of Bradley Birkenfeld's coworkers tipped him off to look on the bank's intranet. There he found a document tucked away, out of casual sight, called "Cross-Border Banking Activities into the United States." The document, which the traveling bankers had never been shown, was a set of guidelines for UBS employees.

It explained that UBS bankers in Switzerland were not allowed to provide cross-border services to US residents and spelled out several practices UBS was legally forbidden from engaging in. It stated that only products and services that were licensed and registered with the proper US authorities could be offered to US persons. It forbade establishing relationships with new clients residing in the United States as well as maintaining relationships with US clients, if doing so involved the use of mail, e-mail, telephone, advertising, the Internet, or personal visits. In a list of bullet points, the document stated that UBS should ensure, among other things, that

- no marketing or advertising activity targeted to US persons takes place in the United States,
- no solicitation of account opening takes place in the United States,
- no cold calling or prospecting into the United States takes place,
- no negotiating or concluding of contracts takes place in the United States,
- no carrying or transmitting of cash or other valuables of whatever nature out of the United States takes place; the same applies to actively organizing such transfers or attempting to circumvent this prohibition through other means.[2]

In short, the document described the *exact opposite* of what Birkenfeld's team was being trained and encouraged to do. Birkenfeld knew what he was looking at—a "cover your ass" document. If the shit ever hit the fan, UBS management could trot out this document as proof that it had made the law clear to its employees.

Birkenfeld was pissed, and understandably so. As a UBS banker who routinely conducted business in the United States, he felt he was in a highly compromised and vulnerable position. He and his

---

[2]   whistleblowers.org/storage/documents/Birkenfeld/initial_whistleblower_e-mails_and_memos.pdf.

colleagues were being encouraged to break the law. And yet, management had this document on file that it could use to throw them under the bus whenever necessary.

Birkenfeld confronted his boss about this, nearly getting in a fistfight. He was told not to rock the boat. He fired off memos to the heads of the compliance and legal departments at UBS, but got no response. After three months of deafening silence, Birkenfeld resigned from the bank. UBS followed up by sending him vaguely threatening letters reminding him that he was legally bound to keep bank secrets.

After leaving UBS, Birkenfeld had a disagreement with his former employer over a bonus he was owed. When UBS refused to pay it, Birkenfeld invoked whistleblower protection under the company's guidelines and demanded UBS look into its own cross-border banking practices. UBS did an internal investigation, agreed to change some of its policies, and also agreed to try to resolve the matter of Birkenfeld's bonus.

While that matter was still under dispute, Birkenfeld went to several US government agencies, including the DOJ, the IRS, and the Senate Subcommittee on Investigations. Now, it happened that at that time, the US government was already conducting a probe into several Swiss banks. To make a long story short, the information Bradley Birkenfeld was offering, including pointers to thousands of potentially tainted bank accounts, gave the US government some strong ammunition against UBS. The United States sought and gained permission from the Swiss government to travel to Switzerland to question UBS executives directly.

In a closed-door meeting on October 17, 2008, UBS admitted to wrongdoing in its international business practices and to helping defraud the IRS of tax money. UBS made it known that it wanted to settle the case and avoid a public international trial. The US government, for its part, made it known that it wanted UBS to give up the names of the American account holders. Of course, giving up the names of customers runs directly against Swiss banking law and is antithetical to everything Swiss banking stands for. So that was a major sticking point.

Finally, in February of 2009, UBS agreed to a settlement. It would pay the United States $780 million in fines and unpaid taxes. It would also give up the names of about 250 Americans who had accounts at UBS (even though it was illegal for them to do so under Swiss law and illegal for the United States to ask them). In return, UBS executives would be granted a "deferred prosecution" deal in which none of them would be tried or serve jail time.

How and why those 250 names were chosen will never be known, but—you probably guessed it—that's how I got drawn into the whole mess. I'll go into more detail on that shortly, but let's finish up the UBS story first. There were a couple of additional plot twists that indirectly affected my story and show you the kind of corruption and influence that was at work in this case, from top to bottom.

The day after UBS's settlement offer was put on the table, the IRS announced that it was suing UBS to cough up more names. The United States knew—thanks to Birkenfeld and others—that there were some fifty-two thousand accounts at UBS belonging to US citizens, including some highly prominent people. It wanted them all.

UBS now faced a tough choice: break Swiss law by giving up the names or endure a major lawsuit by the US government.

In early 2009, Hillary Clinton, a few weeks after being sworn in as secretary of state, was called in on an emergency basis to help resolve the dilemma. Although the dispute was between the IRS and UBS, Hillary persuaded the parties to settle the issue through the US-Swiss *treaty* process, rather than through the courts. In other words, the case was treated as an issue between the US and Swiss governments. The Swiss government made several diplomatic concessions to Hillary, and the United States agreed to accept a greatly reduced number of account holders' names—4,450 instead of 52,000. The final compromise—which was classified as a "peace treaty" (ha!)—allowed the deferred prosecution to stand, which meant that no one at UBS would have to answer for their actions. It also allowed—in my opinion, which I can't prove—thousands of politically connected and influential Americans to avoid having their accounts looked into. (According to Birkenfeld and others, American account holders at UBS included A-list movie stars and top politicians who were designated as PEPs—politically exposed persons—and given added secrecy and kid-glove treatment at the bank.)

The "treaty" was also patently illegal by Swiss law, but no one seemed to care.

Shortly after the deal was made, according to an article in *The Wall Street Journal* ("UBS Deal Shows Clinton's Complicated Ties," July 30, 2015), Bill Clinton received $1.5 million in speaking fees from UBS. Donations to the Clinton Foundation went up from less than $60,000 prior to 2008 to a total of $600,000 by 2014, and UBS lent out $32 million through programs launched by the Clinton Foundation.

Just a coincidence, I'm sure.

And what happened to Bradley Birkenfeld? Well, that's a fascinating story that's worth telling, at least briefly. It doesn't *directly* relate to my story, but it illustrates the deplorable conduct of the Department of Justice, conduct that played out in spades in my case as well. Birkenfeld's story also served as a cautionary tale for me as I tried to navigate my own case.

Birkenfeld's big mistake, it turned out, was going to the DOJ. He soon discovered, as I later would, that the DOJ is a lazy and inept agency that is more interested in getting easy convictions than in serving the greater good or conducting meaningful investigations. According to the CNBC article mentioned earlier, Birkenfeld says he offered to wear a wire for the DOJ, to give up the names and phone numbers of UBS bankers doing business in the United States, and to meet regularly with DOJ staffers. The DOJ didn't take him up on any of these offers. Rather, they treated him with hostility from the start, figuring he was an easy target to prosecute—after all, he had walked right in their door. Instead of recognizing him as an absolute *gold mine* of valuable inside information on the Swiss banking industry, they made him do a "proffer." A proffer is a formal offer of information made by someone who is under criminal investigation by the feds, with the understanding that the person will receive some protection from prosecution.

During the proffer process, Birkenfeld gave up the names of *some* of his clients at UBS, but, the DOJ alleged, he failed to give up the name of his biggest client, a California-based Russian billionaire named Igor Olenicoff, who was believed to owe the IRS vast sums of money. And so the DOJ indicted *Birkenfeld.*

Under pressure, Birkenfeld pled guilty to one case of defrauding the US government. Despite a well-publicized wave of opinion that sending Birkenfeld to prison would discourage an entire generation of whistleblowers from coming forward, the DOJ stuck to its nearsighted agenda and pushed for jail time for him. On August 21, 2009, Birkenfeld was sentenced to forty months in prison and a fine of $30,000.

So, just to recap: None of the UBS execs involved in the crime of hiding money from the IRS were charged. Olenicoff cut himself a walk-free deal by writing a check to the IRS. Most of the influential account holders at UBS never had to face exposure or prosecution. And the over fourteen thousand Americans with Swiss accounts who voluntarily came forward in the wake of Birkenfeld's whistleblowing were given amnesty-type treatment. The one person who had the balls to come forward at the expense of his own career—*and* who gave the government inside information that led to billions of dollars in recovered taxes for the United States—was sent to prison.

And here's the real stinger. Birkenfeld *tried* to tell the DOJ about Olenicoff and, in fact, *did* tell the Senate subcommittee about him. When Birkenfeld first came forward, he asked the DOJ to subpoena him so that he could turn over names. Why? Because he was living in Switzerland and it was *illegal* under Swiss law for him to turn over bank customer names. Only a subpoena would free him to do so. But the DOJ failed to subpoena him.

There is, however, clear evidence that Birkenfeld *did* talk to the Senate Permanent Subcommittee on Investigations in 2007 and that he did reveal Olenicoff as one of his clients. Well, then, you might ask, how is it possible that the DOJ was able to jail Birkenfeld on the basis of withholding information that the evidence clearly shows he did not withhold? And why would DOJ prosecutors choose to make an enemy of the goose that could have kept laying platinum eggs for them?

How and why indeed. I think you'll find yourself asking the same kind of mind-boggling questions after you see the evidence in my case.

As for Birkenfeld, he got the last laugh. The government, you see, offers a whistleblower reward "to people who provide specific and credible information to the IRS" about noncompliant taxpayers. How much? According to the IRS's website, "If the taxes, penalties, interest and other amounts in dispute exceed $2 million, and a few other qualifications are met, the IRS will pay 15 percent to 30 percent of the amount collected." And so Birkenfeld's lawyers immediately went to work trying to secure him his earned reward. Needless to say, the government fought them tooth and nail, claiming that because Birkenfeld did not "give complete and truthful disclosures" (source: *Wikipedia*), he was not entitled to whistleblower status. The government, however, lost its bid. Five or six weeks after Birkenfeld was paroled from prison, having served thirty of his forty months, he was presented with a check from the US Treasury for $104 million.

This amount was based on his share of the $780 million that UBS had ponied up. Of course, it should have been more, a *lot* more; the IRS has reportedly collected over $7 billion in unpaid taxes, thanks to the Birkenfeld affair. But it's not bad for a last laugh.

Will I have my own last laugh? Only the future will tell.

But in late 2009 / early 2010—the part of the story we're going to look at next—I hadn't yet had my fateful collision with the DOJ train. That train was still steaming down the track, headed straight for me.

CHAPTER NINE

Showing Up on the Radar

I started hearing about the UBS story the same way everyone else did: on the evening news. It didn't register as a cause for concern, at least at first. But then it started tickling something in the back of my mind. I remembered meeting with some banks when Steve Kerr and I had gone to Switzerland back in '06, and I thought UBS might have been one of them, but I wasn't really sure. I hadn't given Switzerland much thought since the financial meltdown. And now, in late 2009, Smart Safe Homes was enjoying a banner year, and I was trying to put the past behind me. I'd hired several employees, and we were going full steam ahead. We had taken over half of the office building I owned and were getting TV coverage and more customers than we could handle. I was focused on the here and now.

Still, the news stories were troubling. There was talk of UBS handing over five thousand American names associated with Swiss bank accounts. I talked to Steve Kerr, and he echoed my concerns. It was probably nothing, but still…

We called Chris Rusch and put him on speaker so we could talk to him together. I don't remember the exact conversation, but the gist of it was this:

"Chris, we've been hearing some pretty scary stuff coming out of Switzerland. We're just calling to make sure we don't have anything to worry about."

"Oh, we're fine," said Rusch. We heard him get up and quickly close a door. "They're only targeting the accounts of Americans who are hiding assets. Not people like us."

"Are you sure about that?"

"Absolutely, guys," he said. "Don't give it another thought."

I grilled him on a few specific aspects of the corporate paperwork, and he seemed to have ready answers.

"All the i's dotted and t's crossed, then?" asked Steve. "Nothing that can come back and bite us in the ass?"

"Nothing. We're good. Go golfing. Eat a cheeseburger. Relax."

Rusch sounded calm and confident. Besides, he knew the ins and outs of the Swiss operation a lot better than we did, so we basically had to take him at his word.

"If you want," he offered, "I'll double check with Pierre Gabris, make sure he hasn't picked up anything through the grapevine."

"Yeah, would you do that and get back to us ASAP?"

Pierre Gabris was the money manager in Switzerland. He was the one who handled the actual assets—the stocks and the cash from the conversion of the stocks—so he was the person closest to the actual UBS accounts.

Within a day or two, we heard back from Rusch, either by phone or e-mail; I don't recall. He said Gabris had confirmed his opinion that we had nothing to worry about. The DOJ was looking only at specific cases of people who'd been flagged for having specific issues. We didn't fit the profile. Also, our accounts were corporate accounts, and the DOJ was looking mainly at personal accounts.

I was relieved to hear that we were in the clear—there was no reason we *shouldn't* be, as far as I knew—and that Rusch's opinion was backed up by Pierre, the guy who had actual boots on the ground in Switzerland. But still, my Belize experience had left me a bit shellshocked and leery. I knew that government agents were capable of grossly misinterpreting paperwork and that problems could snowball as a result. I feared that if our documents weren't 100 percent in order, we could have issues.

Rusch and I had many, many of the same kind of conversation. I probably called him two dozen times in late 2009 and early

2010. Every time I heard a new piece of news or rumor on the UBS front, I'd call him again, and he would assure me that everything was kosher. I believed him, but at the same time, I was worried that our business setup over there was one that could invite government snooping. At one point I even flew to San Diego to talk to Rusch in person. I grilled him on what he was doing to ensure our safety.

"I can jump on a plane to Switzerland right now," he said, "and nail down every last tiny piece of paper, if you want."

"Then why haven't you done that already?" I asked, raising my voice at him for the first time I can recall. His lack of urgency was baffling to me, and I didn't feel good about it.

You might be wondering, then, why I didn't get a second opinion on the Swiss situation. A logical question. In fact, a couple of years later, as we were preparing for trial—in 2012—we did a mock trial to try to anticipate the kinds of issues a jury might have, and that was a question that came up repeatedly for the mock jurors: why didn't you guys get a second opinion?

Well, you have to understand a couple of things. Number 1, we didn't have any reason to think there was a problem. We were understandably nervous about having Swiss accounts, but we kept getting assurances from our lawyer—the person we'd hired to make sure there *were* no issues—that everything was fine. And when your lawyer tells you it's all good, there's no reason to run out and get a second opinion. Number 2, we were not the owners or managers of the Swiss corporation. The way I sometimes explain it to people is this: Imagine you've bought shares in a money market account. One day you find out *you're* under investigation for tax evasion because one of the companies the fund is invested in has come under fire. Does that seem reasonable? Our situation was very similar. We had a small minority investment in a vehicle that someone else was running and that had been inactive for some time.

In retrospect, of course, I wish I had been more aggressive and gotten copies of *all* our Swiss paperwork a lot sooner, but I was busy growing Smart Safe Homes and my hedge fund, and I still had faith in Rusch.

Hindsight is...well, you know.

* * *

Toward the end of 2009, Mike Stuck questioned me about how we were going to handle the taxes on our real estate gains for Smart Safe Homes. I explained to him the "phantom gains" concept that Rusch had laid out for me. "Fine," he said, "but we're going to need an opinion letter we can put on file for the IRS."

I asked Rusch to provide me a letter stating his legal opinion about the tax situation. "I've already reported over a 30 percent return for our fund," I reminded him. "Your letter had better confirm that we're handling our taxes the right way."

"It will and you are," he said. "Don't worry about it."

He wrote the opinion letter. Stuck thought it looked fine—he and Rusch were talking directly to each other by this time—and we filed our 2009 taxes accordingly. Our hedge fund investors were delighted with the year we had.

I continued to feel some mild anxiety about the UBS situation, but Rusch and Gabris continued to send us assurances that we were fine. So all was good.

In March of 2010 I got a phone call from Mike Stuck that sent my life spinning in a whole new direction.

"Mike," he said to me, "I've got something I need to talk to you about, and you're not going to like it."

"So what else is new?" I joked. "I never like what you have to say."

"No, this is serious. You're probably going to want to sit down."

Oh, jeez.

"You're under investigation by the DOJ," he said.

"What?" My heart did a little swan dive into my belly. *DOJ* is not a set of letters you ever want to hear paired with your own name.

"An agent by the name of Lisa Giovanelli came to my office back in November," he said, "and asked to see some records. She specifically instructed me not to tell you she was here. I'm sorry, Mike, my hands were tied. I didn't know what to do."

"It's okay. You did what you had to do. Why are you telling me now?"

"Well, the whole thing hasn't been sitting right with me. I like you, and I value you as a client. So I asked my lawyer for a legal opinion. He said I'm in the clear, legally, to discuss this with you. As soon as he told me that, I called you."

"So what are these DOJ people looking into?"

"Mostly your offshore stuff, the account at UBS specifically."

Exactly what I'd been afraid of ever since I'd heard the UBS story. Had my name been among the 250 that had already been handed over as part of UBS's settlement with the United States?

I went into a panic.

After hanging up with Stuck, I jumped on the phone with Rusch. He continued to act annoyingly calm and collected.

"You have nothing to worry about," he assured me. "They're only looking into certain kinds of accounts."

"Then why the hell are they knocking on my door?" I demanded to know. "Just because they're feeling neighborly?"

"It's just a fishing expedition," he explained. "They're sniffing around a lot of people right now. When they don't find what they're looking for, they'll go away. Our accounts are all in order."

"Can you go see them and tell them that?"

"I'll talk to them when and if it's appropriate, but now isn't the time."

"What do you mean now isn't the time?" I shouted. "They're prowling around my accountant's office behind my back. Just go talk to them and clear the whole thing up."

"That's not how it works, Mike. You don't go to these people and *talk*. They can use anything you say against you."

"Come on, Chris. Please, I *need* you to do this."

There was an uncomfortable pause. "Let me look into it," he said. "Maybe I'll reach out to them if it seems like a good idea." He was trying to end the conversation. There was something he wasn't telling me.

After my conversation with Rusch, I started looking at the whole situation with a fresh pair of eyes. For the first time, I began to realize what a mistake it might have been to put Rusch in a position where he was both managing the Swiss bank operation and also serving as my lawyer. At the time I hired him, I thought his wearing both hats would be a way to ensure that everything was done to the letter of the law, but now I could see the seeds of a possible conflict. If the government found problems with the way he was handling things over there, mightn't Rusch take steps to save his own ass? In that case, mightn't he start doing what was best for himself, not for his client—namely, me?

I began to get a bad gut feeling about Rusch. The wheels hadn't come off that bus yet, but a couple of the lug nuts were definitely loose. I suddenly felt very stupid for having put so much faith in him. Not only had I placed millions of dollars' worth of stock in his hands, but I had also relied on his guidance for setting up the Cayman Islands entity and for giving me the tax strategy from which much of the success of the real estate venture was now flowing. I began to see how easily my whole life could come apart at the seams if it turned out Rusch was just a charlatan or a conman, or both. Why had I trusted him so much?

I found myself rapidly losing faith in the opinion letter Rusch had written for the real estate venture. I realized I'd better get a second opinion on that, and so I contacted an attorney named Steve Silver, a local tax attorney with a good reputation. He reviewed my materials and, just as I feared, reported back to me that Rusch's opinion letter was flawed. In *Silver's* opinion, which he was quite adamant about, the sales of the houses to the clients of Smart Safe Homes *did* trigger a taxable event for us. Therefore, we *did* owe tax on all the value the properties had gained while we held them.

Fuck.

Not to put too fine a point on it.

Silver told me I owed $670,000 in additional taxes for 2009— $550,000 to the federal government and $120,000 to the state of Arizona. (As a side note, Silver also told me that because the mortgages had since decreased in value, he could roll the losses back to prior years. I paid the $670K in taxes, only to later learn that Arizona had stopped allowing rollbacks six months before Silver gave me that advice. Ah, lawyers—that's why we say they're only "practicing." As a result of Silver's mess up, I vastly *over*paid my 2009 taxes. I now have a huge credit with the IRS, which, by the way, I have never requested to be paid back.)

Anyway, the bottom line was that Rusch had hosed me. In more ways than one. As you know, I had already told my Real Estate Venture Fund investors that we'd posted a great return for 2009. Now, thanks to Rusch, I was under criminal investigation and also had to redo my 2009 taxes, which was going to substantially lower the return on the fund. I could see the writing on the wall. The fund was in trouble. It wasn't going to attract any big investors. The Luxembourg deal was probably dead. That meant I would have to go to my investors and come clean. Remember, these people were my friends and close business associates. I couldn't let them take the hit for my misjudgment in hiring Rusch.

Vicki and I discussed the situation, and we both fully agreed: We would have to make our hedge fund investors whole. I went to each of them and told them I didn't know how I would do it, but I would pay back their initial investment, plus interest. I knew my reputation was my greatest asset, and I didn't want any of these good people regretting doing business with me.

The reactions of many of the investors surprised me. One, for example, said to me, "Mike, I invested in your fund because I have faith in you. I knew it was a risk, like all investments are. It's not your fault this Rusch character took you for a ride. As far as I'm concerned, you don't owe me a penny." Others echoed this sentiment.

While it may have been *technically* true that I didn't owe them money, leaving my investors high and dry would not have been the right thing to do. So I didn't feel it was an option. I'm not tooting my own horn here, but throughout my career, I have always bent over backward to do what I believed was right. I was always aware that the securities and investing businesses had a slightly shady reputation, so I felt I had to go the extra mile to distance myself from the bad players. I felt I had to be *more* honest and forthright than anyone else. And that was how I intended to handle this situation.

88

After I paid the $670K in taxes, the fund, of course, went backward. It dropped about 40 percent from its highest point, which meant it was down about 25 or 30 percent overall. Over the next year or so, I had to let all my Smart Safe Homes employees go. I had to move my business back to my home office, from the big office building where we'd taken up half the space. Finally I had to shut the fund down completely.

But even in the face of this, Vicki and I went to each of the investors and wrote them a check—with our own money—for their stock, adding in a 5 percent return. This was incredibly hard for us to do because our income was uncertain, we didn't know if the government was going to seize our assets, and we didn't know if men with guns were going to burst into our house to arrest me (and/or Vicki) at any time. But we felt that paying our investors back was the right thing to do. I believed then, as I continue to believe now, that if you do the right thing, everything will come out in the wash.

It might take a while, though.

Which brings us back to early 2010:

In April of that year, Rusch pulled a head scratcher of a stunt that sent us caroming off in yet another bad direction. Unbeknownst to me, he received a grand jury subpoena from the DOJ. The legal notice demanded he turn over records on our Swiss accounts and stocks. Without telling me he was going to do this, he sent the DOJ a huge pile of my records. This was the wrong move on so many levels.

When I found out what he had done, my head nearly exploded. The phone conversation, to the best of my recollection, went something like this:

"What the hell were you thinking, Rusch? Why did you comply?"

"It was a subpoena, Mike, not a request for charitable donations."

"But those were *my* records, not yours. You had no right to make that decision for me!"

"I did what I thought was in all of our best interests," he replied, then paused for just a hitch. "After all, we're all in this together."

I didn't like the sound of that. "What about attorney-client privilege?" I asked. It was my understanding that the government was not supposed to be able to subpoena a client's records from a lawyer without a court order. "As my attorney, I thought you were supposed to *avoid* providing testimony against me!"

"Sometimes the best strategy is to give them too much information, not too little. Overwhelm them with paper. Then they don't know where to look."

"Where to look for *what*? Didn't you tell me all our paperwork was clean?"

"It is, it is. And by giving them a little of everything, they'll be able to see that. They'll see that we ran a clean ship and did everything right."

"What do you mean by 'a little of everything'? What the hell did you send them, Chris?"

He hesitated for a moment. "Well, an assortment of stuff—on all of our dealings together."

"You sent them records on the family trust? The charitable foundation? The Cayman fund? All of it?"

"It's just white noise to them, Mike. They don't care about all those things."

"But, Chris, think about it. Now the DOJ has information on my family, on my Cayman fund, on everything. The DOJ, for crying out loud! Have you ever read anything about these guys? They'll use anything they can get their hands on to *create* a case against you. You should never, never send the DOJ 'bonus materials'!"

"I'm sorry, Mike, I—"

"Send me copies of everything you sent to them. Can you at least do that for me? I am very fucking pissed at you, Chris, very fucking pissed."

I hung up, my head spinning. I still couldn't figure out why, as a lawyer, Rusch had rolled over so easily. It was almost as if he had *volunteered* my records to the DOJ! His actions didn't make any sense.

At that time, though, I thought all I was dealing with was incompetence. I still trusted the guy's basic integrity. I'd worked with him for four years and thought I knew him pretty well. It didn't occur to me that my own lawyer could be actively plotting against me.

CHAPTER TEN

Under Investigation

Being under criminal investigation by the DOJ is not as fun as it sounds.

In my case, the investigation went on for about two years before charges were brought by a grand jury. (A grand jury, in case you've never had the pleasure of being criminally indicted, is a group of citizens that oversees an investigation and recommends whether or not to bring criminal charges.)

When a criminal investigation is going on, your peace of mind takes a hike and anxiety moves into your life like a guest who won't leave. You know the investigation is plodding along, but you are powerless to affect the process in any way. In fact, you are legally prohibited from doing anything to interfere. The closest thing I can compare it to is being diagnosed with a serious medical condition. You can't control the outcome; all you can do is arm yourself with good information, take care of yourself, talk to your loved ones, prepare for any eventuality, and try to live your life as normally as you can. Meantime, you know the disease might sneak up on you anytime, anywhere, and stop your heart.

It was important for me to try to control the things I could control. That's why one of the first things I did, when I learned I was under investigation, was take my computer to a security specialist to have the hard drive backed up. I wanted to make sure there was a dated record of the exact contents of my computer, one that would stand up to forensic examination, so that I could not be accused of altering my records in any way, shape, or form. I knew I hadn't done anything wrong, and I wanted to have undoctored evidence of my e-mails, my financial records, my personal writings, and my tax history available to the court. (Contrast this with Hillary Clinton's behavior. Upon learning that her e-mails might come under investigation, she promptly deleted her computer's contents.)

I also began a habit of doing online research. I wanted to gather as much "intelligence" as possible so that I could be mentally and emotionally prepared for what lay ahead, and also so I wouldn't make any stupid, easily avoidable mistakes. I researched the law; I researched the IRS, the DOJ, and the federal court system. I compulsively searched the Internet to learn more about other people who were having run-ins with the DOJ.

One of my go-to sources was a website called Federal Tax Crimes, a blog run by an attorney out of Texas named Jack Townsend. Townsend was a former DOJ prosecutor—so I took his advice with a grain of salt—but he seemed like a pretty honest and forthright guy. Townsend's site posted a public record of federal tax crime prosecutions, including the most detailed information on offshore tax cases that I could find anywhere. He was trying to track the cases of some of the other people whose names had been surrendered by UBS.

Townsend posted alarming statistics on his site, such as the fact that in 2009 and 2010, the government had almost a 90 percent conviction rate in tax crime cases, and in roughly 80 percent of those cases the defendant served jail time. *Jail time!* I learned that federal tax cases typically dragged on for years, usually without a happy ending for the defendant. This was far from encouraging news.

It became clear to me that my preconceptions about how alleged tax evaders are treated in the legal system were dead wrong. I had always heard, among friends and attorneys, sentiments like, "It's all about the money for the IRS. They're not interested in sending people to jail; they just want their back taxes. The IRS is *always* open to settlements."

Well, that may or may not be true when your case is still in the *hands* of the IRS. But once the DOJ gets its mitts on you, all it cares about is prosecuting you criminally to the fullest extent of the law. As far as the DOJ is concerned, you are in the same category as mobsters, murderers, drug dealers, and counterfeiters.

It's not "all about the money" to the DOJ. The people at the DOJ have absolutely zero interest in filling the government's tax coffers; they want to get *you*. But yet, in another sense, it *is* about the money: the money in their paycheck envelopes. And the way they get more of that is through high conviction rates. DOJ prosecutors, I was learning through my research, earn their stripes—i.e., their raises and promotions—by sending people to jail.

Before I came under investigation, I knew nothing about the DOJ except that it existed, and knew very little about the IRS either. I had no idea how the two agencies worked together. But as I did my research, I began to learn how they're *supposed* to work. Every IRS or SEC case is supposed to begin with an internal review to determine whether anything in fact has been done wrong. Pretty logical, right—before charging someone with robbing a bank, you should first find out whether a bank has actually been robbed. The process is supposed to be *in*ductive rather than *de*ductive. In other words, they're not supposed to start with the supposition that wrongdoing has taken place and then gather evidence to prove it; they're supposed to look at the facts and the evidence. And then *if*, and only *if*, a problem is discovered to exist, they're supposed to make a referral to the DOJ.

If that process had played out for Steve and me, our whole nightmare would have been stopped in its tracks. The IRS would have seen that we did everything 100 percent correctly and would not have had an issue with us. Assuming Steve and I each owned only 4 percent of the Swiss corporations—which was factually the case—then we did all our tax filings right. Period.

But because our names popped up on UBS's list, and because US prosecutors were willing to deprive American citizens of due process so that UBS bankers in Switzerland could continue golfing and sailing without interruption, our case went straight to the DOJ.

Once a case is in the hands of the DOJ, I was learning, it is treated purely in a criminal light. The DOJ has neither the means, nor the desire, to do an internal review. It doesn't *want* to hear evidence that might exonerate you. It operates in "let's send them to jail" mode, not "let's examine the facts" mode. And here's the worst part: *No mechanism exists* for throwing the case back to the IRS for a review. Once the DOJ gets the case, it is on a one-way track: the criminal track. The DOJ is going to try to prove you robbed a bank, regardless of whether a bank has been robbed or not.

Learning this kind of information was a double-edged sword. On one hand, it opened my eyes to reality and helped prepare me to face any attack the government might mount against me. On the other hand, it threw a hardball at my mental and emotional health. It spelled the end of peaceful sleep and the end of the illusion that this problem might go away with minimal disruption to my family and me.

Some of the most disturbing research I did involved actual tax crime cases. Reading reports about real people's real experiences with the IRS and DOJ revealed to me the depths to which the government was willing to sink in order to bag suspected tax evaders. A couple of the cases I read still stand out in my mind.

One of these was the case of Robert Kahre. He was a businessman who had a clever idea to help him and his employees reduce their tax burden. He decided to pay his employees as contractors, using gold and silver coins *at the face value of the coins.* For example, he might pay a worker four fifty-dollar gold coins at a face value of $200. This meant the pay amount fell below the reporting requirements for 1099 employees, so Kahre didn't report it and neither did the employee. Of course, the fair market value of these coins was around $5,000, and the employees would cash them in for that amount. A sleazy tactic? Well, it depends on your political opinions.

Kahre knew what he was doing; he was testing the government's double standard. You see, gold and silver coins are clearly marked, *by the US mint* itself, as legal tender with specific denominations. You can legally spend a $50 gold coin at a store, and if you do, you cannot demand the store give you $1,500 worth of merchandise—nope, you're using the coin at its face value, not its market value. If that's true, then shouldn't an employer be entitled to pay his employees with coins at their legal face value? Kahre thought so. Of course, he knew the government would probably disagree, so he hired an independent legal researcher who provided him with well-documented support that what he was doing was legal. So Kahre claimed he was not intentionally breaking the law.

Not surprisingly, the IRS disagreed. What *is* surprising, though, is how it handled the case. A government SWAT team broke down Kahre's gates *with an armored vehicle*. On a swelteringly hot day, his employees were handcuffed and held in the sun without water, while agents with guns drawn searched Kahre's premises and seized his business records. Kahre was convicted of hiding assets, tax evasion, and conspiracy to defraud the IRS. He was sentenced to fifteen years in prison, a sentence he is currently serving. Holy guacamole.

You might agree or disagree with what Kahre did, but a SWAT team and fifteen years in prison for following the letter of the law? Really?

Another case involved a CPA named James Simon. While he was away on a business trip, his wife Denise was helping their ten-year-old daughter get ready for school when about a dozen armed IRS agents wearing flak jackets stormed their home without warning. According to the website RememberDenise.org, the Simons "had not been contacted by any government representative about any legal concerns before the raid, nor had they received any summons or subpoenas requesting documents or questions to be answered. They had not been in trouble with the federal government before" and "simply were unaware the IRS had any concerns about their income tax returns."

The raid of the Simons' home went on all day. Three days later, Denise Simon typed a suicide note and took her own life. The final line of the note, written by hand, was, "With my dying breath, I swear Jim and I are innocent." Whether the Simons were innocent or not—and I, for one, am willing to give them the benefit of the doubt—it is tough to justify the heavy-handed tactics of the IRS agents.

These stories, and others like them—Bradley Birkenfeld's, for example—were scaring the living crap out of me. My biggest fear was that government agents with AK47s would bust down my doors and drag me out in front of my family. I'm not kidding. I worried about being ruined financially too, of course, but my main fear was that I or Vicki or both of us would be arrested in front of the kids and that we'd end up in jail, leaving our kids parentless.

These fears gave way to generalized feelings of paranoia. I started thinking I was being followed. I found myself eyeing strangers at the grocery store and taking evasive routes when driving my car. Our house at Firerock was finished by this time, and we were trying to live in it. But it was perched on a hill and had a lot of glass. We started to feel like we were living in a fishbowl and often kept the blinds down instead of enjoying the view (which had been our main reason for building the house where we did). There was one three-month period where we kept the blinds drawn the entire time, night and day; we felt like we were living in a cave. At one point, I became sure that the place was bugged and had it swept by a security team. Another time, Vicki caught someone on a nearby hill taking photos of our house. We reported it to the security people at our development, but were never 100 percent satisfied with the answer they gave us. Steve Kerr caught someone taking photos of an aircraft he owned around the same time.

It was hard to know whether our concerns were real or imaginary or a little of both. In the end, it made no difference; they were having the same effect on our lives.

Another factor stoking the flames of fear and paranoia was that many of my former shareholders were being contacted by the DOJ. These were people I had done business with a few years earlier. These folks had sold their stock to me, and in many cases, their names were still on the stock certificates that had been sent over to Rusch in Switzerland. Though I had legally purchased the stock from them and owned it outright, the stock went overseas with their names on it, and this was stirring up suspicion in the DOJ ranks.

Again, it came down to the fact that the investigators didn't understand the world they were dealing with and weren't interested in talking to me so I could enlighten them. Here's the deal. Every stock has a title. When you buy a stock, you might not bother transferring that title to yourself, at least for a while. So you own the stock, but the title might still carry the former owner's name. It's kind of like what happens in the used-car business. A dealer buys a car from someone, and he throws the title in a drawer, figuring the name on the title will get transferred later when someone else buys that car. Most dealers don't go to the bother of transferring the title to themselves, only to transfer it again to the customer who buys the car.

Handling car titles this way is perfectly legal. Same thing with stocks. I often wouldn't bother to transfer titles. Why? Because it costs money and effort to do so. So I'd just hold the certificates in their original names, figuring I was only going to transfer them again at some point anyway.

Much of the stock I sent to Rusch was in other people's names, and I would tell Rusch to transfer it directly from that name to whatever name he needed to put it under. Again, perfectly legal, no big deal. But when the government saw stocks being transferred from various names directly to the Swiss entity, they inferred all kinds of crazy notions, suggesting it was evidence that we were trying to hide money. If they'd bothered to look at our tax returns, they would have seen that we had *already declared that stock to the IRS*. It was fully owned by us, there was no attempt to hide it, and there was nothing shady going on. But, of course, the DOJ wasn't interested in facts; it was only interested in getting a conviction.

So now the government was trying to question all the original owners of these stocks. These were people I knew and had done business with, and the DOJ was knocking on their doors. I felt terrible about putting these folks through that kind of hassle, and embarrassed about the whole situation. Worried too. As I've said, I've always done business honestly, and I had no "buried bodies" in my past. But still, I had no idea what kinds of questions the DOJ might be asking these people or what the people might say that could be misconstrued by the DOJ or open new cans of worms. So I was extremely anxious about the situation.

From what I heard later, some of these good people slammed the door in the DOJ's face; others invited them in for tea and cookies.

One of the worst aspects of being under investigation was that—and I hate to admit this—on some level, I almost felt like I "deserved" to be in trouble. Even though I had done nothing wrong and had always gone the extra mile to prove my honesty, part of me still held on to beliefs from my ancient past. I'm from Spokane, and the people I grew up with were mostly working class and professional people. Good people, but people whose dreams for wealth were limited to buying lottery tickets. There was a strong belief among "my people" that anyone who made his living by moving stocks and money around was probably doing something illegal or immoral. Growing up, I believed the same thing. So deep down in my psychological makeup was this core belief that people who did *exactly what I did for a living* were somehow illegitimate. I didn't *consciously* believe that anymore—I *knew* I wasn't a cheat—but the investigation was tapping into deeply buried feelings about my line of work and was eroding my self-worth and confidence. And that was only making me feel even more vulnerable.

When I tried to share my concerns about the investigation with Steve, his attitude was, "Let's negotiate a deal and move on." He still seemed to feel the solution was to just write a check.

"You don't get it," I'd try to tell him. "It might not be as easy as you think to get past this. The legal process might drag on for five or eight years. People are going to prison for this kind of thing. People like us are getting hit with huge fines and losing *everything they own.*"

"Well, I can't worry about that," he'd say. "Let's talk to Rusch, bite the bullet, and try to get it behind us as quickly as we can."

That option was officially taken off the table when I received a phone call from Chris Rusch...

CHAPTER ELEVEN

The Lawyer Shuffle

"I can't represent you anymore," said Rusch when I answered the phone.

"What do you mean, Chris?"

"The government tells me I have a potential conflict of interest here," he replied. "I need to stop giving you legal advice and start getting some of my own."

"But you're our attorney in this mess. It's your advice we've been following all along. We're counting on you."

"Not anymore."

Rusch explained that the stack of documents he sent the DOJ—which I was still furious about, by the way—had raised some questions among the government people, and they had recommended he no longer serve as attorney for Steve Kerr and me.

When I expressed surprise at this, Rusch said something like, "Let's face it, Mike, the writing was on the wall. We knew at some point they were going to go hard at me for my role in this thing."

"Maybe *you* knew that," I said, "but I didn't."

"Mike, I'm the one who set everything up in Switzerland. Obviously, if they have issues with our operation, there they're going to need to talk to me."

"Should I be worried about that?"

"No. Absolutely not. I've told you a hundred times, and I'll tell you again: Everything was done perfectly legally. After the feds have sifted through all the documents and tramped down all the dead-end streets, I'm sure they'll come to the same conclusion. But in the meantime…"

"Right. What do we do now? Steve and I just want to get out of this thing as quickly and cleanly as possible. Who do we get to represent us? Do we need someone with a criminal background? A litigator? A negotiator? Do you have anyone you can recommend?"

"Actually, I do. Guy by the name of Richard Carpenter. He's in my office building. He was my professor in law school. He's an excellent attorney; I've gone to him a couple of times with tricky cases or questions about how to handle things in my own practice. There's no reason we can't all talk to him, at least for now. After all, we're in this thing together."

There he was, using those annoying words again.

"You trust this Carpenter guy?" I asked.

"Yes."

"Then set up a meeting."

I flew out to San Diego, and Rusch met me at the airport. I had expected to meet with Carpenter alone, but Rusch stayed in the room as we talked. I went over the basic facts of the case with Carpenter, as Rusch chimed in occasionally to amplify or clarify a point. I could tell by Rusch's body language that he really wanted me to choose Carpenter as my attorney. But this didn't quite sit right with me. After all, if the three of us—Rusch, Kerr, and myself—were going to use this guy, but Rusch was the only one who had a long-standing friendship with him, how would things play out if we all got indicted?

I asked Carpenter several questions about the case, trying to get a sense as to whether he thought he could help us avoid criminal indictments. He hedged and dodged in classic lawyerly fashion. In short, he didn't exude confidence about being able save our asses. I was looking for an attorney who could see a strong angle of attack and formulate a game plan with optimism. I wasn't getting that from Carpenter. Rusch pressed me for a thumbs-up/thumbs-down on the spot. I felt a little awkward about turning the guy down with the two men sitting right there staring at me, but I wasn't ready to make a decision.

Shortly after my visit, Steve Kerr went to see Carpenter. He hired the guy and wrote him a check. I didn't agree with that move, but there wasn't much I could do about it. Steve was free to hire whomever he wished. After all, we weren't official partners, and if the shit really did hit the fan at some point, we might face different charges and have diverging legal interests. So we might need our own attorneys. But I still felt it was extremely important that we work as a team on this thing.

After Kerr went with Carpenter, there was a period of a week or two where I didn't have an attorney at all, and I felt pretty lost at sea. I was still listening to Chris Rusch and relying on his advice to a certain extent, but I knew I needed to find some real legal representation.

It didn't take Steve Kerr long to figure out that Carpenter was primarily an academic who would not be able to do the job we needed done. One day he called me and said, "Hey, Mike, I talked to this attorney by the name of Paul Charlton. A friend of mine recommended him. I think you should come down and see him right away."

"You got it."

I jumped in my car and drove to the office building of Gallagher & Kennedy, a prestigious Phoenix-area law firm where Paul Charlton worked and was a shareholder. As soon as I saw the building, I knew what I was in for. You know the type of firm: company name carved in stone outside the building, whole floor of an office building to itself, office furnishings worth more than a paralegal's annual salary. I could feel my wallet shrinking as I rode the elevator to the G&K floor. Not that I minded paying good money for good services, but I was never a big fan of professionals who sunk more money into their signs and suits than they did into their services. As a securities broker and investor, I'd always shied away from that kind of thing, preferring to let my performance speak for itself. I'd spent most of my professional life in a pair of shorts and a golf shirt. Most of the smartest people I'd ever worked with were that way too.

While I waited to see Charlton (he seemed like the kind of guy who liked to make you wait), Steve filled me in on his background. He certainly had impressive credentials, and there was a reason his name sounded familiar to me. He was the former US attorney for the Arizona district, appointed by George W. Bush himself. In that federal job, he had overseen a staff of over two hundred employees and, in 2006, had ranked as the number 1 US prosecutor in the country for convictions. (I hoped he was equally as skillful at *avoiding* convictions.) Now he did a lot of white-collar criminal defense and cases that involved interacting with government agencies.

I won't say I hated Charlton right from the start—that's putting it too strongly—but there was something about him that irked me. He looked like he stepped right out of a Hollywood casting agency. With his hundred-dollar salt-and-pepper haircut and his Tom Cruise teeth, he struck me as someone who tended his own image very carefully. I started referring to him, almost immediately, as the Movie Star. The more I got to know him, the more convinced I was that he preferred being in front of a camera to being in front of a judge or behind a desk.

But at our first meeting, he said a lot of the right things. He asked some decent questions and seemed to have solid experience when it came to negotiating with government people. He also had some connections *within* the government, so that was a plus. Maybe he could get to the right people and stop this investigation in its tracks before it gathered any more momentum. Maybe.

After I met with Charlton, Steve and I went down to the building's lobby, and he asked me, "So what did you think?"

"About Charlton? Well, when he stopped posing long enough to answer questions, he seemed to know what he was talking about. His government connections fit the bill, I guess. But I don't know, there's something about him—"

"Well, get used to it, 'cause I hired him," said Steve.

"What?" I couldn't believe my ears. "Why would you do such a thing without even consulting with me first?"

"Look, I'm sorry, I felt certain you'd be impressed with the guy."

"If I was *casting a soap opera*, I'd be impressed with him. But as for hiring him as an attorney, we should have talked about it first. Did you already give him a check?"

"Not yet."

"Good, then nothing's official. Until he accepts payment, we're free to take our business elsewhere."

"There's one little problem with that," said Steve.

"Oh?"

"He's already reported in with the DOJ as the attorney of record."

"What!" I screamed, seeing red. "You had no right to allow him to do that! We're in this together when it comes to the DOJ!" Yelling at Steve was not something I normally did—especially in the lobby of a public building—but I was ripping mad. "Who gave you permission to speak for both of us?"

When I finally calmed down, I realized the die was cast, like it or not, and I needed to live with the situation. Charlton was our guy. It was important that Steve and I present a unified front to the DOJ.

When we went back upstairs to Charlton, we agreed that he would serve, more or less, as the lead attorney, but that I would have independent representation for myself. Charlton recommended a gentleman he'd worked with in the attorney general's office, Fred Petty.

Petty's office was half a block down the street from Gallagher & Kennedy, and far more modest. It took up only *part* of the first floor.

Petty seemed a lot more down to earth than the Movie Star. He reviewed my case and agreed to represent me and do all the necessary work for a one-time flat fee of $25,000. I liked the guy and wrote him a check for the entire amount, right on the spot.

One of the first tasks to be handled by our new legal team was to try to get all the materials Chris Rusch had submitted to the DOJ thrown out. Our argument was that Rusch should never have sent the DOJ those materials because he was our attorney. As such, he was covered by attorney-client privilege and was barred from sharing materials given to him confidentially by his client. Therefore, those

materials should be disregarded by the investigation team and grand
jury.

Paul Charlton wrote up the motion. This was our first legal
action to go before a judge, and—wait for it—we lost. Because Paul
Charlton, the Movie Star, messed it up, plain and simple. What
you're *supposed* to do when submitting a motion that covers multiple documents is create a *log* in which you list and identify each of
the documents separately. That way, the judge may decide that *some*
of the documents are allowed into evidence while others are not.
Because Charlton didn't do this, the judge had no choice but to dismiss the whole motion. As a result, *all* the documents Rusch sent the
DOJ were allowed into the investigation as evidence.

On what basis, you might be wondering, was attorney-client
privilege overruled regarding Rusch? Well, the answer to that question is an important one, and it carries through this entire case in a
significant way: There is an exception to attorney-client privilege. It's
known as the crime-fraud exception. It stipulates that communication between a client and an attorney is *not* privileged if that communication is made with the intention of committing or covering up a
crime. Sounds reasonable, right?

BUT...

There's a built-in problem with this exception; do you see it?

Until a verdict is delivered, the government *has not yet proven
that there* was *an intention to commit or cover up a crime.* So, you
might ask, what happens in a case when (1) attorney-client privilege
is denied through the crime fraud exception, (2) the attorney testifies
against his client(s) and/or submits evidence against them, and then
(3) the court later determines that no criminal intent existed? Should
not all the testimony and evidence given by that attorney against his
client(s) be stricken from the record? And should not any convictions
that resulted from that testimony be automatically overturned?

These are vital questions that loom large over this case, as you
will see. We'll get into them more later.

As for now: Thanks, Paul Charlton. Nice job. At this point,
most of the "evidence" the DOJ had against us was material our
own attorney had mailed to them, special delivery, and that Charlton

had failed to suppress. The prosecutors didn't seem to have much else on us. Under the Freedom of Information Act, we requested all the documents the government had obtained from UBS and Pictet banks. The government complied and sent us the documents, but of course, they were all redacted to the point of uselessness. (We later found out, by hiring a Swiss attorney to get the original records, that most of the stuff the government redacted was not in fact privileged information but was information *favorable to our defense* that it didn't want us to see. By sending us these comically redacted documents, I guess they were trying to scare us into assuming the government had all sorts of secret information on us. But it was all a giant smoke-screen, designed to intimidate and mislead.)

Things were not looking good. Less than thirty days after hiring our crack legal team, not only had Charlton let us down, but my individual attorney Fred Petty was already asking me for another $25,000 on top of what I thought was a "one-time fee." At this point I was feeling thoroughly disgusted with our lawyers and not sure what to do. Our shareholders were reporting back to us about their visits with the DOJ, Rusch was acting secretive and strange, and I had this terrible feeling that everything was drifting out of control. I kept trying to *think* my way through the moving parts, but I knew I didn't have all the information.

In the midst of this, just to add some spy-movie drama to the situation, Chris Rusch showed up at my office one day, fresh from a flight from San Diego.

"We can't talk on the phone anymore," he told me, looking around as if my office might be bugged. "You, me, and Steve. We have to assume they're monitoring our conversations and tracking our phone records. Anything you say on the phone can be used against you at trial."

"I'm still hoping there won't *be* a trial," I said.

"Yeah, well..." He gave me a look as if to say, *and I'm still hoping reindeers can fly*. "The fact remains that we can't officially talk anymore. Don't worry; I'm not abandoning you guys—we're in this together—but we need to get some burner phones."

"What the hell are those?"

"I guess you weren't a big fan of *The Wire*."

Burner phones are cheap, prepaid cell phones you use when you're looking for privacy and lack of traceability. They come with their own phone number (not yours) and are popular among cheating spouses and drug dealers. The idea is that you buy the phone with cash, so there are no credit card records, you use it for a specific purpose, for a specific time period, then you "burn" it.

Rusch went to Walmart and came back with three cheap cell phones, one for each of us.

For some reason, being the proud owner of a burner phone did not make me feel more secure. But it wasn't long before I used mine to call Rusch in San Diego.

"Chris, I don't like the way things are going—with the legal team, with the investigation, with anything. I'm very worried and very confused. What the hell do we do next?"

"Well, of course, you know I can't advise you legally anymore. And I've had to get my own representation." Rusch was now with a firm out of San Diego called Coughlan, Semmer & Lipman LLP.

"I understand that, Chris—why do you think I'm calling you on this fucking *Bourne Identity* telephone—but, off the books, what would you do if you were me?"

"Let me get back to you on that."

Rusch called me back on the burner phone with a list of four or five lawyers he thought would be good for me. I wasn't ready to pull the plug on our present team, but I started calling the names.

Most of his referrals could be ruled out within sixty seconds, but there was one whose background and pedigree—not to mention his distinctive name—made him hard to ignore. If you're a politics junkie, you might recognize his name; he was appointed by President Obama in 2015 to head up the Tax Division of the Attorney General's office.

His name was Cono Namorato.

CHAPTER TWELVE

Domo Arigato, Cono Namorato

Cono Namorato worked for a firm in Washington, DC, called Caplin & Drysdale. With over fifty years of experience and a prestigious DC address, C&D is a self-described "boutique firm" made up of "lawyers' lawyers." It was cofounded by a former commissioner of the Internal Revenue Service and has a history of hiring former IRS and DOJ attorneys. C&D's website boasts that its "style of practice is aimed at minimizing our clients' liabilities without compromising the ethical principles that are essential to the integrity of the legal system." Gives you a little sense of how they view themselves.

Namorato himself had a long track record of working for the DOJ and the IRS in positions such as director of the IRS's Office of Professional Responsibility, deputy assistant attorney general for the Tax Division of the DOJ; and chief of the criminal section of the Tax Division. The man was steeped in criminal tax law, though most of his experience was on the prosecution side. (His has since returned to his comfort zone; he now heads the Tax Division of the US Attorney General's office.)

I called Mr. Namorato from my home in Spokane and got Steve Kerr on the line with us. When we asked Cono to describe his experience and expertise to us, he characterized himself as a "negotiator." He summed up a couple of cases where he'd been able to win favorable settlements and keep his clients out of prison.

"That's excellent," I said, "but do you know how to *fight* these guys?" I meant the DOJ; was he able to challenge them in court if need be? I probably should have been more specific with my question.

After a brief pause, Namorato said, "I've fought them before."

"That's good," I said, "because it might come down to that."

I later learned that Namorato had never been in a trial, at least not on the defense side.

Negotiation was his thing. Personally, I was not in love with the idea of negotiation, but as a practical matter, I had to keep an open mind about it. Steve and I were still trying to coordinate with Chris Rusch—not as our attorney, but as our fellow business associate who was also under investigation—and we were "all in this together," defense-wise, at least up to a point. So the possibility of a negotiated solution that all three of us could live with had to be kept alive. I had no intention of pleading guilty to something I didn't do, but I thought that by exploring the negotiation route, we might get a glimpse of the cards the prosecution was holding.

So it was a good thing that Namorato could negotiate with the DOJ. Or so I thought.

In June or July of 2010, at Cono's request, I started sending him some of the correspondence I had on file about the case. We talked back and forth a few times over the phone, and then he said we should meet in person. Rather than fly him out to Arizona, I decided I would travel to DC. I had never been there and thought it would be a good excuse for a family vacation. And boy, did we all need one.

Namorato applauded the idea of my bringing the family along with me and said, "Make sure you visit the Spy Museum."

In the middle of the summer of 2010, we flew out to Washington together as a family. The trip was a pleasant release from all the stress and anxiety that had been pressuring the family for the past several months. It was a fun and educational experience for the girls. Educational for me too, but in a different way.

On the first day, the family went sightseeing while I paid a visit to Caplin & Drysdale at their offices a few blocks from the White House.

When I entered the reception area, I was greeted by Cono's assistant, who, after dispensing the usual pleasantries, escorted me to the conference room, where the man himself was waiting with a few of his associates.

Cono Namorato.

With his gaunt face, grayish complexion, and thick Abe Vigoda eyebrows, Namorato could have been cast in a movie as either a Mafia don or a funeral director. The first thing I remember saying to him was to make a little joke about the DOJ. "Are these people even Americans?" I said, referring to the heavy-handed tactics they were known for using.

Cono didn't laugh. "You'd better be careful what you say, Mr. Quiel," he said with his funereal face and without a trace of a smile. "*We* were with the DOJ." He looked around at his associates, who nodded solemnly.

In retrospect, I think Namorato was making a declaration about his loyalties that day. He was telling me he valued his connections with the DOJ more than any one client. I should have paid attention. I should have turned around and walked right out the door. But I didn't. You have to understand. I was starving for information at this point, hungry to talk to anyone who might understand the inner workings of the DOJ and the type of case that was shaping up against me. I was a complete neophyte, at the mercy of anyone who knew the system better than I. Namorato was an authority on the DOJ, and I wanted to pick his brain. I wanted him on my side.

Namorato offered a preliminary analysis of my case that was as grim as his face. "They can charge you on a 7206 and a 7201," he said, rattling off the relevant statutes, "and probably get you on securities fraud too." He went on to describe the massive fines I might face and even mentioned prison time. If his eyebrows weren't enough to terrify me, his words certainly were. But I guess that was the point. He wanted me to be scared to death, I believe, and ready to accept whatever solution he offered.

"So what do we do?" I asked.

"We set up a negotiation meeting, and we negotiate."

"What are our chances?"

"I think we can do pretty well," he said. "It'll end up costing you some money, and they may want you to plead to a few things, but I think we should be able to keep you out of prison, and that's the main thing, right?"

"Right. But look, Mr. Namorato, just so we're clear," I said as we settled in over our bottles of designer water, "I'm not guilty of any crimes here. If I broke the law at all, I didn't do so intentionally; I did it by following the directions and advice of my attorney."

Namorato stared at me like a wax museum exhibit.

"You *know* these DOJ guys, right?" I said. "Can't we just meet with them informally, talk it out, explain the situation?"

"Mr. Quiel," said Cono (and again, I'm paraphrasing from memory), "let me explain something very carefully. You need to remember this, whether you decide to hire me or not: Never, *ever* 'talk' with government prosecutors. Is that clear? Keep your mouth shut and keep all of your cards in your pocket."

That was probably the most helpful advice I ever got from Cono Namorato.

"And what *you* need to understand," I told him, "is that I'm not guilty, and I won't plead to anything I didn't do."

Namorato furrowed his considerable brow. "Why don't you just let me do what I do best here, Mr. Quiel? You're paying for my negotiating skills."

"But I want to proceed from a standpoint of innocence."

He nodded. It was *not* a nod that said, "I will abide by your wishes." It was a nod that said, "I acknowledge hearing the noise that just came from your face."

* * *

Here's something I know now but didn't know at that time: Defense attorneys hate innocent clients. They are, in fact, much more comfortable with guilty ones. I'm not just talking about Cono Namorato here; I'm talking about lawyers in general.

Most of us operate under several illusions about innocence and the law. One of these illusions is that if we are innocent, the truth will come out, and the system will protect us. Another is that our lawyer will be more committed to defending us if he knows we are innocent. The biggest illusion of all—and I certainly believed it before this nightmare happened to me—is that lawyers *prefer* to defend innocent people.

Wrong.

It's *innocent* clients that make lawyers lose sleep at night. You have probably heard someone ask the question of a defense lawyer, "How do you in good conscience defend clients you know are guilty?" If that lawyer is answering honestly, he will probably tell you, "Give me guilty clients any day of the week."

Here's reality from a lawyer's point of view: The vast majority of clients who walk through his door *are* guilty—if not of the exact crime they're charged with, then of something in the neighborhood. Lawyers know how to deal with this kind of client. Their only real concern is whether the *prosecution can prove* the client's guilt or not, and how strong the prosecution's case is. Their job is to attack and weaken the prosecutor's case to the greatest extent possible and then get the client the best outcome possible, given the prosecution's case. They may not get their client *exonerated*, but they try to get a deal that everyone can live with.

As a general rule, their clients know they are guilty and are not really expecting to get off scot-free. They are happy with anything their lawyer can do to get *some* of the charges dismissed and *some* of the punishment lessened. Therefore, the lawyer has all kinds of compromises and strategies at his disposal. If his client gets ten months in prison instead of four years, the lawyer can sleep well at night; he did his job.

Not so with the innocent client.

With the innocent client, the lawyer knows that a not-guilty verdict is the only acceptable outcome. His options are limited, his hands are tied, and there is little room for compromise. He can't use most of the negotiating tactics he has in his bag of tricks; his client is depending on him to *set him free*. Big burden there.

It's the *innocent* client that worms into a lawyer's conscience, making the lawyer work late into the night, thinking and rethinking every angle of the case. The lawyer knows that if his innocent client goes to jail, he—the lawyer—will have to live with the knowledge that he failed the client. Every night an innocent client spends in jail is a night the lawyer sleeps a little less soundly in the bed his client paid for. And if, heaven forbid, an innocent client gets the death penalty, the lawyer has to deal with that forever.

Try carrying *that* on your conscience.

That's why defense lawyers avoid innocence as if it were a communicable disease. And why they typically don't ask you if you're guilty or innocent. They sleep better, in fact, when *they* have their doubts.

I hadn't yet learned this sobering truth, so I was annoyed by the fact that Cono Namorato seemed totally uninterested in my protestations of innocence. But I *was* impressed by his experience and his connections.

* * *

I decided to take a gamble with Namorato and gave him a check for $70,000 to review all my materials and get started on a strategy.

Meanwhile, I was still trying to coordinate with Steve Kerr and Chris Rusch and their lawyers. Steve still had the Movie Star as his attorney. I was still working with Fred Petty—I hadn't yet terminated with him—and Chris Rusch was working with a couple of attorneys from Coughlan, Semmer & Lipman. This thing was getting complicated. How should all these attorneys work together? Who should take the lead, if anyone? What should their respective strategies be?

It seemed wise to get everyone together in the same room.

I proposed a meeting of all the attorneys and clients in San Diego, where Rusch and his team were located. Everyone agreed, so we scheduled a date.

Of course, *I* had to pay for everyone's airfare and hotel accommodations. That meant flying Cono—first class, of course—from Washington, and flying the Movie Star first class from Phoenix. Steve and I flew Southwest, as we typically did.

When the day of the meeting arrived and we walked into the conference room, Chris Rusch was conspicuously absent. His attorney, Michael Lipman, strode in and addressed Steve Kerr and me.

"Chris Rusch will be attending today's meeting," he said, "which means that you gentlemen can't be present."

"This meeting was my idea," I protested. "I paid for everyone to be here."

"Regardless, you can't be here if my client is to attend."

I felt like a kid being asked to leave the grown-ups' table at Thanksgiving, but I decided it was more important that Rusch attend the meeting than that I attend. He had more of the critical inside information that the other lawyers would need.

Steve and I drove over to the US Midway Museum and spent several hours walking around an aircraft carrier. When we got back, Rusch's team had already departed, and we learned that the meeting had quickly devolved into a shouting match between all the attorneys. Rusch had said very little, and absolutely nothing had been accomplished.

Adding up the plane fare, hotel costs, and attorneys' time, the meeting had cost me around $25,000. I would have been better off spending it on scratch tickets.

The hope of planning a coordinated attack with Rusch and his lawyers, it seemed was no longer on the table.

* * *

Cono continued to work the negotiation angle. He set up a formal meeting with the DOJ and began formulating a strategy.

As part of that strategy, he wanted me to proffer. I didn't agree.

I've already explained briefly what a proffer is, but let me explain why an attorney should be extremely reluctant to advise his client to do one. As I mentioned before, a proffer is an offer of information you make to the government with the hope that the prosecutors will give you some kind of immunity or plea-bargain arrangement. I say "hope" because the government can basically do whatever it wants. *It doesn't offer any of its promises in writing.* In fact, the written language on a proffer sheet specifically states that no assurances are being given.

In a proffer, the government essentially puts you in a room where it expects you to sing like a canary for hours. But if for any reason it decides you're not being 100 percent forthcoming, it can back out of any assurances it has given you. And here's the dangerous part: Anything you say in a proffer can open up new lines of investigation against you and/or be used against you in court. Proffers can even lead to new charges being filed against you.

The government loves proffers, because the government gets all the goodies with none of the risks. Not only do they get a free preview of the kind of testimony you will offer in court, they also get new information from you that can aid their investigation, as well as learn what you'll be like under examination on the witness stand. Proffers are a very high-risk venture for the person offering the information. The only time it makes sense to do one is if you are royally screwed by the evidence and/or you really, really, really trust the prosecution team.

So I was pretty distressed that Cono was coaxing me in the direction of a proffer right out of the starting gate. Knowing how eagerly the government misinterprets information, I could see all kinds of ways that a proffer could get me in trouble. Remember, I worked in the securities industry, where any legal black mark on your record can be a career ender.

Cono seemed very cozy with his DOJ contacts, but here's a small illustration of his attitude toward clients: When I knew he'd be flying to Arizona for the negotiation meeting with the DOJ, I offered to put him up at my house (a 6,000-square-foot house with plenty of space, comfort, and privacy), and he told me, "I never stay with clients. I'll require a hotel."

The night before Cono was due to come to town for the big DOJ negotiation meeting, I was talking to Steve Silver—he's the attorney who was giving me tax advice on the real estate venture after I stopped working with Rusch. When I told him about Cono's idea of proffering, Silver said, "I never do proffers for clients."

114

"Really?" I said. "You know how to do settlements with the DOJ without proffering?"

"Absolutely."

"Great, then I want you on my team."

Silver said fine; he was happy to help.

"Cono Namorato's flying in tomorrow," I told him. "Why don't you pick him up at the airport—that'll give you guys a chance to talk—and then we'll meet at my office?"

By the time the two lawyers got to my office, I could already observe a change in Steve Silver's behavior. He was fawning and acting like a groupie around Cono, laughing at his jokes and agreeing with all his comments.

When we sat to talk, I told Cono, "Steve Silver is here because he says I don't have to proffer."

Silver suddenly looked as if he'd been tasered in the ass. In the presence of the big Washington attorney, he immediately lost all his bravado and said, "Well, I don't *call* it proffering, but we do need to offer the DOJ something concrete."

"WHAT!" I shouted at Silver, shocking the two men with my anger. "You told me I didn't have to proffer! What gives you the right to lie, when I can't?"

The two lawyers sat there staring at me, not quite sure how to respond to my outburst. I should have thrown them both out right then and there, but I was still starving for information and trying to figure out my best strategy.

After I calmed down, I said, "I don't want to proffer because it's like admitting guilt, and I don't want to admit guilt."

"But you *are* guilty," said Cono.

"Like hell I am," I replied, getting testy.

"You *did* do some things wrong with the selling of the stock," Namorato reminded me.

"No, *Chris Rusch* did. And I didn't know it at the time. Anything I did or didn't do was based on the advice of the attorney I hired to set everything up for me." I then explained the concept of *mens rea* to Cono—a concept *he* should have been explaining to *me*. *Mens rea* means, essentially, that in order for a crime to take place, there must be an *intention* on your part to do something wrong or illegal. Sometimes the law gets broken even when people are acting with good intentions. In that case, the "wrongdoing" does not rise to the level of a crime. "I'm not going to say things to the DOJ that I can't take back. What if this case ends up going to trial?"

"Well," said Namorato, "that *is* an issue. You can't 'admit guilt' through a proffer and then later claim you weren't guilty if the case goes to trial."

"Then we've got a problem here," I said. "Because I'm not going to perjure myself by saying I did something wrong, just so that we can cut a deal."

Cono steepled his fingers and looked pensive. "If you're telling me you would have to perjure yourself in order to admit guilt to the DOJ," he said with a sigh, "then, as your attorney, I obviously cannot recommend that you commit perjury."

"So, no proffering?"

He shrugged agreement and sighed.

I didn't know where that left us for strategies, but I was glad he had heard me. I got the sense, though, that he still hadn't given up on the idea of proffering.

On the day of the meeting with the DOJ, Cono and Silver decided they didn't want me in the room for the negotiations. The Movie Star, who was also in on the meeting, told the same thing to Steve, his client. And so, as Cono, Steve Silver, the Movie Star, and his secretary met with the DOJ behind closed doors, Steve and I sat outside, biting our fingernails, drinking coffee, and waiting to hear what kind of deal the DOJ was going to offer us.

CHAPTER THIRTEEN

Fight or Fold?

As I waited to learn what sort of offer Cono Namorato would land me through his negotiating skills, my mind kept drifting to a much graver situation my family was wrestling with. In the fall of 2010, a man I loved and respected, John Lee, was waging a parallel battle to mine, and that battle was forcing him to ask himself the same question I was grappling with: "Should I fight or should I fold?" But John's battle was for stakes much higher than mine.

To understand the way our stories intertwined, we need to go back a couple of months.

As I mentioned, it was in the summer of 2010 that Cono Namorato stepped into my life. Right from our first conversation, his vision was laser-focused on making a deal with the DOJ. I guess that shouldn't have surprised me. Negotiating was his tool of choice. And, as the saying goes, when your only tool is a hammer, every-thing becomes a nail. Cono wasn't interested in *fighting* the DOJ, because that would have required a tool—litigation skills—that he didn't possess, at least as far as I could see. So he wanted to turn my case into a nail.

Cono and I had many phone conversations over the course of that summer, and in every one of them, he tried to convince me of my guilt and of the overwhelming advantage the US government had on me. It didn't matter how many times I told him I was innocent;

his message to me was always the same: you did something wrong, you got caught, and Uncle Sam's going to ruin your life if you don't cooperate.

I think his message was intended to scare me. And I have to admit, it worked. As I said earlier, I had read many accounts of armed IRS and DOJ agents storming people's houses and of people going to jail and losing all their assets. I knew the same thing could happen to me. Knew it.

But that didn't mean I was ready to roll over. In fact, every time Cono would point out specific "evidence" against me, I would research the statutes and show him how I had not, in fact, behaved illegally. And we would argue back and forth. My words always seemed to fall on deaf ears.

One of Cono's favorite scare tactics was to talk about the redacted portions of the bank account documents the government had sent me. He'd say things like, "Whose names have been blacked out there, do you know?" or "Are you 100 percent sure that's not *your* signature on that document?"

And the truth was, no, I wasn't 100 percent sure. I didn't *think* I had signed anything shady, but I wasn't dead certain. Back in the days when the Swiss venture was being launched, if Rusch, my attorney, had told me to sign something, I probably signed it without too many questions. I had trusted him to be my legal guide, and at that time, I had *much* more important issues on my mind—my house construction, my pancreas, my business.

So in the summer of 2010, my state of mind was massive confusion and indecision. On one hand, Cono's pleas to make a deal with the DOJ made logical sense. A deal would be expedient and would get this nightmare behind me in the quickest way possible (but would likely include prison time). A deal would also, Cono assured me, result in more lenient sentencing than if I were to go to trial and lose.

On the other hand, my gut was screaming out to fight back. I was mad as hell about being charged with a crime I didn't commit—all because some federal prosecutors wanted to play politics. There was a huge part of me that wanted to stick it to the DOJ, to clear my name of all wrongdoing, and to see actual justice served. And I sure as hell didn't want to go to jail.

So, fight or fold? I went back and forth on a daily—an hourly—basis.

As I was wrangling with this decision, Vicki and I went to visit her parents in Spokane. We had spent the summer at our lake house there, with the girls, as we did every year, and before returning to Phoenix that August, we went to the Lees' house for dinner.

Up until that point, we had not told Vicki's parents about my legal dilemma. We hadn't wanted to worry them and had been hoping to get the matter resolved. But now the time had come to speak.

I remember the four of us sitting together in their living room over coffee. "John," I said, looking my retired colonel father-in-law in the eye, "something pretty serious is happening to us. I'm under investigation by the DOJ."

Vicki's parents did their best not to react in shock. I let the news settle in on them before continuing. "I didn't do what they're accusing me of, but if I choose to fight them, it's going to be a hell of a battle. I don't know whether I should take a deal or not. If I take it, I'm going to have to plead to some charges."

John nodded slowly, taking it all in.

"I just want you to know," I continued, "that if I cut a deal with them, it's not because I'm guilty. It's because I think that will be easier on Vicki and the girls and on everyone concerned."

"But you'll end up with a criminal record?" John asked sharply.

"Yup. Believe me, that's not something I take lightly. But these government agencies can run all over you and take everything you own. I don't think I could live with myself if I let that happen to my family."

John put his hand on my shoulder, looked at me hard, and said, "Mike, I believe you're innocent. I can't tell you whether to fight or take a deal. But if you decide to challenge this, it will be the biggest and hardest battle you'll ever fight. You'll be going up against the US government, and believe me, those boys play for keeps."

He was trying to tell me that he supported me, no matter which choice I made. That meant a lot to me.

It didn't make my decision any easier, though.

Vicki's parents didn't know a lot about the world of finance, so I tried to explain some of the fine points of my legal issues to them, to help them better understand the decision we were facing.

In the middle of the conversation, John stood up and announced, "Excuse me, I don't feel very well." He proceeded to walk across the room and lie down on the floor. We all looked at each other in worry and went to him. He looked pale and disoriented and a bit panicked. He wasn't breathing right. I thought my news might be literally killing him. "John, did I do this to you?" I asked.

He put his hand up and waved off the question.

When he was finally feeling well enough to make it to the bedroom, Vicki's mom explained to us that John had had a few bouts of dizziness recently. We all agreed he needed to get some medical intervention.

My family and I flew back to Phoenix for the start of the school year. We returned a few weeks later. It was typical in those days for us to fly back to Washington a few extra times during the course of the fall to enjoy the lake house before the cold weather came. We did that for the three-day Labor Day weekend. While we were there in Spokane, Vicki's parents invited us over. They wanted to host a cookout for the whole family.

John looked much better than he had when he'd been lying on the floor, but he seemed to have lost some weight. Still, his energy was up, and he seemed determined to make the day a special one. I remember he dragged out this ancient meat smoker—a cheap aluminum thing from K-Mart that looked like it had been sitting in his shed for forty years—and smoked a brisket for five hours. John and I sat and drank martinis, as we had done many times early in my marriage, and talked about various things, both important and trivial. As all this was going on, Vicki and I exchanged frequent smiles. We took his high spirits as a sign that he was feeling better.

Looking back, though, I now believe what was happening that day was that John wanted to have one last perfect day with his kids and grandkids, because he knew his time was running out. Somehow, he summoned the will to create a memorable Labor Day. But it was the last time we ever saw him healthy.

A few weeks later, we received a call from Vicki's mom. John had cancer. It had started in his lungs and metastasized to his brain.

* * *

After Cono Namorato's big meeting with the DOJ—which to this day, I wish I had insisted upon attending—I sat down with him and Steve Silver.

"So, what's the verdict?" I asked the men, dreading their answer but hungry to hear it too.

Cono rubbed his hands together as if he were about to present a gourmet feast, while Silver looked on with a proud paternal smile. "You should be happy with this deal," Cono said. It sounded like a command. "We got you a great offer: You plead guilty to one charge only, you pay a fine and back taxes of 1.5 million dollars, and you get a maximum of three years in prison."

"Three years?" I repeated, checking my hearing.

"That's correct." He could see I wasn't happy. "Hey look, they made us *two* offers, I want you to know. The first one involved *five* years, and I rejected that one."

I leaned back in my seat and let out a long breath.

"You don't seem thrilled," observed Namorato. Give the man a gold star.

"Listen, Cono, I'm glad you negotiated with them," I said, "and I will definitely give this offer careful consideration. But I'm telling you right now, I don't like the idea of taking a deal. I didn't do anything wrong, and it's going to be very hard for me to say that I did. Are they still expecting me to proffer?"

Cono shrugged as if to say, "Hey, it is what it is."

I tried to explain to him, once again, that it was the idea of proffering that scared me more than anything. I didn't trust the government. I'd read stories, including Bradley Birkenfeld's, about people who'd gone to the government with proffers and gotten themselves into much deeper trouble as a result. I was especially nervous about saying something that could trigger a securities investigation, because I knew that could lead to another twenty years in prison. On top of the tax charges, we could be talking thirty-five years here. Remember: What you say—or don't say—in a proffer can cause the government to renege on any deals it has offered you.

Namorato, as I recall, said something to the effect of, "Look, Mr. Quiel, it's your life and your decision. But I've gone to great lengths to get this deal for you, and I've put my DOJ relationships at risk."

I wondered about the truth of that, frankly. I wondered just how hard Cono had sparred with his DOJ buddies to get me a "great deal." I called Steve Kerr and was talking to him about it when he mentioned that his legal team had taken notes during the DOJ meeting. So I took a little drive over to Gallagher-Kennedy and requested a copy of the notes from Paul Charlton's secretary, who was happy to furnish them to me.

Without telling Cono I had the notes, I asked him to summarize the DOJ meeting for me. There were three or four glaring inconsistencies between Cono's version of the meeting and what the notes said. The notes made no mention of a first offer that Cono rejected. No. What was obvious from the notes was that Cono had simply taken the first deal the DOJ offered. In essence, he had walked onto a car lot and bought first car the salesman showed him, at the asking price. From what I could see, he didn't negotiate *at all*. Behind those closed doors, a good ol'-fashioned love fest had gone down, and the DOJ had made all the moves.

I now believe that Cono was more interested in getting invited to the DOJ Christmas party than he was in helping me. I can't prove that, but it's what I believe. I think that's the way it is for most DOJ alumni; they remain in the DOJ's pocket forever and are more motivated to preserve their old relationships than to protect their clients.

At this point I felt like I was being fed to wolves—by the leader of the pack. But I still couldn't tell Cono to take a hike, though. Right now, his deal was the only offer I had in hand, and I might yet be forced to take it.

So as the fall of 2010 went on, I had to continue listening to his doom and gloom phone calls, telling me how screwed I was if I didn't take the deal. Steve Silver wasn't any better. After he joined my defense, he went over all my documents with a fine-tooth comb, including all the work Chris Rusch had done. He bitched and moaned the whole time. "How could you have worked with such an incompetent?" "How could you have done things so stupidly?" His attitude echoed Cono's: I was an idiot who had botched everything up, and I should cut a deal and be done with it.

My lawyers were making my decision a tough one. In my heart and in my gut, I wanted to fight the DOJ, but in my head I wondered if Cono and Silver were right.

A couple of things happened that helped me make a decision.

One was that I got a letter from my dad. He said he wouldn't be comfortable, as my father, seeing me plead guilty when I wasn't guilty. "If you do that," he told me, "your whole life will change. You may think you'll be getting past this trouble faster, but you'll have to live with that decision for the rest of your life. Remember, once you sign an admission of guilt, there's no going back. You're guilty forever. It's a one-way street."

He was right about that. I knew it in my belly.

The other thing that happened was we heard from Vicki's mom and learned that John Lee had opted for a full round of chemo and radiation therapy. He was planning to fight his cancer aggressively, no holds barred.

That hit me powerfully. If John Lee, a man who had served as a fighter pilot in the air force, who had done three tours in Vietnam, who had fathered the woman I loved and raised five children to be decent, caring adults, could find the courage to endure the blows of chemo and radiation, at his age and in his weakened condition, then how could I, in the prime of my life, simply fold my cards and give up my battle? If John could fight, then, damn it, so would I.

I called Cono Namorato and said, "If I decide to fight this thing, what do we need to do?"

"Well, we...*you* need to find a litigator."

Right. Cono was a negotiator. A lover, not a fighter. When I asked him to refer me to a litigator, he said he couldn't help. No names came to mind. Right.

I started doing some research of my own and found the website of an attorney named Michael Minns out of Houston, Texas. His credentials impressed me. But even more impressive were his track record and testimonials. There were quotes on his home page from congressmen, authors, and law professors, saying things like, "Minns is a giant," "The finest legal mind in America," "If I were ever charged with a criminal tax issue, Mike Minns would be my guy," "Michael Minns blasts corrupt judges, champions the underdog, and even beats up on the IRS," and "If you are accused of a tax crime and you don't have Michael Minns…pack your toothbrush and tell your family you're going to be a guest of the Feds for a while."

Minns was described by his clients as having great integrity, caring deeply about the people he served, and being an "anti-lawyer." It all sounded great to me. I must have read every word on his website a hundred times.

Finally I picked up the phone and gave him a call.

I honestly don't remember what we talked about that first time, but I remember that he passed my gut test with flying colors. I liked the guy immediately and felt I could trust him. But, of course, I still needed to vet him—I'd been burned by websites before.

I went back to Cono and asked, "Do you know a lawyer named Michael Minns? He's done some pretty high-profile tax cases."

"Can't say as I've heard of him."

I called Minns back and shared Cono's response. Minns burst out laughing. "That's rich," he said. "I had two IRS lawyers disbarred in a very high-profile case. It was the only time in US history that active IRS attorneys have ever been disbarred in the course of duty. And *Cono Namorato* was the one who had to fire them. He *damn well* knows who I am."

I didn't know what kind of game Namorato was playing, but I knew for sure that I didn't trust him at all anymore.

By this time I was leaning very heavily toward working with Minns. Every instinct was telling me that he might be the one guy who could help me here. But at the same time, I was coming to a stark realization: Just as admitting guilt would be an irreversible decision, so would deciding to fight. There was no middle ground here. The moment I made the decision to fight, I would have to ride this thing out to the bitter end.

Win, lose, or draw. The die would be cast.

Maybe it was time to meet this Minns guy in person.

CHAPTER FOURTEEN

Meeting Michael Minns

In November or December of 2010, Vicki and I packed up my records to go see Michael Minns in Houston. It was a ridiculously huge assemblage of paperwork. We had six or eight fat binders packed with tax returns, banking records, e-mails and other correspondence, info on the shareholders who'd been contacted by the DOJ, materials on my hedge fund and charitable foundation—anything Chris Rusch had put his hands on—and more. Everything was organized according to the way I thought the government would likely go after me.

We met Michael Minns at his Houston office, dragging the binders behind us in wheeling suitcases. He introduced us to Ashley Arnett, his partner. She was a younger attorney who helped him with all his litigation cases. Smart, capable, no-nonsense.

As for Minns himself, we learned some intriguing things about him. He was a *literal* fighter. He boxed in the ring and had won the Golden Gloves competition in Houston. Having started his career as a high school English teacher and single parent, he knew what it was like to struggle and had a reputation for fighting for the underdog, even when there was no money to be made for him. He was fearless about taking on the government and had written two books, *How to Survive the IRS: My Battles Against Goliath* and a best-seller called *The Underground Lawyer*, which had become a bit of a bible for defense lawyers. Many of his cases had been publicized in the press, and he'd appeared as a guest on *Geraldo*, *The Today Show*, CNN, CBS, and NBC. More importantly, he had a record of winning roughly half of his cases against the government. That might not sound impressive until you consider the fact that in federal court, the government wins about 97 percent of the time.

Mike Minns was proud to say he'd never worked for "the other side."

This guy knew how to fight, he knew the law, and he wasn't afraid.

Minns was also very scrupulous about money. He explained that he carefully documented his spending on each case and always tried to save clients' money whenever possible. The money aspect wasn't especially important to me, but I was glad to see that it was important to *him*. Since the investigation had started, I had spent well over $100,000 on attorneys, with almost nothing to show for it, and Steve Kerr was over half a million in the hole to Paul Charlton, who had done nothing thus far but botch a motion and mousse his hair.

Minns had the whole day blocked out for our meeting and wasn't charging us for his time. That impressed me, after dealing with so many lawyers who wouldn't cross a room to shake your hand unless that hand was holding a check.

When Minns recovered from the shock of seeing all the binders, I kicked off the meeting by going over the basics of the case, even though I'd already done so by phone. "In 2006," I said, "I was approached by my attorney, Chris Rusch, who proposed the idea of starting a bank in Switzerland so that my partner, Steve Kerr, and I would have easier access to foreign investment money. We paid Rusch $45,000 apiece to keep us in compliance with offshore tax rules. We agreed that Steve and I would own no more than 4 percent of the Swiss corporation, and then we sent Rusch some of our assets, in the form of stock we owned, to get the bank started. After that, some things may or may not have been handled incorrectly, but I don't really know all the details because I wasn't an officer, director, or control person. I was an investor, and I had bigger things to worry about at the time."

Minns patiently combed through the binders as I recounted my history with Rusch, blow by blow, over the next couple of hours. It was the first time that Vicki had heard me tell the whole story from the ground up, and she listened with rapt attention. Minns acknowledged that he did not understand much of the financial material—such as the hedge fund stuff—so he skimmed it only lightly, but the e-mails clearly grabbed his interest.

After reading several of them carefully, and scanning through the rest, he snapped the binder shut decisively and slapped it down on his desk.

"All you know is that you own 4 percent," he said. "That's all you asked for, and that's all you know. Period. You weren't required to report that holding. Therefore, you've done nothing wrong." Minns had distilled the contents of the binders down to the one key fact that he thought was the cornerstone of the case.

"So can you help me?" I asked, feeling a rush of relief.

"I believe I can. So…" He sat up straight and looked me in the eye. "Are you going to hire me?"

I hadn't expected to be asked to deliver a decision so quickly. "I don't know why you're asking *me*," I told him. "Ask her." I pointed to Vicki.

Vicki turned to me. "After what I've heard today," she said to me—remember, this was the first time she had heard the complete account of the case—"I don't see how you can *not* hire him."

"There's your answer," I said to Minns. "Yes. I am going to hire you, but first I need to clean some things up. I need to talk to Steve Kerr, my partner. He's doing his own thing, and he's all over the place. He still thinks he might settle with the DOJ. If he's doing one thing and we're doing another, this won't work. So I need to get him on board. I also think it's still possible to get Rusch to work with us."

"Nah," said Minns, "Rusch is going to roll over."

"What?" I said, surprised. "I don't see that happening."

"Mark my words. Not only will he roll over," insisted Minns. "But he'll be the lead government witness."

I didn't agree with Minns's prediction but kept my comments to myself for the moment.

Minns told me I'd need to hire a local attorney as part of the legal team, to handle routine court appearances and other matters. He also asked me what my budget was for fighting this thing.

"I want to say it's unlimited," I replied, "but at the same time, I don't want to go crazy."

"Understood."

"And *your* fee?" I asked.

"It'll be $200,000 for now," he said, "which may or may not cover everything. It probably won't—not if this goes to federal court." Well, at least he was honest about it. That was a refreshing change.

"And what do you think will happen to me?" I asked, explaining my fears of being arrested publicly or in front of my family.

"They may charge you with securities violations," he answered, "which means they might show up at your door. It's unlikely they'll seize your assets. And they probably won't wake your kids in the middle of the night with guns in their hands. But if you hire me, we'll get ahead of that kind of thing. We'll talk to the prosecutors and make sure they don't pull any stunts like that."

I told Minns I'd send him $25,000 as a good faith gesture but that I'd have to make sure the Kerr piece was going to fall into place before pulling the trigger on the rest of the $200,000. And with that we parted ways.

It felt great to have a path toward possible victory.

* * *

After being back home for a few days, my resolve to fight began to wane, and I found myself reassessing my hand of cards yet again. Cono Namorato, whom I was still working with, continued pressing me to take the deal. When I talked to Kerr, he hemmed and hawed, didn't seem at all convinced that fighting was our best play.

Kerr told me I should get Minns to come to Phoenix, to meet with his people. Then he would be better able to make a decision. Minns agreed to come. Of course, the holidays were now upon us, and it was going to be tough to get a bunch of attorneys together in the same room. So Minns and Kerr's legal team agreed to a meeting in Phoenix immediately after the New Year.

In the meantime, I continued to drive myself crazy with uncertainty. Fight or fold? My decision was not yet carved in stone, I realized.

A family trip back to Spokane for the Christmas holiday didn't help. We went to see John Lee and found him hiding in the back bedroom of his house with his oxygen tank. He didn't want to come out. He had begun his chemo and radiation in November and had dropped from 180 pounds to about 110. The radiation was diminishing his capacity to think, and he was a ravaged man.

I was shocked and shaken by the changes.

"John," I said to him. "You don't have to do this." I meant fight. He didn't have to fight anymore. Not if the radiation and chemo was doing *this* to him.

"Yes, I do, Mike," he answered. "The doctors told me this is my best hope, so I'm going to do it, all the way through to…the end. I have to try to beat this thing."

Suddenly I didn't find John's resolve as inspiring as I had before. I wondered, in fact, if he might be delusional. Was fighting *really* his best course of action at this point? Might not the treatment be causing him more harm than the illness? Had his judgment been compromised by the radiation? Was he capable of thinking straight anymore?

I realized, of course, that I was asking the same kinds of question about myself. When we returned to Phoenix, I felt sadder and more confused than ever.

It was a phone call that finally pushed me off the fence once and for all. A few days before the end of 2010, Cono Namorato called. He launched into his usual spiel about how the government was going to pulverize me and I stood no chance. I wasn't in the mood for it. With New Year's Day just around the corner, I was looking for some way to feel optimistic about 2011. And Cono wasn't helping.

I said to him, "Cono, here's what it all boils down to. You're telling me to take a plea simply because there's a big, bad government out there."

I'll never forget his response. "Son," he said, "that's the way it's always been, and that's the way it will always be."

No. I refused to accept that. The government didn't get to ruin a person's life, just because it had all the power. Sorry.

I was done with that kind of thinking. I was done with feeling like a victim in this. I was done with compromise.

I was done with Cono Namorato.

A mental switch flipped in my brain. I was going to fight. I was all in. No turning back. No more doubt. "It's you and me, John," I thought to myself. "You, me, and Michael Minns."

* * *

A couple of months later, I got all the confirmation I needed that I'd made the right decision. In late February / early March of 2011, Vicki and I got word that her dad's treatment had taken a turn for the worse.

Back in January, when he was due to begin the second round of chemo and radiation treatment, the doctors had had to postpone it because he was so weak. But John had convinced them to start it back up again. About three weeks into that second round, he had lost so much weight and was in such bad shape physically that they had to call off the dogs. The writing was on the wall. John was not going to win this battle. He was transferred to a terminal care center.

That's where he was staying when Vicki and I and the girls went to see him for the last time. We learned that he had become extremely confused and incoherent. According to the nursing staff, he no longer knew where he was or what day or year it was. The radiation and the brain cancer had been a one-two punch that had finally robbed him of his beautiful mind.

Vicki's younger sister Nicole approached us before we entered his room and tried to temper our expectations. "He stopped talking to anyone about a week ago," she said, "so he won't be able to communicate with you, but I think some part of him will know you're here."

We stepped toward the room and froze inside the doorway. Neither of us could believe how quickly the cancer had done its work. As frail as he'd looked back in December, he was now little more than a living skeleton. It was hard to imagine what was keeping him alive. I had trouble connecting the gaunt frame on the bed with the robust and vital man I'd always known.

In the few seconds we stood there in the doorway, my entire life with John played out on the movie screen of my mind, from the first time I'd shown up at his door, at age seventeen, to pick up fifteen-year-old Vicki for our first date and he'd refused to let her get on my motorcycle to the sight of him bent over his K-Mart smoker, cooking that final Labor Day meal.

John Lee had always been strong in body and mind. During our early years together, when he was still in the air force, he ran his household with military precision, barking orders at his children as if they were airmen under his command. A lot of people found him intimidating because of that. But for some reason, I never did. Maybe it was because I had served in the military too. I had always been able to see the gentler and more thoughtful man behind the facade. John did a lot of things for me, I remembered. He paid for Vicki's and my wedding. When I left the service and couldn't find work, it was John who hired me to cut grass or shovel snow, so I'd be able to put food on my newlywed table. And often, when I just needed advice or someone to talk to—before Vicki and I moved to Scottsdale—it would be John and me sitting in his living room for hours, talking and drinking martinis.

After he retired, John's more genteel side began to emerge. He became quite the literary man, working on his writing and helping others with theirs. One thing that John understood, and shared with me, was the dual-edged sword that the government represented. John loved his country, but he also knew how powerful and dangerous the government could be. As I stood there inside the door of his room, I recalled a poem he had written—my favorite of his—that somehow captured both the sacred duty of serving one's country and also the danger of jumping to the government's tune unquestioningly.

I include the poem here in its entirety, because it says a great deal about who John Lee was and why his opinion and his advice mattered so much to me.

Someone Said
by Colonel John W. Lee

As someone said, in '62,
"Seek not the fame your fathers knew.
Go, find a better way to give
And teach the world a way to live."

Then someone said, "Go far away.
Go, take this torch, and do not stray
From purpose bold, from purpose brave,
And take our love to those you save."

And as on other shores we toiled
And fought for lives we often soiled,
Our souls recoiled and wept for dead
Who'd never heard what someone said.

And soon our glowing purpose bold
Became the bane of battles old.
And someone said, "You've gone too far."
And others feared a larger war.

Then someone said, "Let's end the fight.
Bring home our torch, bring home the light.
Seek not a better way to give,
Teach not the world a way to live.

Bring home your hearts, there's naught to gain,
Forget your dead, forget your pain."

And someone said it all was wrong;
That our brave purpose took too long.

So back we came, to home returned,
Brought home the torch that all now spurned,
Saw the flame fade, as our light fled,
And all forgot what someone said.

Now years have gone, a black wall grown,
And blossomed names from seeds we'd sown
On other shores, in others' stead,
They'd tried to do what someone said.

Now mourners come, and spread the pall,
And seek our souls locked in that wall,
And never question, in our stead,
"Why did we do what someone said?"

Why, indeed? Why did we humans so often do what "someone said" instead of following our own deepest beliefs and instincts?

Vicki stepped close to John's bed. As soon as she did, he opened his eyes. I had a sense he wanted to say something, so I went over to him. He took my hand, looked at me, and said, as clearly as he'd ever spoken in his life, "You've got to fight them, Mike. I believe in you." Then he faded into unconsciousness again.

I promised him I would take his words to heart.

John W. Lee never spoke to anyone again, and he never came back to mental clarity.

Several days later, on March 13, 2011, he died.

And with his death, I vowed to fight to clear my family's name until every last option had been exhausted.

CHAPTER FIFTEEN

The Battle Begins

On January 4, the second working day of 2011, attorney Mike Minns and his associate Ashley Arnett arrived in Phoenix for our meeting with Steve Kerr's legal team.

The meeting was held at Gallagher-Kennedy, where Paul Charlton, the Movie Star, was employed. Attending the meeting were Minns, Arnett, Steve Kerr and I, and Joy Bertrand, the local Phoenix attorney I had hired at the urging of Mike Minns. Hiring her set me back another $25,000—but, hey, what was a few bucks when you were having fun?

Here was the annoying thing. Everyone who'd had to fly or drive to the meeting was there on time; the only person late was the Movie Star himself.

Fifteen minutes after the scheduled start time of the meeting, the Movie Star marched into the room with five attorneys from Gallagher-Kennedy, all in single file, and they took their places at the table. The delayed grand entry seemed intended to impress and intimidate the rest of us. All it managed to do was piss Mike Minns off. He hated that kind of lawyer theatrics.

Minns politely listened to everything Kerr's legal team had to say—we didn't want a repeat of the screaming match that had taken place in San Diego—but I think after the Movie Star's "grand entry," Minns's mind was already made up; he would try to persuade Steve to find another lawyer. Minns had already suggested an excellent local attorney to Steve, but Steve wasn't sold on him yet.

After the meeting, Minns spoke to Steve again. Steve was clearly having doubts about working with the Movie Star. As I said, he had already spent over half a million dollars—probably closer to $700,000—on Gallagher-Kennedy, and this was *before charges had even been filed yet in the case.* But at the same time, he felt invested in his team. Minns again suggested that Steve talk to the local attorney, a man by the name of Mike Kimerer (too many Mikes in this story, I know, but what can I do?). In Minns's opinion, Kimerer was one of the best lawyers *in the country*, and he had an office nearby. Steve agreed.

Kimerer was an older gentleman, a solo practitioner with a ton of trial experience. He had won some awards and had a lot of other feathers in his cap: former president of the American Board of Criminal Lawyers; service on several state bar and supreme court committees; former state bar president; a listing in Best Lawyers in America; and an "AV Preeminent" designation from Martindale-Hubbell, the lawyer-rating organization.

Minns took Steve Kerr to Kimerer's office and introduced the two men. Kerr and Kimerer immediately got along well, and it turned out that Minns had already prenegotiated a flat-rate deal for Kimerer to represent Kerr. It was a lot less than Minns was charging me, but I didn't care. (Again, this thing was never about the money for me, and I gladly paid far more than my share of the legal expenses all the way through the process.) I was just glad to see Kerr, Minns, and Kimerer singing in three-part harmony. The price was right, so Kerr pulled the trigger. He hired Kimerer on the spot and was officially finished with the Movie Star. Good riddance.

With that piece of business behind us, I told the new team, "Now that we're all here in one place, I bet we can get Chris Rusch to join us."

I called Rusch (on the burner phone). He was happy to jump on the next available flight—San Diego to Phoenix takes only a little more than an hour. I picked him up at the airport, and within a few hours of making the call, we were all sitting together in Kimerer's conference room.

At this point, a meeting took place that would turn out to have major impact on the trial. Though Rusch would later try to put his own spin on the nature and purpose of this meeting, Minns viewed it, correctly, as a "passing of the torch," where one lawyer hands off a case to another. Rusch had been Steve's and my previous attorney, and now that he could no longer represent us, Minns and Kimerer wanted to hear his summary of the case, ask him questions, and gather any other insight, background, and information he might provide.

Rusch started the meeting by making the disclaimer that government prosecutors had named him as a "subject" in the investigation. However, he said, he'd had no further communication with them. He'd had no offer of immunity and had not been tendered a deal of any kind. He didn't know what the government's legal angle was. He said he believed that he, Steve, and I would be better off working together as a team and said he was happy that we all finally had this opportunity to talk in person.

Rusch went over the basics of the case from his POV. His version was pretty consistent with what I'd already told Minns. Rusch explained that he was the person who had set up the corporations in Switzerland, that the Swiss structure was never intended to be a tax-dodging tool, and that all the actions taken in Switzerland were his doing and his responsibility. His intention all along, he said, had been to establish an overseas banking corporation, one in which all operations and all decision-making took place outside the USA. By setting up the business that way, he explained, the company could earn money as a freestanding entity. The only time a US investor in the company, such as Kerr or I, would create a taxable event would be if he or she drew dividends or income from that company.

Rusch told the lawyers that he had never set up an offshore corporation before this one, though he admitted that he had pitched himself to Steve and me as an expert in such matters. Still, everything had been done legally, Rusch insisted, and at no point did he, Steve, Kerr, or I commit any actions with illegal or fraudulent intent. All the paperwork was handled correctly, including the initial transfer of the stock to fund the company.

Any problems that *may* have occurred, he said, arose later when the original business plan got stalled. Rusch explained that he'd had difficulty getting the Swiss business off the ground. The two investment advisors he'd hired over there were charging high fees, losing money, and failing to attract investors. The company just wasn't getting any traction. As a result, the startup money essentially just sat around in the UBS holding accounts for a couple of years, and because of that, it began to generate reporting requirements—such as FBAR filings—that would *not* have been necessary if the business had gone forward actively as planned. (There were also, he noted, a couple of stock transactions that, in retrospect, should not have taken place at all.) But Rusch clearly stated that neither Steve nor I were aware of any potential tax/legal issues, and at no time did we withdraw any money from the Swiss accounts. In fact, the accounts were set up in such a way that we could not have accessed the money even if we wanted. The few times we were paid money from the accounts, as a result of transactions he did, we reported the money on our taxes and paid the full income tax rate of 35 percent on it. And because we never had any interactions with the holding banks—never saw any statements from them or had any communication with them—we would not have known that FBARs needed to be filed, unless Rusch specifically told us. Which he acknowledged he had not.

Essentially, Rusch confirmed for our new attorneys that Steve and I had done nothing wrong and that if mistakes had taken place, they were his doing. We had simply followed the instructions he had given us as our tax attorney. If indeed the Swiss venture had "fallen out of compliance" with the tax laws, this was a passive failure, not an active one. And it was not something Steve Kerr or I could have been expected to be aware of, as non-attorneys not actively involved in the operation.

Chris was more open than I imagined he'd be, given his somewhat tenuous legal position.

What Rusch did not realize—nor did I or Mike Minns at that time—was that the entire meeting was being recorded. Yup, someone in the room (I never found out who) had taped the whole thing.

More on that later.

*　*　*

With our legal teams finally set in stone, we entered a waiting game. Much of the year 2011 was spent in "calm before the storm" mode. As I described earlier, this was a year of intense emotional ups and downs. I lived in constant fear of being arrested and was deeply worried about what was going to happen to my family. Still, I had to wall off those concerns so that I could continue to function and earn a living. There were long stretches where it seemed that nothing at all was happening with the investigation, but then I'd hear from friends and associates who'd been questioned either by Stockwell, the main prosecutor in the case, or by Monica Edelstein or by the grand jury, and/or by DOJ agent Lisa Giovanelli.

These friends all reported that they hadn't told the government anything incriminating—mainly because there was *nothing incriminating to report*. In the past I had done business with these friends, honestly and transparently, and had acquired stock from them in perfectly legal ways. The government's notion that I was guilty of securities violations seemed to be a dead-end street.

I actually started to think that all this DOJ questioning might be a good thing, that it might lead the feds to abandon the idea of charging me. "The more they dig into this," I said to Minns, "the less they're going to find. I didn't do anything wrong. At some point, aren't they just going to take their marbles and go home?"

"No," said Minns, bursting my fantasy bubble. "The government *never* invests this kind of time and money in an investigation without bringing charges." He was, however, fairly confident that the government would not physically arrest me. When and if charges were filed, he believed, the government would allow me to turn myself in. Monica Edelstein had, in fact, personally assured him of this.

We know how *that* went.

On January 29, 2012, I was arrested on the golf course and hauled to the 4th Avenue jail. And here's where the story picks up from where I left it in chapter 1.

As you may recall, I was taken in shackles from the US Marshal's office to my arraignment hearing, where I was ordered by a marshal not to make eye contact with Vicki. During that hearing, Monica Edelstein argued passionately to the magistrate judge that I should be held in custody until trial. The stone-faced marshal stood by me, ready to whisk me out the back door and into the prison shuttle. I was terrified about the prospect of going to jail because, as I said earlier, I knew that in Arizona, cases often took eighteen months between arraignment and trial.

The heavy-handedness of the arresting team was what saved me. When the judge learned that I had been handcuffed by armed officers at a golf course and thrown in jail, he was quite angry about the overkill. And so he set bail and allowed me to walk free on my own recognizance, pending trial.

Getting out on bail was an enormous relief.

But that relief was soon tempered by the barrage of news stories that hit the press and the Web. These stories were told in an entirely one-sided way—the government's side. There were headlines such as, "Hiding a Golf Course and Millions," "Lawyer Helped 2 Hide Millions in UBS, Other Banks," and "Three UBS Clients Charged with Hiding Money in Offshore Accounts." The articles were full of unproven accusations that the average reader would undoubtedly accept as fact. Let me tell you, seeing those articles forever changed the way I read and watch the news. They said things like these:

> It's one thing to hide a few dollars. It's quite
> another to hide a few million dollars…[T]hree
> individuals involved in venture capital are alleged
> to have hidden away millions of dollars and

RIGGED

a golf course in Colorado through secret Swiss accounts.[3]

Kerr and Quiel filed false tax returns with the IRS in 2007 and 2008, hiding their overseas accounts, and failed to disclose overseas assets to the U.S. Treasury Department as required by law.[4]

Three ex-UBS AG clients, including two who ran venture capital firms, were indicted on charges of hiding millions of dollars in assets from U.S. tax authorities through the use of secret offshore accounts.[5]

Unless you've had false information printed about you, you probably can't imagine how infuriating it was to see pure conjecture reported this way. I felt like the victim of a smear campaign, one that had the full sanctioning of the US government. I wanted to respond immediately by publishing my own press releases. But of course, Michael Minns ordered me to do no such thing.

All I could do was suck it up and hope to salvage my reputation by winning at trial. Even if we *did* win at trial, though, I knew that most of the damage had already been done. Half the people who read about my arrest would never read about my acquittal, and of those who did, half would probably still think I was guilty.

The DOJ's own press release was, unsurprisingly, the most damning of all:

---

[3] http://www.taxabletalk.com/2012/01/30/hiding-a-golf-course-and-millions.

[4] http://www.law360.com/articles/304706/lawyer-helped-2-hide-millions-in-ubs-other-banks-doj.

[5] http://dorotbensimon.com/2012/02/three-ubs-clients-charged-with-hiding-money-in-offshore-accounts.

Department of Justice
Office of Public Affairs

FOR IMMEDIATE RELEASE Monday, January 30, 2012

UBS Clients and Tax Attorney Indicted in Phoenix for Hiding Assets in Secret Foreign Bank Accounts

Phoenix-area businessmen Stephen M. Kerr and Michael Quiel and former San Diego attorney Christopher M. Rusch were charged in Phoenix with conspiracy to defraud the Internal Revenue Service (IRS) for concealing millions of dollars in assets in numerous secret Swiss bank accounts held at UBS and elsewhere, the Justice Department and Internal Revenue Service (IRS) announced. The charges are contained in an indictment returned by a federal grand jury on Dec. 8, 2011, which was unsealed today. Kerr and Quiel were each also charged with filing false individual income tax returns for tax years 2007 and 2008 and failing to file Reports of Foreign Bank and Financial Accounts (FBARs) for those same years. Rusch was arrested yesterday by U.S. law enforcement agents in Miami after being removed from Panama by Panamanian authorities at the request of the United States. Quiel was also arrested yesterday in the Phoenix area.

After providing some background information on each of us, it continued...

Beginning in or before 2004, and continuing through at least December 2007, Kerr and Quiel obtained control of shares of stock of publicly traded domestic companies in a way that concealed their ownership of the stock. Kerr and Quiel then deposited the stock, or proceeds from the sale of the stock, to multiple undeclared bank accounts set up with the assistance of Rusch at UBS in Switzerland and at another Swiss bank. These accounts were all held in the names of nominee entities to further conceal Kerr's and Quiel's ownership. Kerr and Quiel also used the accounts to conceal income earned from the subsequent sale of this stock from the IRS. In 2007, the combined total net assets in Kerr's accounts exceeded $5.6 million and Quiel's accounts exceeded $2.6 million. Rusch maintained signature authority over the secret accounts and, with the assistance of a Swiss account manager and financial intermediary, facilitated transactions on behalf of Kerr and Quiel.

...In addition, Rusch utilized his client trust account to transfer funds to Kerr's and Quiel's undeclared Swiss accounts and to repatriate funds back to the United States for the benefit of Kerr and Quiel. None of the three defendants disclosed the existence of these offshore accounts, or any income earned through these offshore accounts, to the IRS for the years charged in the indictment.

The conspiracy and FBAR charges each carry a maximum potential penalty of five years in prison and a $250,000 fine. The false return charges each carry a maximum potential penalty of three years in prison and a $250,000 fine.

This case is being prosecuted by Trial Attorneys Timothy Stockwell and Monica Edelstein of the Justice Department's Tax Division and was investigated with the assistance of the IRS.

At the end, it added the almost comical tag line:

> An indictment is only an allegation of criminal conduct and is not evidence of guilt. A person is presumed innocent until and unless proven guilty beyond a reasonable doubt in a court of law.

Right. Thanks, DOJ. We're sure you mean that sincerely.

News stories weren't the only damaging thing that got published in the wake of my arrest. One day I was talking to my brother-in-law in Spokane, and he said to me, "Hey Mike, did you know your tax returns have been posted online?"

"You're joking, right?" I replied, realizing I should have known better by this point.

"Wish I was," he said. "You might want to check it out. It's on this site called Scribd. They've got your whole family's social security numbers out there for anyone to see."

I immediately went on the site and discovered that indeed my tax returns were posted there. Because they were evidence in a federal case, they were considered public information. The court's electronic records system, PACER, routinely posts such documents online. Then there are outside sites, such as Scribd, that republish the documents and make them public.

The uploading rules on PACER, however, clearly specify that all personal information must be redacted from documents before posting them.

The government hadn't bothered to do that. Instead, it had carelessly posted my tax returns with all my family's *real social security numbers* still on them. It took a while to clear this up. I was finally able to get the source website to redact the numbers, and the outside sites eventually followed suit, but not before one of my daughters became a victim of identity theft. We learned about this when someone tried to open a DirecTV account and a credit card using her SS number. After that, I had to get LifeLock accounts for all my kids.

When I brought the situation to the government's attention, of course, they offered no apology and no accountability. I got the government version of a "Hey, shit happens." Monica Edelstein even claimed in court that the numbers *had* been redacted, which was simply untrue. Accountability and truthfulness, you see, are required only of private citizens.

* * *

The year 2012, after my arrest and release on bail, was another year of waiting and preparing. We were given a November trial date—ten months out, not bad for the state of Arizona. But then, thanks to various motions and continuances, it ended up being pushed to March of 2013.

One important thing that happened during 2012 was that we finally learned, once and for all, that Chris Rusch was not going to be our ally. Up till this point, believe it or not, I still didn't think Rusch would turn on us. I guess it's the mark of a true conman that you want to keep believing in him. Or maybe he really *didn't* want to turn on us; maybe the feds just put him in such fear for his own ass that he felt he had no choice but to cut a deal.

At the time of Rusch's arrest—the same day as Steve's and mine—he had been living in Panama. He had moved there (leaving his family behind, I'm told) to run some new offshore businesses, such as a tax prep business that used Panamanian preparers at a fraction of the cost of US employees.

The DOJ, in typical fashion, did not bother to try to legally extradite Rusch to the United States. What fun would that have been? Rather, they went for drama and intimidation again. They waited for a plane he was on to land in Panama, captured him at gunpoint on the tarmac, and flew him to Miami. From there they did a little "diesel therapy" and had him bused to the jail in Florence, Arizona. That's one long ride in which to do some thinking.

No "personal recognizance" for Rusch, though. They kept him locked up for five months. I heard he was beaten up by the authorities before he even made it to Florence, though I can't swear for a fact that happened. I am pretty sure, though, that they did find ways to pressure him, intimidate him, and "break" him while he was in jail.

After he'd been in prison for three months, his parents put up their house for bond money, and a motion was made to let him out on bail. Inexplicably, it took the court two months to decide on the motion (maybe because they liked having ready access to him), but he was finally allowed to return to California to live with his parents pending trial. He had to wear an ankle bracelet and was basically under house arrest.

Sometime later, he appeared in court again in Phoenix. This time he pled guilty to several charges, including conspiracy to defraud the US government and failure to file an FBAR. When he entered that guilty plea, I knew he had turned. He had cut a deal with the government. My suspicions were further confirmed by the fact that after he entered his plea, they removed his ankle bracelet. Why would you remove someone's ankle bracelet *after* he pled guilty? Wouldn't he be *more* of a flight risk now that he knew he'd be going to jail? Apparently, the government didn't think so.

Hmm, I wonder why.

Rusch's plea deal was an extremely troubling development. Not that I was afraid of what he might reveal. I was afraid of what he might *invent*. I figured the DOJ was getting frustrated with the way its case was developing. It knew it was going to need some dramatic evidence or testimony if it hoped to get some traction here. And I knew the DOJ would stop at nothing once it had decided it needed a guilty verdict.

Therefore, the only reason the DOJ would cut Chris Rusch a deal was because it expected something juicy from him in return.

Which meant Chris Rusch was about to embark on a new career as a fictional storyteller. And that might be very bad news for Kerr and me.

CHAPTER SIXTEEN

Pretrial and Jury Selection

I gave my defense team a blank check to pay for whatever resources we needed, so we were able to pursue some options that aren't on the table for many defendants, such as staging a mock trial, flying in a team of expert witnesses, and hiring a jury consultant. In the end, I'm not convinced any of this stuff helped us very much, and in some ways, it worked against us. If I had it to do over again, I'd probably skip some of the bells and whistles and rely more heavily on the wisdom of my core team.

The mock trial, which we held many months before the real one, was an eye-opening exercise in several ways—though, again, I'm not sure it accomplished much in the long run except add to my frustration and worry.

A mock trial, in case you've never seen one, is a staged rendition of a real trial that you present for a group of volunteer jurors. The purpose of the exercise is to show you strengths and weaknesses of your case (and the prosecution's), and to test-fly the way your case will play with a jury. Of course, a mock trial is quite condensed and abbreviated and full of guesswork about what the prosecution will do, so it's not an accurate reflection of a real trial. Not even close. Still, it can give you information that helps you strategize your real defense. Theoretically, anyway.

In our case, the mock trial was limited to two days. My testimony and Steve's was taped ahead of time, and then the most damaging parts of our testimony were shown to the fake jury. This was deliberate; you want to see how your most problematic evidence and testimony sits with a jury so you can make adjustments before the real trial.

Our mock jury was broken into three groups, so essentially we got three sample juries. The fascinating part was that we got to observe from behind a one-way glass as each of the juries went through its deliberations. One thing I learned from doing this was how absolutely brutal people can be and how willing they are to pull the "guilty" lever. There's an underlying assumption that if you are accused by the government, you are guilty. That was a scary thing to witness.

I was equally surprised by my own judgments. I thought I could guess the way jurors would vote, based on their ages and the way they looked and dressed. Again and again they fooled me. Probably the most shocking thing I learned was how arbitrary the whole jury process is, and how your verdict really depends on the hand of cards you happen to draw. One group of jurors may see things one way, the next group may have a completely different take on the same evidence, based on nothing more than their collective personalities.

In our case, all three of the mock juries ended up hung, though I think we got more "not guilty" than "guilty" votes overall. In one group, ten people were going for guilty, but then a young woman in her twenties stood up and said, "These are people's lives you're talking about and you're willing to convict them based on *this*?" She turned whole group around. If she'd been on the real jury, I'm convinced I would have walked free. It was so arbitrary.

Several issues came up in the mock trial that I wished we could have done a better job addressing in our actual defense. One of these was the prejudicial attitude jurors had about Swiss banking. In their minds, Switzerland was strictly a tax haven, and anyone who banked there could be assumed guilty. We heard remarks like "He knew better than to put his money there" and "Come on, the guy stashed his money in *Switzerland*." I wish we could have found a way to convey the idea that Switzerland, as a nation, is all about quality, not secrecy—look at its knives, its clocks, its chocolates. That Swiss obsession with quality and precision carries into its banking industry, and that's one of the main reasons Switzerland *became* the banking hub of the world. Secrecy is only a minor aspect of Swiss banking. If you're involved in moving money internationally, you inevitably get involved with Switzerland. It doesn't mean you're a criminal! I wanted the jury to understand that.

Another key issue was the jurors' ignorance about stocks. It was clear from the mock trial that they didn't understand stocks in general and certainly didn't understand my ownership of them. People hear about stocks on the news—terms like stock margins, stock trading, and penny stocks—and they form all kinds of half-baked ideas. I wish we could have presented the analogy of the house I mentioned earlier. That is, if I had given Chris Rusch a house to sell instead of a pile of stocks, no one would have indicted me. But because *stocks* were the asset in question, everyone was confused about them, including the prosecution, defense, and jury.

The mock trial also revealed a mind-set that I knew would be almost impossible to combat: most people consider $2 million a crapload of money. I remember at one point the mock prosecutor asked me, with an incredulous tone in his voice, "Mr. Quiel, do you routinely give two million dollars to someone and then give up control of it?" I replied, "Yes," which threw him for a loop. No one involved in the trial could grasp the idea that as a business investor, I was used to losing millions of dollars on deals, and there was no way I would put a business that was generating over a *hundred* million in investments at risk in order to save taxes on a couple of million dollars. People just couldn't wrap their heads around that.

I could see these attitudes were going to work against us, and I tried to communicate my concerns to Minns, but he didn't seem to take them as seriously as I did, or maybe he just thought there was nothing we could do about them. That's not a criticism of Minns. A defense lawyer has a zillion aspects of a trial to juggle, and he knows better than you do what needs to be worried about.

It took me a while to accept that fact. Stepping back and letting Minns manage my defense *his* way—when *my* life and *my* freedom was at stake—was one of the hardest things I've ever had to do. But a lesson I have learned in business is that if you're going to hire people to do a job, you need to let them do it their way. You can't micromanage them. So the way I learned to work with Minns was that I would voice my concerns to him, sometimes arguing passionately for my point of view, then I would walk away and let him make the final decision. This wasn't easy, but I believe it was the right way to go.

Minns earned my confidence by doing a lot of things right in the pretrial phase. For example, one of the first things he told me was, "If you owe any taxes to the IRS, you should send them in now."

"I don't *know* if I owe them anything," I said. "Isn't that going to be determined by the court?"

"Well, if it turns out you *do* owe them money," he replied, "and you haven't paid it, that will only be credited against you."

"Okay," I said. "I'll send some money in."

In March of 2012, I sent a $500,000 check to IRS. This turned out to be good advice from Minns; in October of 2012, the IRS sent me a refund check for $500,000, which was held as evidence and I had to retrieve after the trial. That check was a thing of beauty. What better way to prove to a jury that I didn't owe any tax money than to show them an actual refund check from the IRS, recently dated? If a picture is worth a thousand words, I figured, a check must be worth a million.

Late in 2012, Minns did another smart thing. He filed a motion to prevent the prosecution from calling expert witnesses. The way that happened was this:

As the trial date drew closer, the discovery process was going on, and lots of motions were being filed back and forth (and posted on the court's electronic PACER system). We were also preparing our expert witnesses, flying them to Phoenix so we could strategize with them before the trial. In the midst of all this, the prosecution filed a motion that contained *their* expert witness list—and it was *blank*. This was one of Stockwell's tactics that he had used at past trials. He figured he'd have an opportunity to fill it in later. Minns alertly noticed the missing information and filed a motion stating that the prosecution should now be forbidden from using any expert witnesses at trial. Judge Teilborg agreed.

The prosecution freaked out and filed an emergency motion, saying they had a woman, Deborah Saparata, they *needed* to use at trial as a tax accounting specialist. But the judge was adamant: no expert testimony for the prosecution. So that was a big win for us, and it happened before the trial even started.

There were a number of pretrial hearings in late 2012 / early 2013. To be honest, I don't recall what happened at any of these. What I do remember was being overwhelmed by the setting itself. The Sandra Day O'Connor United States Courthouse in Phoenix is a grand and sobering place. The courtroom we were assigned was huge, with multitoned wood paneling, recessed lighting, and an oversize federal seal of an eagle hanging over the judge's bench. I was in awe, frankly. I didn't want to be sitting in that seat, but I was still in awe. Earlier in my life I might have viewed the grandeur of the courthouse as an example of government waste. But now, as a defendant, I saw it differently. I understood that the timeless architecture and imposing structure were meant to communicate a message: shopping malls may come and go, but truth and justice are lasting. What happens within these walls *matters*. I felt comforted by this message somehow.

This was a place where lies could not survive, I thought.

Silly rabbit.

* * *

At last the trial date arrived. March 5, 2013. The first piece of business before opening arguments was, of course, the selection of the jury.

The mock trial had shown us some of the challenges we'd be up against in finding twelve suitable jurors. I don't mean to sound "classist"—I'm from a working-class background myself, and I washed and repaired airplanes as a young man, you'll recall—but I knew it wasn't going to be easy to find a dozen working-class people who could (a) understand stocks and the business model I used in my investing work, (b) grasp the idea that I earned enough income that a couple million dollars was not a major amount to me, and (c) keep an open mind about the guilt or innocence of a hedge fund manager who had assets in a Swiss bank account.

You're supposed to be tried by a jury of your peers, but looking around the room, I could see that wasn't going to happen. I guess I shouldn't have been surprised. After all, what kind of people can take five weeks off to sit through a lengthy trial? Not the movers and shakers, sorry to be blunt about it. As I once heard a comedian express it, "When you go trial, your fate rests in the hands of twelve people who are too stupid to get out of jury duty." Now, I'm not saying that people who serve on juries are stupid—far from it—but I do think it's fair to observe that juries consist mainly of retired people, teachers, and other government employees; people who are able to take unlimited time off when they receive a jury summons. Social Security recipients and civil servants. Not exactly an ideal jury pool for a trial that's going to involve complex financial concepts that I had a hard time explaining to my own defense team. (You also have to wonder whether government employees might have a *slight* pro-government bias.)

On the day of jury selection, about 150–200 potential jurors showed up. Each was given a number. We were supposed to start with number 1, then work our way through the pool in order until we had sixteen jurors (twelve regulars and four alternates). Normally, what happens is that jurors are given a questionnaire to fill out ahead of time, and the attorneys on both sides can study these, but Judge Teilborg wanted to do it "old school." He conducted the voir dire verbally. The process began with general questions like, "Does anyone have a family member or friend who's been prosecuted?" Later the lawyers were able to ask more specific questions of individuals. Of course, there's no way to do any fact-checking during voir dire, so you basically have to take everyone's word for whatever they say. One of the jurors we ended up with, for example, said he was a convenience store clerk, but we later learned that he owned three Cricket cell-phone retail stores. So he lied to get *on* the jury. For what reason,

I don't know. He later ended up being the lead juror. Other folks gave answers they obviously hoped would disqualify them.

At the end of the day, we still hadn't nailed down a jury, so we had to continue into day 2 of the trial. Normally, judges don't like to have a night carryover during jury selection, but it couldn't be helped in this case. I thought the situation could actually work in our favor; it would give us the whole evening to strategize.

Not so fast. As I mentioned, I hired a jury consultant to help us. But he surprised us all by announcing that he had a strict eight o'clock bedtime and he wasn't willing to compromise on it—even though I was paying him seventeen grand to be there. So we had to settle for a short strategy discussion over dinner. And here's where I wish I had just kept it simple and trusted my lawyer.

The way jury selection works—at least in this case—is that the defense gets to strike six jurors; the government gets to strike three. Neither side knows which jurors the other side is striking. Both Minns and my jury consultant agreed that there were three particular jurors that needed to be excluded. Minns's thinking was that the government was going to exclude the same jurors, so we should let the prosecution "spend" its strikes on those three; we could go then deeper into the pool with our strikes. The consultant disagreed. He thought it was so important to exclude those three jurors that we couldn't take any chances. Minns finally gave in to the consultant.

The next day—you guessed it—the government excluded the same three jurors. So we, in effect, squandered three of our strikes. The jury consultant was worse than a waste of money; his advice actively worked against us. Who knows how the case would have gone if we'd had a better jury.

The jury we ended up with included a bus driver who kept falling asleep, the Cricket store owner masquerading as a convenience store clerk, and the usual assortment of retirees, teachers, and civil servants. If I had been accused of murder, this might have been a fine jury, but I had serious doubts that these folks were going to be able to understand fine points of securities commerce the government's own investigators and prosecutors couldn't seem to grasp.

Now that we had a jury in place, Minns felt even stronger about a strategy he had already been leaning toward—namely, that he didn't want me to testify at my own trial. For a variety of reasons, he felt I might not come across as believable or trustworthy under fire on the witness stand. I disagreed with him on this. I knew that the one quality that had enabled me to succeed as a broker and investor was that I *was* trustworthy, and people knew that.

"Michael," I said to Minns, "everyone I've ever done business with—friends, partners, clients, coinvestors—likes me, trusts me, thinks I'm a good person, and would be happy to do business with me again. That's why the DOJ hasn't been able to dig up any dirt; no one has anything bad to say about me. Your job is just to make the jury see me the way my friends and associates do. What's so complicated about that?"

"The witness stand is a whole different world," he told me. "I've seen some of the nicest, most honest people get obliterated on the stand and some of the sleaziest jerks come off like Mother Teresa. The fact is, *most* people don't make very good witnesses on their own behalf, and they don't stand up well to cross-examination, especially in a case like this."

"Why's that?"

"Because this case requires a lot of complicated explanations that only a lawyer or financial scholar can give clearly. If *you* try to explain this stuff on the stand, you'll hem and haw and go off on tangents. It will come off as dishonest or misleading, even though it isn't. The prosecution will pick you apart about what you knew or didn't know and will manage to make you look like an idiot or a liar."

"But if Rusch lies about me," I said, "I'm going to want a chance to refute his testimony."

"I know you will, but I don't think that's a good idea. You have a constitutional right not to testify against yourself, and as your attorney, I advise you to avail yourself of that right. Of course, you also have a right to take the stand if you want to. Ultimately it's your decision."

Crap.

No one ever said being a criminal defendant was easy.

CHAPTER SEVENTEEN

The Trial Opens

As the actual trial got rolling, our decision not to have me testify sat heavily in my gut. Although we could still change our minds based on what the prosecution did, both Minns and Kimerer felt pretty committed to the strategy. I had agreed to the decision, but still, it was making me feel scarily out of control. It meant my fate was now *completely* in other people's hands—the prosecutors, my attorneys, the witnesses, the judge, the jury. That was not a position I typically found myself in. As a so-called self-made man, I liked to be the one driving the car in my own life. Now I was strapped into the passenger's seat, and I didn't like it one bit.

The trial, as I've mentioned, was presided over by James A. Teilborg—a thoughtful and knowledgeable jurist, as it turned out. On the prosecution side, the attorneys were Timothy Stockwell and Monica Edelstein. They were smart, ruthless, and from my point of view, wholly uninterested in the truth. Their job was to win, period. The possibility of our innocence was of no concern to them.

Steve Kerr and I were to be tried in tandem, we'd decided. That was because our cases overlapped to a large degree and because we faced the same five charges. However, we each retained our own defense team. Throughout the trial, the jury would be given "limiting instructions," meaning that they could only consider certain evidence for my case or for Steve's.

Michael Kimerer was Steve's main attorney, assisted by Rhonda Neff. I was, as you know, represented by Michael Minns and Ashley Arnett. I also had local attorney Joy Bertrand in my camp, as well as Michael (yes, another Michael) Ware, whose role was to observe the proceedings with a cool head and give the other attorneys objective advice, if needed, during the heat of battle.

Judge Teilborg kicked things off by giving a very thorough set of instructions to the newly impaneled jury, then uttered the fateful words, "At this time the government may present an opening statement."

I found myself clenching my fists and holding my breath. Here we go. This was the first time we would get an official preview of how Stockwell and Edelstein intended to prosecute the case. From the witness list and evidence that had been submitted, we had a general idea of where they were headed, but now we would get a look at the roadmap.

Monica Edelstein rose and faced the jury. I'll never forget her first few words…

"How do you get away with millions tax free?" she asked, then paused and answered her own question: "Well, if you're Defendant Stephen Kerr and Defendant Michael Quiel, you assemble a small army of colleagues, golf buddies, a stock transfer agent, business contacts, tax return preparers, foreign money managers, and even a lawyer to help you first acquire assets—in this case stock—then sell that stock for cash, and finally, hide the money in secret Swiss bank accounts, all so that Defendants Kerr and Quiel could spend and enjoy the millions of dollars they hid away without paying a dime of tax." Whew. Breathe, Monica, breathe.

She then proceeded to explain the charges we faced. She promised that the prosecution would prove that Steve Kerr and I conspired with Chris Rusch to conceal money from the IRS by hiding it in Switzerland and informed the jury that Rusch had already pleaded guilty to this conspiracy. She claimed that after Steve and I laid a careful and scheming foundation for our crimes, we brought our conspiracy to fruition by omitting our Swiss income from our tax returns and failing to file FBARs (reports of foreign bank and financial accounts). The latter was a "big deal," she pointed out, and the government would prove that we knew we were supposed to file these forms but deliberately neglected to do so.

Our motive? Greed. Good, old-fashioned, biblical, timeless greed.

And how did our crimes come about? Well, all prosecution cases rest on a good story, and the story she spun was this:

Steve and I were successful businessmen who were good at making money, and one of the ways we did that was by acquiring stock in companies we were helping to take public. Because we made a *lot* of money, we paid a lot of taxes, she said, and that did not sit well with either of us. My Belize tax situation was the straw that broke the camel's back. After paying that huge IRS bill (which was *not* actually huge to me; I didn't even bother taking the deductions I could have taken), I decided I would now seek new ways to deliberately hide *even more* income from the IRS by using offshore structures. (The idea that I would use offshore accounts to trick the IRS after just having been *nailed* by the IRS for having an offshore account made no logical sense. But Ms. Edelstein, I was soon to learn, was no slave to logic.)

Within three months of resolving my Belize dilemma, she claimed, I began scheming with Chris Rusch and Steve Kerr to find ways to hide money in Switzerland. The way we elected to do that was by creating fake companies. These companies were nominee entities run by nominee individuals—"nominees" being another name for puppets put in place to do our bidding. There were no real companies in Switzerland, she stated, just bank accounts, and all the transactions in those accounts were controlled by defendants Kerr and Quiel.

In order to pull off a conspiracy like this, Edelstein said, a "small army" was required. The way we worked was (1) we illegally and unethically acquired stock from people we were doing business with; we then (2) moved either the stock or the money from the sale of that stock to Switzerland and then (3) used our "untaxed secret money to buy whatever [we] wanted without reporting the money."

Most of the people who played a role in our scheme, she noted, had no idea they were participating in something illegal. The only ones who knew the whole story were Steve Kerr, Chris Rusch, and Michael Quiel. As evidence that we knew we were doing something wrong, we failed to tell our accountants and tax preparers anything about our Swiss accounts.

She put up a nice-looking chart—at least Kinkos was getting rich on this thing; that made one of us—showing the way we disguised all the money supposedly coming and going from Switzerland by creating these dummy companies not in our own names.

"Everything that happened here," she said, wrapping up her opening statement, "happened because of greed. Defendant Michael Quiel and defendant Stephen Kerr orchestrated this entire scheme because they did not want to report their money to the IRS and they didn't want to pay their fair share of tax."

Done.

Now it was our turn. Mike Kimerer and Mike Minns each had an opportunity to make his own opening statement.

I'd like to say that our guys opened brilliantly.

I'd also like to say that the Easter Bunny lives in Scottsdale.

One thing that became immediately obvious was that although our two defense teams were supposedly working together, there hadn't been much coordination between them. (When you get down to it, attorneys in cases like this never *really* work together; each is more concerned about his own client, and maybe that's as it should be.) This lack of apparent coordination resulted in opening statements that were, I thought, pretty weak and disjointed.

Kimerer, in my opinion, was terrible in his opening. I don't mean to discredit him; he is a gifted attorney and he did a good job, overall, for us during the trial, but I thought his opening approach was seriously off track. I believe it left the jury feeling lost and intimidated.

He started out fine. "[L]et me tell you what this is a case about," he said. "What this case is about [is] two successful businessmen, prominent businessmen, who had great reputations, who decided to expand into the international financial market, and they looked to an expert to give them that information, and that...was a lawyer and that lawyer was Chris Rusch...This is a man that said he was an expert in international finance...And what this case is about is a greedy, an unethical, and incompetent lawyer who gave them the wrong advice, either negligently or deliberately, stole money from them, ended up becoming a defendant in this case and, when was charged, immediately made a deal with the government as fast as he possibly could to negotiate a way of escaping from prison. And the case here really is going to be more about...Chris Rusch than it's going to be about anything else."

Not F. Lee Bailey-level stuff, but not terrible.

He then went on to explain in detail how his client, Steve Kerr, got started in business. Still sounding good, though maybe a bit on the long-winded side. One thing he brought up that was extremely important was the fact that Steve's father had had a *terrible* experience with the IRS and that it had basically ruined his life. Because of that, Steve decided early in life he would never let that happen to him and was extremely scrupulous about staying IRS-compliant in all his business dealings. I knew that to be true about Steve and was glad to see Kimerer play that card.

Where Kimerer got off track was by launching into a complicated and convoluted explanation of how Steve and I made our money and acquired stock. He put a chart in front of the jury with a timeline of events, then began explaining concepts like stock splitting and reverse mergers and hedge funds.

It was *way* too complex for a jury to digest—I could barely follow it myself, and I did this stuff for a living. He then went into an equally complicated explanation of the Swiss corporate structure, how it was set up, how it developed. You could tell the jury had already checked out mentally.

What I think he *should* have done was tell a much simpler story, at least for starters: that Steve and I wanted to expand our global investment opportunities and so we bought a small 4 percent interest in a Swiss investment structure that Chris Rusch agreed to set up and operate in a tax-compliant way. But instead of running the Swiss venture the way we all agreed, Rusch stalled us, misled us, and stole our money while we were busy paying attention to more important things. Then, when trouble started brewing at UBS, instead of telling us, his clients, about what he'd done, he lied to us, sent the government our records without consulting us, and then copped a deal to sell us out and save his own skin.

Kimerer *did* tell that story, more or less, but it was buried under so many details the jury couldn't find it.

Any jurors who managed to stay alert during this opening presentation were surely thinking to themselves, "What the hell have I gotten myself into? I am *never* going to be able to follow this case."

Again, Mike Kimerer is a *terrific* lawyer, but this opening wasn't his best work. Maybe he was just having a bad day.

One great point he did make with the jury, though—and it turned out to be dead-on accurate—was that the prosecution's *entire case* would rest on the credibility of Chris Rusch, a man who was not only an admitted criminal and a soon-to-be-proven liar, but who also had a highly vested interest in making Steve and I look like the guilty parties.

Mike Minns did a lot better with his opening statement, in my opinion, but I still don't think he was quite as effective as his talent warranted. Part of the reason for that, as he explained to the jury, was that he had to follow two opening statements that he didn't have the luxury of screening ahead of time. So he had to revise all his remarks on the fly, based on what had been presented in the previous two arguments.

Minns wisely understood the need for simplicity, though. He began by informing the jury that the accounting firm of Prather Kalman had done a thorough audit of our businesses and had determined that *neither Steve nor I owed anything to the IRS*. All the smoke and mirrors the prosecution would throw at the jury couldn't hide the fact that, in reality, we hadn't scammed the government of a dime.

What was *factually* true, he pointed out, was that Steve and I had donated a fortune to charity in recent years, far more than the prosecution claimed we owed to the IRS. This was hardly the financial behavior of men motivated by greed.

RIGGED

He also pointed out that if we had sold the stock in question in the United States, we would have paid only the long-term capital gains tax of 15 percent on its earnings, but by moving the stock overseas, we ended up paying regular income tax of 35 percent on all the proceeds. Hardly a crafty strategy for outwitting the IRS.

Minns talked about my family life, my service in the military, and my lengthy record as an honest businessman who had a reputation for treating everyone fairly and paying his taxes. He talked about the business model I developed as an investor and the way I often acquired stock through business deals. Though the prosecution would make these stock transactions look fishy, he said, they were always perfectly legal, and the defense would show that.

He explained how in my first dealing with Chris Rusch (the Belize issue), Rusch took me to the cleaners by not claiming business deductions that would have dramatically lowered my IRS bill. When Rusch saw how happily I went along with this crummy deal, and when he learned a little more about Steve and me and how much we earned, he decided he had found himself a potential meal ticket and decided to latch on to us. (Rusch also thought I was dying of pancreatic cancer at that time, said Minns, so he didn't think he'd have to deal with any long-term consequences of cheating me.)

Minns explained how Rusch unsuccessfully solicited us on several business ideas until he found one that grabbed our interest. We could raise a lot of investment money abroad, Rusch told us, if we got involved with Swiss banking.

"And they like that idea," Minns told the jury, referring to Steve and me. "Not for secrecy. *These guys don't want secrecy.* They *want* their clients to know that they own four percent of a Swiss bank. [That's how] you make more sales and get more investments." This was an important point for the jury to understand. The whole reason we became interested in Switzerland was to enhance our image and our global appeal. We wanted to be *seen* as guys with financial connections in Switzerland. Secrecy would have defeated that whole point.

Minns then went on to stress for the jury that *the* most important aspect of the Swiss venture, to both Steve and me, was that it remain tax compliant. I had just survived a nasty encounter with the IRS, and Steve's father had been destroyed by the IRS. The last thing either of us wanted was to flirt with tax trouble.

For that reason, we all agreed that Steve and I would each own only 4 percent of this Swiss venture, a percentage that did not require reporting on our taxes. This was, in fact, the way we always operated in business. When we acquired interest in companies, we never sought to be in control; we always chose to be minority investors. We knew that if we owned 5 percent or more, our reporting requirements would go way up, and neither of us wanted that. Nor did we want the headache of directing and controlling companies. That wasn't our thing. We were investors, not CEOs. The way we did business was to put our money in, hope for the best, and move on to our next investment.

The defense, said Minns, would show that we never in fact had any control over the Swiss accounts or the transactions that happened in Switzerland. The e-mail record would prove that we repeatedly grilled Rusch about tax compliance and that we had contracted with him, for $45,000 each, to keep us tax compliant.

Minns then went on to describe, as Kimerer had done before him, how Rusch deceived us, siphoned off our money, did numerous illegal and unethical maneuvers, and then when cornered by the government, made a secret deal with the prosecution to plead guilty and serve up Steve and me on a silver platter—the most heinous act a trusted lawyer can do to his clients.

There was no dispute on either side that Rusch was guilty. But we, the defendants, were not. We had simply followed our lawyer's advice. And that, said Minns, was an "absolute defense in a tax case."

End of story.

Minns took his seat.

And with that, the prosecution began laying down its case.

CHAPTER EIGHTEEN

The Prosecution's Case

As we get into the meat of the trial—the witness testimonies and cross-examinations—I'm going to have to condense and summarize what happened quite a bit. The trial went on for several weeks, and the court transcripts are over *three thousand pages* long. Most of that material, if I'm being honest, is excruciatingly dull. Let's face it, we're not talking about murder here, or even sex and drugs and rock-and-roll; we're talking about tax forms and stock certificates and bank account documents. There were parts of the trial where even *I* had a hard time staying awake, and my freedom was on the line. So as I describe the trial, I'm going to go light on the details.

Chris Rusch's testimony was indeed the heart of the case, as Kimerer had predicted in his opening statement. Watching Rusch create a story out of thin air, and then spin the known facts to fit that story, was one of the most enraging and heartbreaking experiences I've ever had. The man isn't stupid, I'll give him that. He was smart enough to fabricate just a few small, critical details that he knew would make all the facts look completely different.

Part of the reason he was able to get away with spinning as much as he did—he still ended up looking like a bald-faced liar, in my opinion—was the way the trial unfolded chronologically. Several times, when Rusch appeared to be backed into a corner, the judge would excuse him so that another witness could testify out of turn.

This occurred because some of the witnesses flew in from Europe and other places, so they needed to be accommodated when they were in town. As a result, Rusch often had time to adjust his story before getting on the stand again.

In the end, I don't think the jury believed a word Rusch said, but I think his lies might have been even more baldly exposed had he not been given breaks, at key points in the trial, to think and strategize.

There weren't many Perry Mason-style dramatic moments in the trial, but there were one or two of them, and they involved Rusch.

But before Rusch could take the stand, the prosecution had a lot of work to do. It had to lay its foundation for the conspiracy idea. This took a long, long, long—did I mention long?—time (and was a hugely misguided strategy, in my opinion).

If you'll recall from Edelstein's opening argument, the prosecution wanted the jury to believe the "conspiracy" had three major phases. Phase 1 was that Steve and I allegedly acquired stock in a fraudulent manner from shareholders we did business with. Stockwell and Edelstein had to sell this to the jury by inference more than by fact, because the facts were not on their side. How did they get away with this? Well, early in the proceedings, Judge Teilborg ruled that it was permissible for the prosecution to use the word *fraud*. He also ruled that the term *securities* could be used. So the prosecution put two and two together and began to speak of "securities fraud"—even though they hadn't proven fraud in this case. Many, many times during the course of the trial they used this prejudicial term *fraud* to characterize the way we acquired stock.

What's interesting, though, is that we were *never charged* with securities fraud. One would think that if the government was so convinced that we had committed securities fraud, it would have charged us with that. It's a pretty juicy indictment, after all. But the prosecutors knew they didn't have a prayer of making those charges stick. So instead, what they did was *imply*. Over and over, they tried to paint perfectly legal transactions as fraudulent. They insinuated that routine stock transfers and practices such as stock splitting and forming shell corporations, which are common occurrences in business, were dirty and suspect.

What they seemed to be trying to show—and I say "seemed" because most of the witnesses they put on the stand ended up being more favorable to the defense—was that Steve and I duped people into thinking they no longer owned stock that they, in fact, still owned. We then supposedly misused that stock in nefarious ways without telling the rightful owners what we were up to. The problem (for the prosecution) was that the shareholders all acknowledged they had sold their shares to us and had received full payment for the sale. They testified that nothing inappropriate had happened and that they would invest with Mike Quiel again if presented another opportunity.

The government wanted the jury to believe that this alleged funny business with stocks was something we had been up to since at least early 2005 as part of our elaborate fraud conspiracy. But here's the hilarious thing: *According their own theory, the conspiracy did not originate until late 2006* (remember, I didn't meet Rusch or have the Belize experience that supposedly prompted me to defraud the government until 2006)!

So I guess Steve and I were laying a criminal foundation *just in case* someday we met a crooked lawyer who could help us defraud the government.

As I've said before, the reason so much of the trial revolved around supposed stock fraud was that the prosecutors themselves didn't understand the way stock certificates work. It all came down to the way these documents are titled. I explained this in an earlier chapter. A person can sell stock to another person, but there is no time requirement by which the actual *title* must be transferred. Again, this is analogous to a car dealer who buys a car from one customer, then waits until another customer buys the car before transferring the title. It's a routine way of handling things in the car business. But here's the key point: once the bill of sale is signed, the dealer owns the car, regardless of whose name is on the title. Ownership is not in question.

Often when Steve and I would buy stock, we knew it might be sold again fairly soon, so we would not immediately transfer the title to ourselves. There are a couple of good, and legal, reasons why people handle stock this way, as an attorney and former stock transfer agent testified on the stand. One reason is that transferring titles costs money, and so you don't want to do it repeatedly and unnecessarily. Another is that transferring a title can signal "movement" on the stock, which can affect its market price, something you might not want to do while a deal is still in play.

Several of the prosecution witnesses were friends and associates of Steve's and mine who'd been involved in small, simple, and *profitable* transactions with us. (A key witness, Robert Turner, was involved in a more complex deal, but the stock ownership principle was the same.) The way it often worked—and several witnesses testified to this—was, sometimes, early in a deal, I wanted to raise outside cash so I would ask golf buddies and others if they wished to put in $1,000. When I accepted their small investment, the company would issue them some stock. Then I would come back to them a year or so later and offer to buy the stock back at many times what they paid for it. If they didn't want to sell it at that point, they were free to keep it.

Typically, these folks were thrilled to multiply their money, so they would sell the stock back to me. They understood that from that point on, I owned the stock. I had, after all, paid them for it at a 100 percent profit. They didn't care what I did with the stock after that—split it, sold it, whatever; it didn't matter *because they no longer owned it.* In the case of Robert Turner, we brought him a company and management team to take over his failing business. The new management bought out his ownership for $90,000, and he signed over his stock in a similar way.

Robert Turner's shares remained available after Turner was paid in full. Those shares were offered to Chris Rusch to help the complete funding of his Swiss banks.

While on the stand, Turner testified he had not reported the $90,000 in proceeds on his tax return and had made a private deal with government for immunity if he would testify against us. His testimony helped us and did not hurt us.

What the government tried to prove was that because we didn't transfer the stock titles immediately, the sellers *still owned the stock*. So the prosecution would question witnesses, saying things like, "Did you know that on [such-and-such a date] you still owned 10,000 shares of Company A?" And the witnesses would be surprised and say, "No, I didn't know that."

The reason they didn't know it was because it wasn't true; they *didn't* own the stock anymore. Their name was still on the title; that's all.

The prosecution's approach largely backfired. One witness after another testified that I paid them their money back at a huge profit and that they'd love to do business with me again. A stock transfer agent, Thomas Laucks, testified, despite the government's trying to pull him in the opposite direction, that nothing Steve and I had done with stocks was fishy or illegal. He even volunteered, on the stand, "To be honest with you, I've known these gentlemen for quite a while, and I always liked doing business with them, because they tried to go over the top and do more difficult due diligence than anybody else, and I can't imagine them doing something wrong."

So that was the essence of the stock fraud part of the "conspiracy." Of course, there was a lot more detail to it than that. There was endless testimony about buybacks, stock splits, reverse mergers, medallion signatures, and many other things. But most of that stuff was a smokescreen. The core issue was whether or not Steve and I had done something fraudulent to acquire the stocks we sent over to Switzerland. If we hadn't, then none of the business actions that were taken *with* the stock after we acquired it really mattered. The government offered no credible evidence to prove we had done anything illegal or even fishy.

Phase 2 of the alleged conspiracy—the setting up and running of the fake companies in Switzerland—turned only on the testimony of Chris Rusch. Phase 2, though, would have to wait till the end of the prosecution's case. As I've mentioned, the trial didn't unfold in ideal, linear order for either side.

So let's look at the other charges next—the filing of fraudulent tax returns and failure to file FBAR charges.

When it came to those charges, the government's case was fairly straightforward. They put on some government employees who essentially testified to the fact that I didn't file FBARs for the years in question and that I didn't file accurate tax returns for the years in question, 2007 and 2008. Evidence showed that FBARs were *eventually* filed for those years, but that this was done remedially.

There wasn't a *lot* of contention around the basic facts regarding the FBARs and tax returns, because essentially, both sides agreed. FBARs had not been filed in a timely manner for 2007 and 2008, and the tax returns for 2007 and 2008 might be inaccurate. The real question was one of intent and knowledge. Did we knowingly and intentionally fail to file accurate forms, or were we simply, as the defense teams asserted, following the advice of our attorney at the time (i.e., Chris Rusch)?

In order to show knowledge and intent, the government presented Cheryl Bradley, the IRS agent, as a witness. Both she and, later, Rusch testified that because of my early experience in the Belize situation, I must have known about my duty to file FBARs. Bradley testified that after being audited in 2006, I had filed FBARs for the credit card account in Belize, for the years 2000–2003. Presto: proof that I knew about my FBAR duty.

But here's the interesting thing. It turns out that I *didn't* file FBARs on that Belize account. Why? Because it was a credit card account, and FBARs are not required for credit card accounts (debit accounts yes, credit accounts no). Even *I* didn't realize during the trial that she had testified falsely on the stand. I have since submitted multiple FOIA (Freedom of Information Act) requests for the government to produce these mythical FBAR forms for 2000–2003, and the government has been unable to do so. For one simple reason. The FBARs don't exist. They were never submitted. They weren't required.

So the government's assertion that I knew about my duty to file FBARs rested on the "fact" that I had filed FBARs on my Belize credit card account, an event that *never occurred*. Unfortunately, I did not know this during the trial—that's how ignorant I was about the topic of FBARs—so I was as snowed by Bradley's false testimony as the jury probably was.

I don't know whether Cheryl Bradley committed flat-out perjury in an attempt to get me convicted of the FBAR charges or was just mistaken about the facts. In Chris Rusch's case, I believe the falsification was deliberate. Perjury carries up to a five-year sentence for everyday citizens but apparently not for government witnesses.

As to the charges of filing false tax returns, a fascinating thing happened. On the actual indictment in which I was officially charged, *the government incorrectly identified the section of the tax return I supposedly falsified*. The charge read—I kid you not—"on Schedule B, Part II, line 7b of the Forms 1014, [Quiel] reported that he did not have an interest in, and authority over, a financial account in Switzerland…" Well, guess what? There *is* no line 7b in Part II of Schedule B. That line is in *Part III*. So I was being criminally prosecuted—and facing jail time—for the incorrect filing of forms, while the government tried to dismiss its own incorrect filing as a clerical error. The government, you see, gets to play by its own set of rules.

The prosecution called our accountants as witnesses, and they testified that they had never heard of the Swiss venture or the Swiss accounts. This was supposed to be a shocker to the jury. It was supposed to prove that we had made conscious efforts to conceal the accounts from our tax people so they wouldn't advise us that we needed to report them.

Our argument, in addition to pointing out the glaring error in the government's own indictment, was that I did not have "interest in and authority over" the financial accounts in question, so I didn't need to report them. End of story. Yes, I had an investor's interest of 4 percent in the corporations but this percentage *did not require reporting to the IRS*. Plus, I had no authority over these accounts. The idea of reporting this stuff to Mike Stuck did not even occur to me because I had planned from the start for it *not* to meet reporting requirements. And besides, this was not a matter I *would* discuss with Mike Stuck. I was in the investing business, and I *never* asked my accountant whether I should invest. The prosecution sold the jury the idea that something was fishy because I did not report my minority ownership to my accountant. Sounds logical, but remember, my accountant didn't review my investments, only my tax obligations.

Mike Stuck did, however, testify that I was an honest client and that he would be happy to work with me again in the future. His professional code of ethics, he said, would forbid him from doing so if he suspected I was breaking the law.

And Mike Stuck did, in fact, resume doing my returns shortly after the trial.

There was a great deal of testimony on whether Steve and I had knowledge and control of the Swiss accounts. The prosecution brought in two bank witnesses to prove that we did, but our attorneys got them to testify that it was, in fact, Chris Rusch and a couple of other Swiss "financial intermediaries" who had sole authority to sign on the accounts and to move stock and money within the accounts. Steve and I were "beneficial owners" only, a term that means something different in Switzerland than it does in the United States. In a Swiss bank account, the beneficial owner, or BO, has no control whatsoever over the accounts that are opened in his name. Only the signatory authority (Chris Rusch in our case) can sign checks, make withdrawals, etc., and only the investment manager (Pierre Gabris in our case) can move money around within the accounts. The BO can do neither and, in fact, needs to sign a formal document if he wishes to receive even basic information on the account.

A BO is like a beneficiary of a life insurance policy. The beneficiary cannot access the policy until an "event" occurs. With a life insurance policy, that event is the death of the policyholder. We never did find out what event would have given us access to the Swiss accounts.

The bank people also testified as to how easy it is for third parties—provided they are recognized by the bank as financial intermediaries, as Pierre Gabris was at both UBS and Pictet—to set up accounts for a BO without the BO even knowing about it. All the intermediary has to do is walk into a bank office with a photocopy of the BO's passport (which both Steve and I had given to Rusch early in our dealings with him), and he can set up an account in the BO's name without the BO even knowing about it. The *BO*, however, cannot just walk into the bank with a passport and take the money *out*.

Our contention all along—and the truth—was that we knew next to nothing about the accounts Rusch set up in Switzerland. The bankers testified that they had never met us, which helped back up our version of the story. All we knew was that Rusch told us he needed to set up various accounts over there, including accounts for the two Swiss corporations we'd purchased for doing business. His explanations as to why he needed these accounts sounded reasonable. We relied on him to tell us anything we needed to know about the accounts, and he failed to tell us anything. We didn't pay any attention to these accounts because, as far as we were concerned, *we didn't own them*. They belonged to the corporations. Bottom line: we had many good reasons for not reporting these accounts on our tax returns. But the main and overriding reason was that Chris Rusch, our tax attorney, had advised us that this was not necessary. And as Minns pointed out in his opening argument, following an attorney's advice is an absolute defense in criminal tax cases.

The government, of course, offered its own sinister twist on the Swiss accounts: *of course* we had no *direct* control of them, they said. That was the whole point of setting up the shell companies. We did not *want* our names to be associated with them. So the accounts were set up under dummy names and run by dummy nominees. But these nominees were mere puppets who did our bidding. Steve and I, the prosecution claimed, controlled all the movements of money within, and to and from, these accounts. *We* told the nominees what to do (never in writing, conveniently, because that would create a paper trail), and the nominees obeyed us.

And that goes to the core dilemma of this trial. If you believed, as the prosecution claimed, that Steve and I were nefarious schemers intent on hiding our identities from tax authorities, then most of the facts, and most of our actions, made sense within that context. If you believed we were duped by Chris Rusch, everything made sense within *that* context.

The crux of the entire case came down to whether or not you believed Chris Rusch. If you believed he was telling the truth about a few crucial assertions—for which the prosecution provided no actual evidence—then you were compelled to view all the facts of the case in the prosecution's light. If you thought he was lying about these assertions, the prosecution's entire case fell apart.

Yep, it all came down to Rusch, just as Kimerer had predicted it would.

CHAPTER NINETEEN

Rusch to Judgment

From the moment Chris Rusch opened his mouth on the witness stand, it was obvious he was well rehearsed. He had made his deal with the government, and he knew what the prosecution wanted from him: Mike Quiel's and Steve Kerr's heads on a silver platter. And he planned to deliver them in grand fashion.

He'd had months in prison to think about his story, and he was ready.

Stockwell and Rusch got right down to business. After the opening niceties were out of the way, Rusch began his testimony by informing the jury that he had pleaded guilty to conspiracy to defraud.

"Who did you conspire with?" asked Stockwell.

"The defendants in this case," replied Rusch, "Mr. Kerr and Mr. Quiel."

"And what was your role in the conspiracy?"

"I set up offshore companies and aided them in setting up offshore bank accounts to hide income and assets."

Bam. There it was, out on the table in black and white. Rusch was planning to testify, under oath, that Steve and I had engineered the whole Swiss debacle as a scheme to dodge taxes. The only question was, how was he going to sell it in a way the defense couldn't destroy his narrative?

Here's the thing about great lies: they are mostly true. They fit *most* of the facts but contain one crucial bit of fiction. Rusch realized that if he was going to be believable on the stand, he needed to employ the smallest number of falsehoods possible so that the real facts would play in his favor. But the few lies he *did* tell were going to need to be whoppers.

The lies began with his account of the Belize business. (Minns tried to get this testimony blocked because of attorney-client privilege, but the judge ruled against us, as he had in our motion to exclude Rusch from testifying against us at all.)

Big Lie Number 1 was this: Rusch claimed he learned through his dealings with me on the Belize affair that I was a "player" who cared more about saving taxes than obeying the law—and that I, in turn, learned that he was a lawyer willing to look the other way. Thus, we found a match made in tax-crime heaven.

The way this criminal understanding between us came about was explained by Rusch in the following testimony:

> STOCKWELL: In addition to the Belize account, did you discuss any other offshore accounts with Mr. Quiel?
> RUSCH: Yes. There was another account that I believe was in a Caribbean island that was also in his name.
> STOCKWELL: And was this an account that was known to the IRS and subject to the audit?
> RUSCH: No, it was not.

A short while later...

> STOCKWELL: Did you discuss with Mr. Quiel whether or not to report this second bank account to the IRS?
> RUSCH: Yes, I did.
> STOCKWELL: And what did you discuss?

RUSCH: I explained that it…was required to be
disclosed, but that it was unlikely that the
IRS would ever find it. So…I gave him
the option of leaving it off of the amended
returns or reporting it on the amended
returns.

Rusch was claiming that we both agreed not to report this size-able Caribbean account of mine to the IRS. One minor problem: that account never existed. Rusch provided *zero* evidence that I actually possessed this account or that I even told him I did! His word was his only proof.

A little background on this: At one point when Cono Namorato was representing me, this First Caribbean bank account thing surfaced. So I wrote a letter to First Caribbean, listing my name and the names of all the corporations abroad, and included a copy of my passport. I called the bank several times, and they would not respond. You see, at that time I was afraid Rusch had gone around the world and set up accounts in my name to hide his ill-gotten assets. First Caribbean never told me of any accounts that existed in my name, but in truth, such accounts could very well exist without my knowledge, and Rusch could still be accessing them to this day. Because it's so easy to set up foreign accounts in someone else's name.

Rusch went on to use this fictional conversation about this First Caribbean account—which my team couldn't really *dis*prove—to establish a key premise: that from the beginning, he and I had a wink-wink understanding with each other. I was the type of guy who liked to hide things from the IRS, and he was the type of lawyer who could help me.

So when we later started talking about Switzerland, Rusch contended, we began with that understanding. All three parties involved knew exactly what we were up to—namely, trying to find a way to hide assets from the IRS.

But Rusch had a major problem with this story. There were several e-mails in evidence that made it abundantly clear that Steve and I were *extremely concerned* about keeping the Swiss venture tax compliant. It was obvious from these e-mail exchanges that we were reluctant about getting involved with an offshore entity and would do so only if Rusch could assure us that everything would be IRS-kosher. There was also ample correspondence about our desire to keep our ownership at the less-than-5-percent level, as well as the contract we'd all signed that gave him the contractual obligation, for a fee of $90,000, to keep us tax compliant. It seemed clear from all the evidence that we had instructed him to do whatever was necessary to make the venture function legally and tax compliantly.

So Rusch was stuck with admitting that *at the beginning*, all parties intended to behave in a way that was tax compliant and that he was in charge of making sure that happened. This, however, was completely at odds with his earlier statements that we had conspired from the start to commit fraud. So in order to salvage his conspiracy claim, he had to concoct Big Lie Number 2. He claimed that Kerr and I decided, very early on, that we did not want to go along with his tax compliant version of the plan…

> STOCKWELL: And did Mr. Quiel agree to this structure as you just described in Switzerland?
>
> RUSCH: No, he did not.
>
> STOCKWELL: And why not?
>
> RUSCH: They didn't want to give up control of the entities and the bank accounts and the capital as would have been required.
>
> STOCKWELL: And if they actually controlled these entities, did you discuss with them reporting requirements and other obligations if they actually controlled these entities?
>
> RUSCH: Just in very general sense, that if you control an offshore company, it's taxable in the United States. But we didn't get into specific reporting requirements or what forms would need to be filed or those things.
>
> STOCKWELL: And after Mr. Quiel indicated that he…would not agree with giving up control

in these Swiss entities, what did you do as a result?

RUSCH: I incorporated [the companies] using nominee directors, which were provided to me by Arno Arndt and Pierre Gabris, [whom] I knew that we could control.

STOCKWELL: And was Mr. Quiel aware of this?

RUSCH: Yes.

STOCKWELL: Did he agree to that?

RUSCH: Yes.

STOCKWELL: Did you have discussions with Mr. Kerr specifically about the use of these nominee directors that you could control?

RUSCH: Yes, I did.

Rusch claimed that several discussions of this nature took place—Steve and I telling Rusch that we wanted to retain control. But again, he offered no evidence of these conversations. These alleged conversations were *absolutely critical* to both the defense and the prosecution. If they indeed occurred, as Rusch claimed, then all the activity that went on in Switzerland could be seen as a sham, directed by Steve and me from the United States. The fact that there were entities in Switzerland that *appeared* to function independently would be an expected part of that sham.

If the conversations did *not* take place, however, then Steve and I behaved in a way that was consistent with our innocence and with our understanding of the Swiss situation. We asked for only 4 percent ownership and believed that was what we had been given. When we became aware that a few business transactions had taken place in Switzerland, we also knew that they'd been handled completely by offshore individuals. Therefore, we assumed the Swiss companies were moving in the direction of being "active and real," as planned. When we took some earnings from Switzerland into the United States—which we did on a couple of occasions—we reported that income on our tax returns, as was required, and paid income tax of 35 percent on it.

In order to ensure the jury didn't believe our version of the events, Rusch had to concoct Big Lie Number 3.

As you know, Steve and I always insisted that we had only the vaguest knowledge about the existence of Swiss bank accounts and that Chris Rusch never provided us information on these accounts. Rusch's Big Lie Number 3 was that he'd kept us well informed about what was going on in the Swiss accounts, by sending us regular statements (his records of these communications—surprise, surprise—had disappeared; they were on an old computer whose hard drive had crashed, ahem). Steve and I, in turn, would give him detailed instructions on what to do with the money and stock, and then he and Pierre Gabris and others would dutifully execute our orders. Of course, our orders to the Swiss team were always given only verbally, so there was no record of them.

But of course, that was the way *we* wanted it, suggested Rusch.

As I listened to him spew fiction from the witness stand hour after hour, my blood temperature gradually rose from a slow simmer to a steady boil. Since long before the trial started, I'd been preparing myself to hear him lie, and I'd vowed to remain emotionally cool, but still, as I heard him manufacture facts out of thin air—and worse, paint innocent facts in a criminal light—I wanted to jump out of my seat, strangle him, and shout the truth. I was strongly reconsidering my decision not to testify. It terrified me to think that the jury might be buying some of what he was selling, and I wanted an opportunity to refute him, point for point.

Patience, my attorneys told me. We would have our opportunity to unmask him during cross-examination.

That opportunity finally came. It was on a day when Mike Minns became ill and Mike Kimerer took over the reins.

It was fascinating to watch Rusch's demeanor change the moment the defense took over the questioning. When Stockwell had been asking the questions, Rusch would frequently grow expansive, providing more information than requested, offering lengthy explanations where none had been called for. The moment Kimerer took over, though, he became Mr. Hostile Witness. Kimerer had to pull every answer out of him with verbal pliers, and he tried to avoid giving direct answers to even the simplest questions.

Despite Rusch's resistance, Kimerer was able to establish pretty convincingly that Rusch had sold himself to us as an expert on international taxes and on setting up foreign corporations. Kimerer pointed out—for the jury as much as for Rusch—that there was nothing wrong with a tax attorney trying to help his clients pay the least amount of taxes legally allowable. He recited the famous quote by Learned Hand that guides many tax attorneys: "Anyone may arrange his affairs so that his taxes shall be as low as possible; he is not bound to choose that pattern which best pays the treasury. There's not even a patriotic duty to increase one's taxes…for nobody owes any public duty to pay more than the law demands."

Kimerer got Rusch to agree, kicking and screaming, that when Steve and I spoke to him about setting up a Swiss entity, we were all operating within the spirit of the Hand quote. Yes, we wanted to keep our taxes as low as possible, but first and foremost, we wanted to do so in a way that was completely legal and above board.

"[T]here's a whole series of e-mails," said Kimerer, "where you're telling them about all the different things you can do and how to structure these corporations and how to set them up. Is that right?"

"I informed them how to set it up properly, yes," agreed Rusch.

Rusch then testified about going to Switzerland to do the initial setup work. Kimerer questioned him further:

> KIMERER: And everything you described in those e-mails you described as being tax compliant and there was nothing illegal with any of those things, isn't that correct?
>
> RUSCH: Yes.
>
> KIMERER: So when you went [on] your trip— and that was to meet people you've known for some time. I believe that was to meet… Mr. Pierre Gabris?
>
> RUSCH: Yes.

KIMERER: And also there was an attorney, an Arndt, Mr. Arndt?

RUSCH: Yes. He's—he wasn't an attorney, but yes.

KIMERER: So these were people you had to talk to, to help set all these structures up.

RUSCH: Yes.

KIMERER: And you utilized them to set these structures up.

RUSCH: Yes, I did.

KIMERER: And when you utilized them to do that, in your mind there was nothing illegal about those structures at that point.

RUSCH: At that time, no.

A little later, the following exchange took place:

KIMERER: What they did is they came in to you and said, "We want to set up a foreign business…and we want to do it to attract foreign investors." Isn't that why they came to you?

RUSCH: Yes, it is.

KIMERER: And that's what you attempted to do for them, correct?

RUSCH: Yes, it is, sir.

And at another point:

KIMERER: And as I understand it, Mr. Rusch, you start out doing it right and you were doing it right and then at some point, you decided or felt that it was wrong. Is that right?

RUSCH: Yes.

KIMERER: And you didn't immediately tell them you were doing it wrong, did you?

RUSCH: No, I did not.

This exchange also occurred:

> KIMERER: Well, after you had set up these compa-
> nies and set up these bank accounts, did you
> ever tell them that they had to file FBARS or
> check [on] their personal returns that they
> had a foreign bank account?
> RUSCH: After the incorporation was complete,
> no, I did not.

So Kimerer forced Rusch to reluctantly admit a number of things: (1) that we all believed we were taking a legal approach at the start, as opposed to conspiring to commit fraud, as Rusch had claimed in his initial storytelling; (2) that our intention from the start was to attract foreign investors, which clearly meant that we wanted the Swiss venture to be public, not secret; and (3) that as our attorney, he did not inform us of the need to file FBARs or report the Swiss accounts to the IRS.

After grilling Rusch about his arrest, the stress it caused him, and his motivation to strike a deal with the government, Kimerer began setting a trap he hoped Rusch would walk into. He began to question him about the meeting that was held at Kimerer's office, the one in which Rusch met Minns and Kimerer for the first time. That meeting, by Rusch's own admission, took place before he knew he was a suspect in the case and before he had made any deals with the government.

Kimerer thought he might be able to get Rusch to lie about the meeting as he had lied about everything else, so he asked him questions such as:

> KIMERER: Did you say [at the meeting] that
> everything you did was legal?
> RUSCH: No, I did not.
> KIMERER: Did you say that there was never any
> intention for Mr. Kerr or Mr. Quiel to com-
> mit a crime?

RUSCH: No, I did not.
KIMERER: You never said that?
RUSCH: I don't believe so.

And…

KIMERER: And did you say during the course of that meeting that it was never clear whether we had to file FBARs or not?
RUSCH: Not that I recall.

Also…

KIMERER: And they at all times relied upon your expertise because they didn't understand the structures and everything you were putting together. You told us that [at the meeting], didn't you?
RUSCH: No, I did not.

What Kimerer knew, but Rusch did not, was that the meeting had been recorded in its entirety.

Cut to the chase: The recording of the meeting was played for the jury. In Rusch's own voice, loud and clear for all to hear, he contradicted the statements he had just made under oath. His taped voice said that he *had* told us we were operating legally in Switzerland, that he *hadn't* told us about the FBARs, and that any mistakes that had been made in the Swiss operation were on him, not us. He also validated the defense's version of events through recorded statements such as:

"The corporation—we weren't really focused on ownership, we were focused on base of operation. All the decision-making and work was being done outside the United States. To set this up, I go over to Switzerland…We incorporated two Swiss companies with the intent that we would set up an investment-type business in Switzerland. That business was to find foreign investors…[I]t was going to be

my job to go to Switzerland and operate the business from there…
But the key to the business structure was that it could operate from
Switzerland on its own…in a tax compliant way. Corporations were
formed. They were funded with money in stock, but then they just
kind of…sat around for some period of time…because, you know,
we weren't able to find investors…So at the end of the day, we had
Pierre and Jerome in Switzerland, but we didn't really set up…an
office and an operation, and didn't really start business."

So, no criminal conspiracy, just negligence or failure on his part
to be get the business launched.

On the tape he went on to describe how our problems arose
passively, not as a result of a conspiracy to evade taxes or perpetrate
fraud. "But, you know, the government's going to say, well, you set
up these companies as shells and you put money in there. And, you
know, you intended not to pay taxes on it and you got caught because
UBS disclosed all these accounts. But…that certainly was never the
intent, and that's not what we were attempting to accomplish in any
sense."

He made several statements acknowledging that he was the person who had advised Steve and me throughout the process, that Steve
and I had no contact with the banks in Switzerland, and that he had
power of attorney on all the accounts.

Regarding the FBAR specifically, he said, "To be honest, I wasn't
even clear if you had to file one…but [Mike Quiel] wouldn't know
that he needed to file one on UBS unless I told him…Because, as I've
said, neither of them were interacting with the bank, or doing wires,
or writing checks, which is how you would usually know that, hey,
I've got a foreign bank account over there which I need to disclose
or not."

Later on the tape, Minns says, "But the only person in the room
that he gets tax advice from [is you]. So the only way he would know
how to do this is from you, and you didn't tell him to do it, so he
wouldn't know to do it."

Rusch replies, "Right."

To confirm this, Kimerer says on the tape, "Mike and Steve relied on your expertise...because they didn't know how to do it; correct?"

And Rusch answers, "Uh-huh."

As the recording was playing in court, you could see Rusch doing mental backflips as he tried to think of a way to spin his own recorded words. He was a good actor, but he couldn't disguise his surprise and discomfort at hearing his own voice negating so much of what he had testified to earlier. He even began crying on the stand. At one point, Judge Teilborg became so disgusted with Rusch that he literally "threw the book at him"—picked up a book and hurled it across his desk in Rusch's direction.

After Kimerer was done with Rusch, I thought the trial was over. I really did. I assumed all charges would be dismissed. Rusch had admitted—on tape, in no uncertain terms—that he had been our sole advisor throughout the Swiss affair and that he had not informed us about reporting the accounts on our tax returns and/or filing FBARs. He had also exposed his own conspiracy theory as horse manure.

As I stepped on the elevator with Minns during a break, I said to him with a grin, "It's over, right? We got him. We can go home now."

Minns shot me a cautioning look. He said something like, "Listen, Mike, it's been a good day for the defense, but it's not over yet. The judge is not going to dismiss the case based on what you just heard. The tape was played for impeachment purposes only—to show that he lied on the stand—not for the truth of what was being said on the recording. Be patient; we'll have to see what happens. The prosecutors still have their redirect ahead of them."

Sure enough, Rusch found a way to spin what had happened on the tape. He claimed that the entire meeting had been a *defense strategy* meeting and that everything he had said on tape had been offered as a plausible defense theory. In other words, he had been trying to give our new defense lawyers a credible story on which to base our defense, not telling them the truth. (If that was the case, why did Minns, on the tape, ask him to leave the room for the part of the meeting where they were going to discuss defense strategy?) Rusch also claimed that the reason he never specifically told me and Steve that anything illegal was going on in Switzerland was that *we already knew*. After those phantom conversations in which we allegedly told Rusch we wanted to retain control in Switzerland, we knew from that point on that everything we were doing was illegal, so there was never any need for him to point that out again.

As I said, the man wasn't stupid.

I still didn't think the jury would believe him. The recording had unmasked him as a liar, and all the rationalizing in the world wasn't going to change that.

But one final twist occurred that allowed him to lob the last volley at us. As part of Stockwell's "redirect" questioning of Rusch (the prosecution gets another crack at a witness after the defense finishes its cross-examination), Stockwell asked for, and received, permission to introduce three new documents that had not been previously submitted into evidence. The defense objected vehemently to this—you can't bring in new evidence, late in a trial, that the defense has not been allowed to examine beforehand—but Teilborg overruled.

Three new documents were then entered into evidence, Exhibits 44, 51, and 52. Rusch testified that these were faxes he had sent, one to Pierre Gabris and two to Steve and me. Exhibit 44 contained instructions to Gabris to make a certain stock transaction. The instructions, Rusch claimed, came directly from Steve and me. The other exhibits were copies of e-mails *from* Gabris that Rusch had supposedly faxed to Steve and me. These contained reports of various transactions in Switzerland and showed money being moved among our Swiss accounts.

These exhibits were brought in to support Big Lie Number 3: that Steve and I were calling the shots in Switzerland and that we knew exactly what was going on in the accounts over there. Because Rusch kept us informed.

How did Rusch suddenly come to possess these documents that had not been previously entered into evidence? He had already testified that his records had been lost in a hard-drive crash. But for some unexplained reason, he had saved a paper copy of these three documents? Hmm.

Needless to say, I'd never seen the documents before.

Minns and Kimerer assumed they'd have a chance to grill Rusch about these absurd "faxes"—When did you send them? Do you have a fax receipt? Do you have any evidence to suggest you didn't just create these documents yesterday?—but Judge Teilborg denied them. On what basis? Because the judge had made it clear earlier in the trial that "recross" would not be allowed. In other words, the defense doesn't get another turn after the redirect.

Well, if that was the case, then *new evidence should not have been allowed in on redirect.*

Minns later told me that the members of the defense team had over a hundred years of combined trial experience and that none of them had ever seen a single case where a new piece of evidence was introduced by the prosecution and the defense was not given an opportunity to vet it or refute it.

But that was the hand of cards we were dealt. Rusch left the stand, having had the last word after all, and we weren't able to challenge his final "evidence."

Now we'd have to see what kind of damage this had done with the jury.

CHAPTER TWENTY

Defense, Closings, Deliberations

After Rusch's testimony, the trial was largely over. The prosecution rested. Our defense lawyers made a valiant effort to have all the charges dismissed under a Rule 29 motion. This is a standard request in which the defense tries to argue that the prosecution has failed to make its case and that everyone should just go home. Rule 29 motions very, very rarely succeed, but I thought we had a chance in this case, given the massive absence of evidence against us and the weakness of Rusch as a central witness. But we were denied. Oh well, no surprise there.

It was now time for the defense to present its case.

Minns and Kimerer still wanted to stick to their plan to leave me and Steve off the witness stand. They felt the prosecution had utterly failed to meet its "beyond a reasonable doubt" burden of proof. Putting us on the stand would only risk opening new cans of worms and would probably lead to many more days of court time. The jury had already been impaneled for several weeks now, and it seemed pointless to drag this thing out any longer.

Our attorneys ended up presenting only one witness, a lawyer named Gary Stuart. He was an expert on legal ethics and his testimony was extremely straightforward. He simply listed all the ethics violations of which he believed Chris Rusch was guilty as our lawyer. They included the following:

- Rusch shouldn't have revealed privileged information to the IRS or DOJ without our informed consent and certainly should not have done so without warning us. Once he decided to reveal this information, he should have withdrawn as our lawyer.
- As our attorney, Rusch should not have entered into a business relationship with us, his clients.
- Rusch failed to act competently in representing us and failed to inform us truthfully about his level of competency.
- If Rusch believed we intended to break the law, as he stated in his testimony, he should have withdrawn from representing us.
- If he indeed advised us about ways to break laws, he should not have done so.
- He shouldn't have attempted to minimize his own exposure at our expense.
- Knowing he had multiple levels of conflict of interest, he should have helped us obtain new counsel sooner than he did.
- He didn't follow the rules regarding the purpose, use, management, or reporting of client trust accounts.

After the prosecution cross-examined Stuart, Kimerer surprised the court by announcing that the defense was prepared to rest.

Yikes. It was jury time.

The next step was that the judge, working closely with both the prosecution and defense, began crafting the instructions to the jury. This consumed many hours of court time as the defense and prosecution argued back and forth about the wording of every little phrase. The goal was to come up with a set of jury instructions both sides could live with. I was amazed at how much work and attention went into this document.

The next day, closing arguments were heard. Steve and I had over fifty friends who took time out of their busy lives to show up in the courtroom and give us support on this final day of the trial.

Stockwell gave the arguments for the prosecution. Among the first words out of his mouth were, "We're not talking about a few false deductions here or there. What we're talking about is a vast criminal enterprise that spanned the globe." Yes, he actually used those words: *a vast criminal enterprise that spanned the globe*. Wow, I was impressed with myself.

I guess when you don't have evidence, you have to rely on hype.

I won't go through his lengthy presentation point by point. It was essentially a recap of the opening statement with some dramatic touches thrown in. He talked about how we planned to defraud the government; fraudulently acquired stock through a long, secretive process; and set up sham companies in Switzerland, which we managed from behind the curtain like the Wizard of Oz.

What he didn't want to admit to the jury was that the case all came down to Chris Rusch's testimony. Outside of Rusch's word, there was zero credible evidence that we planned to defraud anyone; that we told Rusch to do anything illegal; that we knew when the Swiss venture began falling out of compliance with the law; or that we had any information about, or influence over, the bank accounts in Switzerland.

What was fascinating, though, was how Stockwell used a simple piece of hearsay "information" as the lynchpin of his conspiracy theory. That was the phantom Caribbean account Rusch claimed I told him about and instructed him not to report on my tax returns. By conspiring to commit that dirty deed together, claimed Stockwell, Rusch and I established a relationship based on defrauding the IRS, and everything that happened afterward fell in line with that conspiratorial relationship.

It was a nice story, but the only evidence that the Caribbean account existed was Rusch's word!

When the defense got its turn to close, our lawyers' arguments were thorough and excellent. Their presentations went on for hours, literally, so I'll only touch on a few of the key points each of the attorneys made.

Kimerer went first. He thoroughly and methodically dismantled the prosecution's story. He talked about the business model Steve and I used and showed how our acquisition of stock was completely legal. He made it clear that the amount of stock we had placed in Switzerland was only a small percentage of the stock we owned, and that the vast majority of it had been kept in the United States and reported on our US tax returns. He showed how Rusch had suckered us in by proclaiming his expertise in setting up tax-compliant foreign companies and how he had systematically kept us in the dark about what was going on in Switzerland so that he and his cohorts could steal from us over time. They did this by "churning" our accounts to generate commissions and by sneakily diverting our funds to their own accounts, he said. He talked about how when Rusch realized he was in legal trouble, he began cooperating with the DOJ to throw suspicion away from himself and make us look like the masterminds.

The government, Kimerer said, knew it had no real case against us, so it was forced to put Rusch on the stand and hope for the best. And now, as Kimerer himself had said at the start of the trial, the government's entire case rested on the testimony of a man who had shown himself to be a thief, a liar, an incompetent, and a scam artist.

Minns, in his closing argument, cleverly brought out a piece of evidence that had been submitted by the prosecution but had never come up at trial. That was the $500,000 refund check I'd received from the IRS. To explain it, Minns presented a letter from the IRS stating that due to business losses, I, in fact, had a $1.4 million *credit* with the government (in addition to the uncashed $500,000 check), which I could apply to past or future tax years.

So the supposed "victim" in this case—the US Treasury—in fact owed *me* over a million dollars.

Minns went on to explain that a person can be held *criminally* liable in a tax case only if it can be clearly shown that he or she willfully intended to do wrong. When deciding whether Steve and I acted willfully or not, he said, the jury must consider the fact that our actions did not even play to our own advantage. We actually lost money by filing our tax returns the way we did.

Minns raised several excellent questions, such as, Why did the government choose to call anonymous bank experts from Switzerland instead of some of the people *actually involved* in the case, such as

Pierre Gabris and others? Could it be because they feared what those witnesses might say? Why did the government, who thought Chris Rusch was a crook and a flight risk, suddenly choose to start believing every word that came out of his mouth? Wasn't the fact the government made a tax-form error on *its own indictment page* evidence as to how complicated these forms were and how easy it was to get things wrong?

And of course, Minns roasted, toasted, sliced, and diced Chris Rusch, calling him an evil man who deserted his own family then continued to claim them as tax dependents, who stopped filing his own tax returns when he realized his criminal enterprises were out of control, who admitted to falsely notarizing documents, who cut a deal to testify against his own clients, who was caught lying in front of the court, and who at this very moment was residing in a hotel at the government's expense, where he was continuing to solicit new scam victims on his website.

The prosecution was given its final rebuttal, which Stockwell, I must say, handled very professionally, and then the court adjourned for the day.

The next morning, Teilborg gave the jury its instructions. As I mentioned, the detail and specificity of these instructions was quite impressive. Some of the instruction was boilerplate stuff about how to weigh evidence and what constituted reasonable doubt; some of it was highly specific to the case, including pages and pages of instructions on how to decide whether a conspiracy had taken place.

Two of the judge's instructions in particular gave me hope. First, Teilborg told the jury that they were allowed to take into consideration the facts that Chris Rusch had pleaded guilty to a felony and had made a plea bargain deal with the government when deciding whether or not to believe his testimony and how much weight to give it.

Second, he told the jury, "One element that the government must prove beyond a reasonable doubt is that each defendant had the requisite intent to commit each of the crimes charged in the indictment. Evidence that a defendant in good faith followed the advice of counsel would be inconsistent with such an unlawful intent."

If the jurors took these two instructions to heart, I didn't see how they could convict us of conspiracy. And if they couldn't check the "guilty" box for conspiracy, I didn't see how they could convict us on the other charges. If there was no proven intent to defraud, then it seemed to me that the charges of filing false returns and failing to file FBARs would become civil matters, not criminal ones.

As the jury was sent away to deliberate, I felt pretty good. I shared my optimistic feelings with Minns, who cautioned me somberly, "One thing I've learned through experience is that you just never know what a jury is going to do."

I guess he knew that better than I did.

So now we waited.

* * *

The jury deliberations were long and slow. One day passed. Two days. The only way the jurors were allowed to communicate with the judge was through written questions, and rumor had it they had asked very few of these. By all indications, they were being extremely diligent and conscientious.

The waiting was driving me crazy, though. After the first couple of days, Vicki and I went and sat on a bench right in front of the jury room so the jurors would be forced to see us every time they entered and exited. We did this for ten hours a day. We didn't want them to forget that they held the fate of a real live person in their hands.

As I sat in the courthouse for days, waiting for the jury to make its decision, I had plenty of time to think. There were so many inconsistencies in the government's case and so many questions that hadn't been answered. I could only hope that the jury would think about these things:

If my Belize tax bill was so huge that it persuaded me to start criminally evading taxes, why didn't I take the basic deductions that would have drastically lowered that bill?

Why, after getting investigated by the IRS for having an offshore account, would I take an even larger *risk by opening an* even larger *offshore account?*

How is it that Steve and I began laying the foundation for our conspiracy before we even met Chris Rusch and before the conspiracy allegedly started?

If Steve and I were watching and controlling everything that was going on in the Swiss accounts, why did we let Pierre Gabris make such lousy investments and milk us for exorbitant fees? As financial experts and criminal masterminds, shouldn't we have known better?

Why would we buy those expensive aged Swiss corporations for marketing purposes if we didn't intend to market the company but planned to use it only as a sham? Why would we pay tens of thousands of dollars to a marketing/advertising company (as was shown at trial) if we wanted to fly below the radar?

If the government thought we were guilty of securities fraud, why didn't it charge us with that?

If we indeed "took extraordinary measures" to conceal income, and carefully crafted a "vast criminal enterprise that spanned the globe," why would we send only a small percentage of our stock to Switzerland, while keeping the rest in the United States? Why invest so much energy and take such huge criminal risk for such a disproportionately small gain? It made no sense.

How could our acts be considered intentional crimes when forensic tax experts agreed that we did not, in fact, owe the IRS anything? Why would we deliberately file false tax returns when we could have paid less by filing accurate ones?

And finally, the biggest question of all: how could the government allow an attorney to testify against his own clients when the crime they were accused of committing together hadn't yet been proven?

Would the jurors ask themselves these questions? Or was I hoping for too much?

* * *

Finally, on the afternoon of April 11, more than five weeks after the start of the trial, the jury returned to the courtroom.

> THE COURT: Ladies and gentlemen, have you reached a verdict?
>
> PRESIDING JUROR: We have, Your Honor.

Judge Teilborg read the verdicts first. He crossed his arms and looked at the ceiling. I didn't know how to interpret what he was thinking.

> THE COURT: All right. If you would hand the verdict to the bailiff, who will hand it to the courtroom deputy. I'll ask the clerk to please read and record the verdicts.

They went through Kerr's verdicts first. Fingers crossed.

> THE COURTROOM DEPUTY CLERK: We, the Jury, find the Defendant Stephen M. Kerr, as charged in Count 1 of the Indictment, Conspiracy to Defraud the United States, not guilty.

Hallelujah. Not guilty on the big one. Logic said that the "lesser" charges should follow suit.

> THE COURTROOM DEPUTY CLERK: We, the Jury, find the defendant Stephen M. Kerr, as charged in Count 2 of the Indictment, Willful Subscription to False Individual Income Tax Returns, for the tax year 2007, guilty.

Guilty? Oh crap.

> THE COURTROOM DEPUTY CLERK: We, the Jury, find the Defendant Stephen M. Kerr, as charged in Count 3 of the Indictment,

> Willful Subscription to False Income Tax—
> Individual Income Tax Returns, for the
> year—tax year 2008, guilty.
> …We, the Jury, find the Defendant Stephen
> M. Kerr, as charged in Count 6 of the
> Indictment, Willful Failure to File FBARs
> (Foreign Bank and Financial Accounts), for
> the tax year 2007, guilty.
> …We, the Jury, find the Defendant Stephen
> M. Kerr, as charged in Count 7 of the
> Indictment, Willful Failure to File FBARS
> (Foreign Bank and Financial Accounts), for
> the tax year 2008, guilty.

I couldn't make sense of these verdicts. How had they found him not guilty of conspiracy yet guilty of all the "downstream" charges? It was totally illogical. I didn't have much time to think about it, though.

> THE COURTROOM DEPUTY CLERK: Okay. The
> verdicts as to Mr. Quiel. We, the Jury, find
> the Defendant Michael Quiel, as charged in
> Count 1 of the Indictment, Conspiracy to
> Defraud the United States, not guilty.

Breath exploded from my lungs. Thank God. I immediately tensed up again, though, clenching my fists as I waited for the other shoe to drop.

> THE COURTROOM DEPUTY CLERK: We, the Jury,
> find the Defendant Michael Quiel, as
> charged in Count 4 of the Indictment,
> Willful Subscription to False Individual
> Income Tax Returns, for the tax year 2007,
> guilty.

What? I was in such shock I couldn't process what I was hearing. The only thing I was aware of was the sounds of my wife and daughters bursting into tears.

> THE COURTROOM DEPUTY CLERK: We, the Jury, find the Defendant Michael Quiel, as charged in Count 5 of the Indictment, Willful Subscription to False Individual Income Tax Returns, for the tax year 2008, guilty.
> …And as to…Count 8, there is no verdict and as to Count 9 there is no verdict.

So…a hung jury on the FBAR charges. Not guilty of conspiracy to defraud. But guilty of filing false income tax returns. It was a crazy combination of verdicts.

Questions swirled in my head. How could I be not guilty of planning to defraud the government yet guilty of willfully filing a false tax return? Why was the jury hung on *my* FBAR charges and not Steve's? (I later figured out that this must have been because the charges weren't written specifically enough. I had, in fact, filed *some* FBARs for 2007 and 2008—on a small Belize account that I'd set up at the advice of Chris Rusch after settling up with the IRS in 2006. So I guess, because of that, some of the jurors couldn't find me technically guilty of not filing FBARs for those years.)

The next piece of business was to decide whether I should be released on bail pending sentencing or thrown in the slammer. Monica Edelstein, bless her blackened little heart, argued that I should be jailed and again had a US marshal on hand for that purpose. Her argument was that because I still had access to those phantom Swiss bank funds, I represented a serious flight risk. (I can think of a couple of one-syllable words that aptly describe Ms. Edelstein, but you would think less of me if I used them.)

My family, once again, was terrified that I was going to be hauled away to prison.

Mike Minns argued that the idea of my being a flight risk was ridiculous. Not only had I surrendered my passport, but my reputation and character were such that my appearance for sentencing was virtually guaranteed. "There's no possibility of him leaving this country, ever, under any circumstances," he said. "I'd quit practicing law before I would believe that."

Luckily, the judge agreed. "[T]he court finds by clear and convincing evidence that neither defendant is likely to flee or pose a danger to the safety of other persons if released."

Mike Minns then made a final plea to the court to dismiss the guilty counts against me. He pointed out that it was the charge of conspiracy that the government had used as its premise to get Rusch to testify against me. That turned out to be a false premise. "For that reason...having been acquitted on the conspiracy," Minns said, "we move to strike all of the evidence that was received from Mr. Rusch, all the evidence that was potentially privileged, and all the testimony of Mr. Rusch...There's nothing left in the record to sustain the remaining counts."

The judge agreed to take the matter under advisement.

The only remaining piece of business was for the court to decide whether I should be retried again on the FBAR charges. Teilborg recommended declaring a mistrial and letting it go at that. No one opposed him.

The US marshal asked me to report downstairs to get fingerprinted again because the government had lost the first set from the day they arrested me on the golf course. Again, the government gets to screw up, but you don't.

Then I returned to the courtroom, retrieved my $500,000 refund check, and walked out the front door of the court house a convicted tax perjurer released on appeal.

A sentencing hearing was scheduled for a few months later.

Until then I was free to go.

CHAPTER TWENTY-ONE

The Real Trial Begins

The real trial for my family and me began after the court trial ended. That was when the strain of all the years of anxiety and stress finally began to catch up to us and crack our armor. In the months following the verdict, Vicki, my wife and the love of my life, who had been a soldier throughout the trial, began to develop a serious case of PTSD. And in trying to help her deal with her problems, I, in turn, developed my own set of symptoms.

PTSD, as you probably know, is short for post-traumatic stress disorder. It's a syndrome common to people who have survived warfare, spousal abuse, natural disasters, and other forms of trauma. So where was the trauma in our case? Some people have implied there was no trauma in our case. After all, Vicki and I only had to deal with a tax situation, a white-collar trial.

To these people, I say, I hope you never have to experience what we did. I hope you never have to be investigated by the IRS or the DOJ. I hope you never have your personal and business records turned inside out and your friends and colleagues interrogated. I hope you are never handcuffed and arrested in front of your friends and neighbors when you have done nothing wrong. I hope you never have to live in fear and uncertainty for years on end, not knowing whether you are going to lose your home, your freedom, your financial security, or precious years with your growing children; not knowing whether armed agents are going to storm your home at any hour of the day or night. I hope you never have to watch overzealous government officials lie about you and destroy your personal reputation and your business. I hope you never have to stand in a courtroom, holding your breath as you wait to learn whether you are going to walk out the front door or be hauled off to prison by an armed marshal. I was facing thirty-five years in prison if convicted on all counts.

These things *are* traumatic. As the website HelpGuide.org points out, emotional and psychological trauma is caused not only by one-time calamities, such as a natural disaster or bombing raid, but also by "ongoing, relentless stress" and "humiliating or deeply disappointing" experiences. An event is *particularly* traumatizing, notes HelpGuide, if it involves deliberate cruelty, if you are unprepared for it to happen, and/or if you feel powerless to prevent it.

Powerlessness is a huge factor. When your safety, your freedom, and your livelihood are being steadily threatened from without, and you have no control whatsoever over the outcome, your mental and emotional reserves begin to ebb away. And when all your reserves are gone…well, something's gotta give.

What many government investigators and prosecutors fail to realize is that their actions affect the real lives of real people. In seeking so-called justice, these agents are so motivated to jack up their conviction numbers that they forget to ask, "Am I sure this person is even guilty? What will happen to this person's family if I wrongly convict him? If the evidence points away from this person's guilt, don't I have an obligation to speak the truth?" Truth doesn't even enter the formula. Winning is all that matters in the DOJ and in federal court. I don't know how these people sleep at night.

From the moment my name was surrendered to the US government by UBS, there was a presumption of my guilt and a single-minded drive to convict me. Nowhere along the way did a single government investigator or prosecutor stop and say, "What if this guy *isn't* guilty? What if there's a more innocent explanation for the facts as we know them? Maybe, God forbid, we should try to find out the truth here." Nowhere along the way did anyone stop to think about the collateral damage they might cause to a real family if they convicted an innocent man. They were too blinded by their own hunger for a "win." The sickest thing is that when the prosecutors finally realized they *were* in the wrong—as I believe they surely must have in our case—they were more interested in saving face than in seeing actual justice served. And my family had to pay the price for their arrogance.

There was no sense of relief or resolution for Vicki and me when the trial ended. Yes, I was able to go home, thank God, but we still had no idea whether I was going to prison or for how long. According to the sentencing guidelines, I could be facing over five years, depending on what they decided my tax bill was.

While the investigation and pretrial stuff had been going on, both Vicki and I, as I mentioned earlier, had developed a vigilance that bordered on paranoia. We thought people were watching our every move. We kept our blinds drawn and guarded our trash. Our chests ached from anxiety as we constantly waited for the next piece of bad news to drop. But by the time the trial was over, I had grown so accustomed to living with uncertainty that it didn't even bother me anymore.

What I didn't realize was that it continued to bother Vicki. A lot.

Vicki was dealing with a perfect storm of mental and emotional issues that were putting her stress level into the red zone. One of these issues was the death of her father. Because he died in the middle of this whole mess, she hadn't really dealt with the event emotionally. Her job, she felt, was to hold the home together and keep life as normal as possible for me and the girls—getting them to and from school, driving to the courtroom on time, putting meals on the table. So she hadn't permitted herself the "luxury" of mourning the loss of her dad. And now, suddenly, she stood to lose the other important man in her life—her husband—and there was nothing she could do about it. She was terrified.

On top of that, one of her best friends had abandoned her after the criminal trial. The hurtful part was that this woman's husband had undergone his own criminal investigation some years earlier—his business partner had turned out to be a scoundrel who was running a Ponzi scheme. At that time, Vicki and I stepped up for this couple, in the face of a government investigation, and helped put him in a new business. And now this woman was treating Vicki like dirt. Vicki couldn't understand why, just as she couldn't understand why the government had come after us the way it had or why the prosecutors had continued to press their case even after they realized Chris Rusch was a total liar and scumbag.

Too many whys. Too few answers.

Vicki's entire belief system had been shattered by the trial. That, I believe, was the real trauma for her. She had grown up in a military family and had always had a deep faith in our government, more faith than I ever had. That carried over to a trust in our justice system. Vicki deeply believed that if you did the right thing and told the truth, everything would work out in the end. She just could not wrap her head around the fact that the system had scapegoated her husband for no apparent reason. She couldn't fathom the fact the government would lie, outright, about me and "pay" a crooked lawyer to do the same. It rocked her world to its core. She simply couldn't process it.

Finally the inner pressure became too much. She started "checking out" mentally. In the middle of a conversation, she would just go blank. Gone. That "thousand-yard stare" you see on the faces of returning soldiers. It was a scary thing to witness. I later realized this was a symptom of PTSD, but at first I didn't know what the hell was happening.

In the weeks and months following the trial, her thought patterns became stuck in a compulsive, repetitive loop. She obsessed over questions she couldn't answer but couldn't leave alone: How could the prosecutors do this to us? What will happen to our family if Mike goes to jail? How can the government get away with treating people this way? Why, after taking my father away from me, does the government now want to take my husband? (Remember, John Lee died from the Agent Orange he was exposed to while serving in Vietnam.) Over and over, she would ask these questions, and I would try to address them with her, playing the role of unofficial therapist. Often I would talk to her for two and a half or three hours at a stretch, always about the same questions. But as soon as we'd start to close in on a fruitful insight, she would go blank and change the subject, so we could never resolve the issue.

The next day, it would be rinse and repeat. Same issues all over again.

At my urging she went to numerous psychologists, psychiatrists, and physicians, but none of them seemed to help very much, at least in the early days. Vicki had doubts about all of them, so she wouldn't commit to their treatment plans. Even worse, she began to doubt *me*. She was losing her ability to trust anyone or anything, and her symptoms were getting worse by the week. The medications she tried didn't seem to help. Her memory and her functioning were deteriorating before my eyes.

I think she wanted help but was also reluctant to genuinely seek and accept it. The reason for that was an underlying fear she had been carrying around for years: her sister had been diagnosed with schizophrenia, and she was terrified she might receive that diagnosis herself. Her fear of her own mind turning against her was probably her greatest stressor of all.

She started having acute "episodes." A couple of times when I was out on the golf course, I got calls from my daughters. "Dad, you've got to come home right away. Mom's acting really confused, and she doesn't even know where she is." The first time this happened, I rushed home and took her to the local ER in Scottsdale. She had a pulse rate of 120. They gave her fluids and calmed her down.

After that, we started monitoring her pulse and blood pressure every day. We realized she was consistently running a pulse over 120 when she was just sitting around the house, doing nothing. Basically, she was a stress bomb waiting to explode.

I think it was about a week after that trip to the ER that I was sitting with her on our patio, trying to talk to her and getting nowhere. It was the first time I began to consciously realize that there were certain triggers that always set off her spiraling thought cycles and that she was absolutely incapable of dealing with those issues once she was *in* a cycle. The triggers were anything to do with the trial, the government's investigation of us, or my incarceration. I remember trying to ask her some simple questions that day, and she just wouldn't answer me. I said to her, "I need to know why you're not talking to me. Are you confused or just angry?"

She looked at me like I was from Mars and said, "I don't know what you're talking about." She meant it. She literally could not understand the words coming out of my mouth.

At that point, I broke down in tears, thinking I had truly lost her, that her mind was permanently damaged. But that was also when I began to really understand that she was suffering from a textbook case of PTSD. And it was a direct result of what the government had done to us. You have to understand, again, the way Vicki was raised. Her father was a career military officer who moved his family around the world so that he could better serve his country. Service to country was a top priority in the Lee household, as was belief in the rule of law. And now the same government John had served all those years had targeted us and lied about us and was planning to put me in a prison cell. Her brain simply couldn't process it, and no amount of medication or therapy was likely to change that.

Not long after the first incident of extreme confusion, she had another one, and I took her to the Mayo Clinic. Mayo doctors had helped me with my pancreas problem, and I hoped they could help her. When we got to the clinic, she had the same physical symptoms as before—high blood pressure, high pulse. I explained to the doctors that I thought she had PTSD from the trial events, but they pretty much dismissed me. I was just the husband, after all; what the hell did I know? They gave her fluids again, along with a potpourri of medications, and sent her home.

I figured this was another temporary "fix" and that within another few days, she'd be climbing the walls again. But lo and behold, twenty-four hours later, she was completely back to normal. Her pulse was under control, and she was functioning and talking like her old self. Wow. The next day we went to a psychiatrist she had been seeing and shared the good news. He was impressed and optimistic.

Then, within another twenty-four hours, she was back in the pit again. So we went to back to the psychiatrist again, and this time he wanted to put her on heavy-duty antipsychotic meds. These were drugs they give to long-term mental patients who have serious psychiatric disorders, chemicals that can put you on the floor and cause long-term brain damage. The fact that the doctor wanted to put her on this level of medication was terrifying to both of us. Needless to say, she became extremely upset. So did I.

I grabbed her by the hand and drove her back to the Mayo Clinic, not realizing how agitated I was myself. I asked to see the records department. "My wife was in here a couple of days ago. We'd like copies of all her records."

They printed up the records, and I looked them over, feeling my agitation grow. "Excuse me, there's no mention anywhere about the meds you gave her," I said, sounding angrier than I intended.

"I'm sorry, sir, that's all the information we can give you."

"That's a bunch of crap!" I snapped at her. At this point, I was having my own PTSD symptoms, though I didn't recognize it. "You need to tell me what meds you put her on right now!"

I stormed down to the to the ER desk, barely containing my anger. "I need to know what you gave her; those meds made her better," I said.

The ER person wouldn't print them up officially from the computer—I'm not sure why—but she finally wrote the medications down by hand and slipped them to me like a secret. Probably just to get rid of me.

It turned out that three of the meds were the same ones Vicki had gotten at the Scottsdale ER. But the fourth was a beta-blocker. Beta-blockers are a mild class of drug prescribed primarily for physical symptoms such as high blood pressure and arrhythmia and secondarily for psychiatric symptoms such as anxiety. Many people take them safely every day; they're a world apart from antipsychotic drugs.

We went back to the psychiatrist and asked for a prescription for the beta-blocker. We filled the script and from that point on—after a little more tinkering with her other meds—Vicki started slowly down the road to improvement. (There's a reason they use the word *practicing* to describe what doctors and lawyers do.)

We made it through the summer. I hadn't been sentenced yet, so we still had that ax hanging over our heads. But we went up to Spokane for a couple of months, as we did each summer, and tried to enjoy the lake with the girls. The beta-blockers were definitely helping Vicki, but she still had a long way to go. A few weeks after we returned to Phoenix, she began feeling confused again, and I urged her to go back to Spokane to be with her mother and sister. I told myself it was because I thought it was what *she* needed, but deep down, maybe it was because I needed a break.

It was around this time I started going to AA meetings three nights a week—not because I was feeling tempted to drink, but because I needed to get out of the house and had nowhere else to go. (And besides, AA was like free therapy.) This was the first time in my life I ever had the feeling of not wanting to be in my own home. I began to dread having more of these long, unpleasant "counseling sessions" with Vicki every time I walked in the door. It wasn't that I didn't want to spend time with my wife; it was just that I knew we'd end up talking about the same things over and over again—the trial, the government, the lies they'd told. And there'd be no resolution. And I didn't know how to help.

This was undoubtedly the most stressful period of my life, worse than the investigation and trial itself. I sure as hell did not want to go to prison, but I'd be lying if I said there wasn't some small part of me that thought even prison would be an improvement over the way we were living.

CHAPTER TWENTY-TWO

Sentenced

The sentencing hearing didn't take place until September of 2013, three months after it was originally scheduled.

The hearing was like a mini-trial unto itself, with government and defense witnesses taking the stand and direct and cross-examinations by both sides. Most sentencing hearings probably don't take very long, but this one ate up the bulk of a day, due to one main issue: The court had to decide how much, if any tax, we owed to the government. This was no trivial matter. The court's finding would determine how much restitution money we had to pay—obviously—but it would also affect the amount of jail time, God forbid, we might be facing. When it comes to tax crimes, the sentence you receive is directly related to the amount of tax you are found to be owing. So this debate on taxes was really a battle for our freedom.

I won't get into the down-and-dirty details. Suffice it to say, the attorneys on both sides had their work cut out for them. They had to make sense of complex tax returns that spanned multiple years for both defendants, as well as understand issues like carryover losses, sophisticated business deductions, and securities tax laws. They had to familiarize themselves with the various accounting systems and models the expert witnesses used. On top of that, they had to be able to sort through the built-in biases on both sides of the aisle.

The prosecutors, needless to say, viewed the whole tax situation from a pro-government position. When calculating our tax debt, they simply *assumed* Steve and I were guilty of many things we had been charged with but which had not been proven during the trial, such as the idea that we had directed the nominees in Switzerland and that we had somehow ended up with all the money Chris Rusch had in fact lost or stolen.

The defense, on the other hand, took the position that without any evidence that we had directed the accounts in Switzerland or had benefitted financially from the Swiss accounts, we ought not be on the hook for most of the taxes on them.

In the end, I think the judge's decision came down to the quality of the witnesses. The prosecutors put on a woman named Debra Saparata. Our attorneys had a field day with her. I almost felt sorry for the woman. Kimerer's relentless questioning revealed that she had no license, wasn't a CPA, hadn't taken the enrolled agent exam, had no experience or expertise in banking taxation, and had been grandfathered into her current position as a "certified fraud examiner." He got her to admit that she hadn't consulted with the CPAs who prepared our taxes, didn't know tax code 367 (covering foreign corporations), and didn't know that the transfer of stock could be a taxable event. On and on it went. A battered Saparata finally presented what she believed to be our final tax obligation.

Our expert witnesses were Sheri Betzer (for Steve) and Ron Braver (for me). Betzer was a CPA with extensive experience working with the IRS, including the training of IRS agents and criminal investigators. Braver was a CPA and certified fraud examiner with a master's degree in taxation and twenty-five years of experience working as a special agent and supervisory special agent for the IRS. Both had reviewed the government's computations, and both had also talked to many of the people involved in preparing our taxes. Using high-level tax accounting methods that Saparata did not seem familiar with, each of them came independently to the same conclusion the Prather Kalman firm had: the tax loss (the amount we owed the government) in our case was *zero*.

Needless to say, the prosecution disagreed vehemently. At one point our witness Braver and prosecutor Edelstein got into a fierce shouting match with each other, and the judge didn't even stop it. In the end, based on the weight of our experts' qualifications versus Debra Saparata's, and on the fact that the government had not come close to meeting its burden of proof, Judge Teilborg found for the defense. Steve and I owed *no taxes*. If the IRS wished to conclude differently in the future, Teilborg said, it could do so through a civil process, but as far as his court was concerned, no financial restitution was due.

So after years of investigation and trial, after millions of dollars spent on both sides of the courtroom aisle, the final upshot was that we didn't owe the government a damn cent. Unbelievable. Maybe if the IRS had been allowed to conduct an independent audit, this whole thing could have been resolved simply and painlessly.

Now the only remaining issue to be settled was the question of jail time. Judge Teilborg said that in deciding on our sentences, he would take into consideration the fact that so many people—over fifty—had shown up in the courtroom to support us. Several of these character witnesses were allowed to give testimony at the hearing, and Teilborg also claimed to have read the many, many letters of support that had been written on our behalves. Each of us had over fifty letters, which our defense lawyers had submitted to the court ahead of time (even though the limit was supposed to be ten). The judge acknowledged that he had rarely, if ever, seen such an outpouring of character support.

I could fill several chapters of this book if I were to print all the letters written for me, but here are a couple that stand out as examples:

June 5, 2013

Dear Judge Teilborg,
   I've known Mike Quiel for my entire life. Ever since I can remember, our families have been very close and have always spent a great deal

208

of time together, enjoying a unique bond that we have always shared. My brother and I have grown up around his kids, and he had never been anything less than a great role model, as well as an excellent father.

In August of 2009, I suffered from a spinal cord injury that left me on a ventilator and paralyzed from the neck down. He helped my parents set up a nonprofit to collect donations to help with the costs of hospital stays, transportation, and rehabilitation. He even took an active role in finding donations for an auction that went towards covering the expenses as well. During that time, he frequently visited me in the intensive care unit in Spokane, as well as when I was staying in a rehabilitation hospital in Denver. He provided much-needed social support for myself, and my parents, during that trying period of my life.

In the time since my accident, Mike has always done everything in his power to support me and whenever I have needed anything, he has been very forthcoming with his help in any way he can. Whenever he was able to, Mike has tried to make it so that I can still participate in things I used to enjoy doing, but are no longer possible. Every summer, I used to go out to his lake cabin, do water sports behind the boat, and swim or fish off the dock. His dock was completely un-accessible to me, but Mike took it upon himself to build a ramp so that I could still be part of the activities that went on down by the water. He also put a railing around the dock to make it so I would not go over the edge. Unfortunately, the path down to the dock is not accessible for a wheelchair either. So to solve this problem, he figured out a way to use a trailer and four-wheeler to get me down to the dock.

To me, Mike has always been someone I look up to and has always done anything that he could to help me keep a positive attitude on life. Through his selflessness and compassion, he has made a deep impact on my life and I will always be extremely grateful for the love, as well as friendship, he has shown me.

Sincerely,
Robert Yamada

* * *

Rypien Foundation
August 14, 2013

Dear Judge Teilborg,

I am writing you today regarding Michael Quiel. Mike has been a dear friend and generous supporter of mine for over 25 years. Mike and I grew up together in Spokane, Washington, and enjoyed our time in High School together. Shortly after High School, I went to Washington State University for football and later went into the NFL. I have two Super Bowl rings and was also Super Bowl XXVI MVP. We have maintained a close relationship through the years, including many trips to the golf course to enjoy conversation about business and family. Throughout my friendship with Mike, I have experienced nothing but respect, integrity, and support from him.

Shortly after my NFL career, I lost my son to cancer. I used my celebrity status and started the Rypien Foundation almost ten years ago with the vision for it to become a premier provider of hope to families with children who suffer from cancer in the United States, and Mike has consistently provided overwhelming support to help us strive towards that vision. Mike has attended and participated in the annual Zak!Charity Open every year since its inception. His unwavering generosity is just one of the many traits that make Mike the wonderful man he is today. I have always known Mike to be a loyal and dependable person with a wholehearted belief in giving back.

My family and I have traveled to Arizona and vacationed with Mike, Vicki, and his daughters, and after spending time with him in a family setting, I can truthfully say that Mike is a loyal husband, devoted father, and compassionate friend. I have nothing but praise for Mike and can attest to his sterling character, as well as our association together.

Sincerely,
Mark Rypien

Judge Teilborg consulted the sentencing tables published by the federal government and concluded that because we didn't owe any taxes, and because there was so much evidence that we were men of high character within our families and communities, our sentence should fall within the lowest allowable range, ten to sixteen months.

As expected, the prosecution argued for the longest possible sentence within that range, the defense argued for the shortest sentence.

The prosecution also argued for immediate detention in jail, the defense argued for release on personal recognizance.

In both of these matters, Teilborg ruled in our favor. We were each sentenced to ten months—the shortest sentence allowable. We were also permitted to go free until such time as we were ordered to turn ourselves in. And because both Steve Kerr and I were both appealing our verdicts, we would not have to turn ourselves in until after the appeals were heard.

Ten months in prison.

It was a shocking thing to contemplate.

Still, to my mind, Teilborg's decision was a major victory. Not only was I happy to get out on bail, I was also confident that we would win on appeal at the Ninth Circuit. Armed with the fact that the federal judge had found we owed zero taxes, along with the great arguments Minns was planning to make in appeals court, I felt hopeful that I would not end up serving any jail time at all.

Maybe, fingers crossed, this thing was actually over at last.

* * *

In 2014, Minns started the appeal process, and life in the Quiel house began to return to normal. At least on the surface. Vicki was attending counseling sessions, and she seemed to be steadily getting better. She still became quite upset whenever she talked or thought about what the government had done to us and taken from us, but she was learning to manage her reactions.

All was not as well as it appeared to be, though. To Vicki, the idea of having an actual jail sentence hanging over our heads represented *added* stress, not lessened stress. She tried to keep a lid on her anxiety, but one day the time bomb that had been ticking inside her since the day she found out we were under investigation finally blew.

It was in March of 2014. Some friends of ours had come down from Spokane to play in a golf tournament. There were three couples all together, and we decided to go out on a Friday evening. Five of us rented a limo (one of the men stayed home), and we went out to a nice dinner in Scottsdale and then to a nightclub. None of us had to drive, so the alcohol flowed freely. More freely than it should have.

On the way home in the limo, Vicki lost it. I mean *lost it*. I don't even remember what triggered her, but she began screaming at me and physically striking me. All the anger over what she had been going through for the past four years came bursting out of her in a torrent. I think part of the problem was that she had recently been put on a new medication, Vyvanse, which reacts poorly with alcohol. It can cause you to feel the alcohol less, which makes you drink more and can trigger extreme mood changes and behaviors. But I truly believe the real problem was the relentless confusion and stress brought on by four years of mistreatment by the government her dad had died as a result of defending. That stress and confusion had finally crystallized into rage, and it needed to come out.

She began hitting me in the face and head, kicking me with her high heels. Our friends tried to restrain her, and I tried to cover up defensively, but she landed a lot of blows. I was scratched up and bleeding from the ears. Thank God there were witnesses to the fact that it was a one-sided attack, or I'd probably still be in jail to this day.

At one point, the limo took a turn to drop one of couples off at the condo where they were staying (the other couple was staying at our house), and I got out of the car. It was less than a mile from our house, so I figured I'd walk home and take myself out of the danger zone.

After I'd walked a ways, the limo came back, empty, and the driver asked me if I wanted a lift. Assuming he had dropped everyone off at our friends' condo, I accepted a lift home. When I got to the house, all *my own* anger came bubbling out of me. I was *really pissed* at Vicki. I started thinking about how hard I'd tried to get her in treatment and how hard she had resisted the help I tried to give her and how it had all come to this.

In one of the poorest decisions of my adult life, I gathered up a bunch of her clothes and belongings, threw them out on the front steps, and locked the door.

About fifteen minutes later, I saw car lights coming down the drive and heard the back door open and close. Then I saw another car back up the drive. I had no idea what was going on. A little while later, the same car returned and pulled into the garage, with Vicki behind the wheel. She walked out of the garage and looked at all her clothes piled at front door. While she was paying attention to the clothes, I ran to the garage and closed its door so she couldn't get in.

But the garage had a keypad. She keyed in the code.

She got the door open a bit, then I shut it. She opened it, I shut it. Open, shut. Open, shut. This Bugs Bunny cartoon went on for a while until she finally managed to enter the garage. At that point, she started screaming at me all over again. The kids were home, and I didn't want a scene. I managed to get her outside again, and we went through the whole process again—she opened the garage door, I shut it. Open, shut, open, shut. She finally got into the house through another entrance and began screaming at me once again as she picked up her clothes from the entryway. We got into a tug of war over one of her clothing items, and one of us released our grip. Vicki went sprawling backward and fell, hitting her head on a concrete step.

Her eyes rolled back in her head. I was horrified. We had a friend—Robert Yamada, whose letter you just read—who had broken his neck and was now a paraplegic; I was imagining the same thing had happened to Vicki.

As I called 911, the couple who was staying with us came running out of the back bedroom, where they'd been packing to leave. I didn't realize that they had come home during all the confusion with the car and limo. They saw Vicki bleeding and having convulsions and called 911 again. We called three times in total, and each time we were put on hold. So we decided to transport Vicki to the hospital ourselves. Before we were able to do so, the fire department arrived, having traced the source of the 911 calls. The police soon followed.

The cops assessed the situation, took hold of me, and marched me to the door. The kids were awake, so I told them to call Michael Minns right away. The cops put me in back of the squad car, suspecting, I'm sure, that I was a wife abuser. I was in shock, thinking Vicki might be dead.

The police kept me in the car for hours as they searched the house, talked to the kids, and did whatever other cop things they needed to do. The whole time they refused to let me in the house and wouldn't tell me what was happening with Vicki. I sat in that car until the sun came up with no word on Vicki. I've never been more scared in my life.

Finally, just to get back inside the house, I told the cops I had to use the bathroom, and they reluctantly escorted me in. I was able to see that the kids were okay, but I still couldn't get any information on Vicki. The cops marched me back out to the cruiser for another two hours, then finally took me to the Fountain Hills police station for processing.

There the police started hammering me with questions. Where did you spend the evening? When did you get home? Who was with you? What happened when you got home?

"I'm not saying anything until you tell me how my wife is doing," I told them. I also asked for an attorney.

The cops continued to grill me and wouldn't tell me anything about Vicki, so I continued to stonewall them. With each passing minute, I was more and more sure that Vicki was dead. My heart was in my throat, and my palms were pouring sweat.

Three times I asked for an attorney, and three times they ignored me, continuing to pepper me with abusive-husband questions. When they finally realized I wasn't going to talk, they gave in and handed me a cell phone. They said I could call whomever I wanted and told me, "Your wife has been admitted to Scottsdale Shea Medical Center. She's in stable condition." That was all I cared about.

After a while, I was taken to my favorite home-away-from-home, the 4th Avenue jail in Phoenix. I was wearing only a pair of jeans and a golf shirt, so when they issued me a receipt for the cash I was carrying, it read, "$0.00." The guards put me through the same routine they had two years earlier, bouncing me from cell to cell. In one of those cells, I found a penny and stuck it in my pocket.

Finally, attorney Joy Bertrand came down, late on Saturday night, and managed to get me in front of a judge, who let me out on my own recognizance.

I walked out of the 4th Avenue jail with the penny in my pocket and my receipt for $0.00, making me the first person in history to ever leave the 4th Avenue jail with more money than I went in with.

I decided to hang on to that penny forever, for good luck.

I was sure as hell going to need it.

CHAPTER TWENTY-THREE

Unlucky Number 9

Needless to say, Vicki and I had a lot of fallout to sort through in the wake of "the incident." I knew charges would be filed in Maricopa County, and I also knew that getting in any kind of legal trouble meant breaking the terms of my pretrial agreement. So I figured I would probably be going to jail sooner rather than later.

I was not allowed to go home yet, thanks to a restraining order the sheriff's office had imposed, so a sheriff had to accompany me to my house to pick up some belongings. When I got there, I found food, clothes, and other belongings scattered all over the floors. The place looked like a bombsite. I didn't know whether it was the police who had ripped the house apart, or Vicki—or what the hell had happened.

The chaos felt symbolic of my life. Of what this trial had done to us.

For the next week or so, I stayed with friends. Mentally and emotionally, I was at the breaking point. My own PTSD was in full bloom. I was super keyed up and couldn't sleep or concentrate. There was a weight in my chest that felt like a block of ice around my heart. Every time anyone would mention Vicki's name, I'd burst out crying, uncontrollably. Shrinks refer to this as emotional lability.

I learned that the sheriff's department had seen skid marks and tire marks driving up an embankment in front of our house. The car had driven straight up the embankment. It then did a speeding U-turn, nearly flipping on its side, and headed straight for a fifteen-foot drop over a neighbor's driveway. Miraculously, the car had come to a sudden stop at the last possible instant before going over the edge. A Hollywood stunt driver could not have repeated this feat. The cops thought it was me who'd been driving the car. They desperately wanted to nail someone for DUI, and based on the tape, I couldn't blame them.

Luckily for me, a friend of mine ran the homeowner's association and had access to all the security footage for our development. The tapes showed clearly that it was I who had been trying to get *away* from Vicki that night, not the other way around, and that it was Vicki who'd done the stunt driving with the car.

But therein lay my dilemma. You see, if I wanted to avoid going directly to jail without passing Go, I needed to clear myself of charges. *But*, in order to clear myself, I would have to throw the blame on to Vicki. And I didn't want to do that. I didn't want Vicki facing charges or going to jail.

I believe the correct term for my position is "between a rock and a hard place."

About ten days after the incident, I got a call from my pretrial officer (similar to a probation officer, but for people who are out on bail before a hearing).

"Quiel, you need to get down here *now*," he ordered.

He was not happy, and I could guess why. Joy Bertrand had advised me not to report my run-in with the local police to the district court. My pretrial officer, it seemed, respectfully disagreed with that advice.

I jumped in my car and drove to his office, where Joy Bertrand was already waiting for me.

"So what the hell happened?" my pretrial officer demanded, the moment I set foot in his office. I didn't insult him by asking what he was referring to.

"My wife had a bad night," I replied.

"Don't get cute with me, Quiel!" he barked. "I want to know exactly what happened. Were you drinking?" What happened?"

"I told you, my wife had a bad night." He waited for me to say more. "Okay, a *horrible* night." He waited again. "Listen," I said to him, "I love my family, and I can't say any more than that, I'm sorry. That's all I can tell you."

"I think you were drinking, and I want to know what happened and I want to know why you didn't call me and report that you'd had a run-in with the police!" He looked like he was ready to burst a blood vessel.

I explained that my lawyer had told me not to report the incident—she was sitting right beside me and verified this—and that I regrettably couldn't say any more about it at this time. I knew my tightlipped stance would go over like a concrete blimp, and I figured I was probably headed straight for jail, but what could I say without throwing Vicki under the bus?

My pretrial officer, to my surprise, let me walk that day, but a "special conference" was scheduled in district court in front of magistrate judge. This had nothing to do with the spousal abuse charges I would probably be facing in Maricopa County; this was strictly about my breaking the terms of my pretrial release.

The conference went on for about five hours, with witnesses, including the sheriff, taking the stand and me sitting in now familiar "defendant's seat." Throughout the proceeding, I kept my mouth shut tighter than a Ziploc bag. I knew the sheriff's department would be just as happy to send Vicki to jail as me, so I couldn't tell them anything that would incriminate her. So I said nothing as the sheriff spoke falsehoods and misinterpreted facts. At one point, for example, Joy Bertrand asked him if Vicki had sustained any other injuries besides the one on her head.

The sheriff replied that she had a scratch on her left shoulder.

Bertrand asked if this could have been caused by a car safety belt when brakes were jammed when her BMW went up the embankment. The sheriff replied no, because when a BMW is in an accident, the seatbelts lock the person into the seat so they can't get out. This was pure fiction, and I think even the judge knew it. The sheriff, of course, wanted to create the impression that *I* had caused the injury to my wife.

Hospital records, however, confirmed that there had been no other injuries to Vicki. The witnesses who had been with us in the car that night confirmed that I had not been the aggressor. Security footage confirmed that I had been trying to get *away* from Vicki that night, not pursue her.

So even though I didn't defend myself during the proceeding, there was plenty of evidence to suggest that I had not committed any felonies. Still, the court nailed me on several violations of my pretrial agreement, such leaving my residence and consuming alcohol. I fully expected to be remanded to jail immediately after the conference, but was surprised once again when the judge let me out on personal recognizance.

Meanwhile, Vicki was still dealing with her own issues. Because of her head injury, she underwent a number of tests while in the Scottsdale hospital. A neurosurgeon on staff proposed that Vicki was experiencing seizures and that these were related to "mini-strokes" that were occurring in her left frontal cortex.

This was a good news / bad news scenario. The good news was that maybe these mini-strokes were responsible for some of the problems Vicki had been having since the trial and that maybe her condition was treatable now that we knew the cause. The bad news was that because of the possibility of seizures, her driver's license was suspended.

When I was finally cleared to return home, Vicki was a wreck. She was still suffering PTSD symptoms, she had fresh stitches on her head, she was stuck in the house because she couldn't drive, she was filled with remorse and confusion over what had happened, and she was trying to figure out how in hell her life had come to this.

That made two of us.

I made an appointment with a Mayo Clinic neurosurgeon to follow up on the mini-stroke issue. The Mayo people looked at the exact same brain scans the Scottsdale team had examined and saw no evidence of mini-strokes.

"And I can almost assure you that no seizures took place," the neurosurgeon said.

So that theory was out the window.

But the good news was that after getting letters from the Mayo and from Vicki's regular physician, she was able to get her driver's license back. Slowly life began to resume a semblance of normalcy. I was attending AA meetings three times a week and getting court-ordered counseling on anger management and substance abuse. Vicki was also getting counseling and continuing to feel better.

We decided to go up to Spokane for the summer, as usual. This turned out to be a major hassle because the judge insisted I remain in court-ordered counseling. Once I was finally able to arrange new counseling services in Spokane and get them approved by the court, I was finally able to join my family there, three weeks late.

During that summer of 2014, Vicki and I worked as hard as we could to return a feeling of stability to the family. We did a pretty good job of it, I think, but of course, there was still a huge shadow looming over us. That shadow was in the shape of a courthouse. Actually, two courthouses. Because now my fate was not only in the hands of the appellate court of the Ninth Circuit, but also in the hands of the Maricopa County court, where a whole new set of charges awaited me.

* * *

Here's how the appeal went.

Mike Minns put together an impressive brief for the appeals court, as did Mike Kimerer for Steve Kerr. Minns's four main arguments for appealing the trial court's decision were as follows:

I. Quiel was denied his constitutional right to cross-examine Rusch on three exhibits entered on redirect.

II. The government's repeated reference to defendants' complicated securities transactions as fraud was prejudicial, and the court's allowing such references over objection was error.

III. 	Quiel was denied his constitutional right to counsel by the trial court's allowing Rusch to testify in violation of Quiel's attorney-client privilege.

IV. 	The trial court erroneously refused to require production of the Special Agent's Report, the defendant's Individual

Master File, and the notes of the government's chief investigator, and refused to review the documents *in camera* or even preserve them for review by this court.

I've talked about the first three of these issues already. To sum them up: we were denied our right to challenge Rusch on those three phony documents he brought in at the end of his testimony, we were treated prejudicially throughout the trial because the court allowed the prosecution to continually refer to our legal stock transactions as "fraud," and we were denied our attorney-client privilege by Rusch's being permitted to testify against us. There were further subarguments to each of these, but that was the essence.

As to the fourth issue, that revolved around a so-called Brady violation. In case you're not familiar with a Brady violation, it has nothing to do with a quarterback under-inflating footballs, but with the duty of the prosecution to share with the defense any evidence it acquires that may be favorable to the defense. In our case, we were never allowed to see the special agent's report (SAR) from the DOJ or notes from the DOJ's chief investigator. The SAR contains key information such as why, when, and how a determination of possible criminal activity is made. In our case, the SAR probably also contained information about how closely Rusch had been working with the government and for how long. This was vital to our defense.

The so-called individual master file (IMF) from the IRS was also a crucial document. The IMF is the complete record the IRS maintains on every taxpayer. The prosecution was allowed to use *portions* of my IMF, but the defense was not allowed to review the full document so as to assess those portions in context. Given the fact that the IRS refunded my $500,000 payment and stated that I was actually carrying a *credit* from the treasury, not a debt, we had strong reason to believe there was information in the IMF that would bolster my claim that I did not owe any taxes to the government. But we were never allowed to see the IMF.

Minns's written brief offered great support for all our arguments, and I was confident we would win on appeal. Mike Minns did not share my confidence. He had a lot of experience with Ninth

Circuit appeals, and he knew that anything could happen in appeals court. His feeling was that when it comes to appeals, luck is a crucial ingredient.

Heading into the appeal hearing in the late fall of 2014, we had reasons to be both optimistic and pessimistic.

On the plus side, we were granted oral arguments. That means the attorneys are allowed to plead their case orally in front of a live panel of three judges, as opposed to simply submitting written briefs. Oral arguments are granted in only about 5 percent of appeals cases in the Ninth Circuit, so Minns felt that by this fact alone, we had a greatly improved chance of prevailing.

On the negative side, we would be facing a very tough crowd on the bench. Of the three appellate judges assigned to our case, one had overturned *only one decision* in twenty-five years, and another had reversed no more than three decisions in ten years. So this was going to be a very, very difficult panel to face. Minns would have to be outstanding in his presentation, and we'd need a lot of luck as well.

Shortly before the appeal case, we had some *great* luck with the Maricopa County case. Joy Bertrand had submitted all the defense's evidence, which was overwhelmingly in my favor, and in a bit of last-minute negotiating was able to get all the charges against me dismissed. This happened the day before I was supposed to appear in court for my trial. I was delighted to have that episode behind me, though angry about all the grief I'd been through—the trip to jail, the meetings and conferences, the court-ordered counseling—for what turned out to be no reason.

But still it was good news. Now all that stood in the way of my life returning to normal was the Ninth Circuit court of appeals.

The hearing was held on the tenth of December in San Francisco. We were given additional reason to feel optimistic when the three judges met us outside the courtroom prior to the hearing. They were respectful and cordial in this informal meeting, and Minns took it as a good sign that they had shown us this courtesy. He was hopeful that because I had not been found guilty on three of the five counts and that because the two guilty counts hinged on those three shady documents that should not even have been admitted, we had a great case for reversal.

Minns argued his case beautifully in front of the judges. I couldn't have asked for more. He also gave an eloquent plea as to why I should not serve jail time. I went away feeling as good as I possibly could, given the circumstances. I really didn't think the appellate judges would send me to prison. Minns agreed; he thought the chances of my serving prison time were slim.

Now it was time to play the waiting game again. Minns told me it would be three to six months before we received a decision from the appeals court.

* * *

Nine days later, on December 19, I was playing the ninth hole at Fire Rock—the same hole where I had learned I was being arrested a couple of years earlier—when the Ninth Circuit weighed in. Ashley Arnett from Mike Minns's office called to inform me. So...was the number 9 going to be lucky for me or not?

"Mike, I've got some bad news," she said. "The appeals court has made its decision. You're going to have to turn yourself in."

"What?"

"We lost the appeal. You're going to have to serve your prison sentence."

My head started spinning. I couldn't believe what I was hearing. And I couldn't believe I was hearing it so soon. My disbelief was soon eclipsed by anger as I realized that in order to render a decision in such a short time, the judges must have already had their minds made up long before the hearing. The granting of oral arguments had been a mere formality.

Why did the appeals judges rule against us? When I later read their decision, it began by stating, "We will uphold a conviction if, 'viewing the evidence in the light most favorable to the prosecution, *any* rational trier of fact could have found the essential elements of the crime beyond a reasonable doubt.'" In other words, the appeals court would overturn the lower court only if no sane person could *possibly* have found us guilty in the absence of the lower court's alleged violations.

As to our specific arguments, the judges' opinion was that we had waived our attorney-client privilege by using an "advice of counsel" defense; that even if Rusch's testimony had been excluded, it was still possible for a jury to have convicted us; that a Brady violation hadn't occurred because we hadn't proven that the state had suppressed evidence or that said evidence was "favorable to the accused" (how we could have known that without even *seeing* the evidence was not explained); and that we had not shown that the use of the term *fraud* had "so infected the trial with unfairness as to make the resulting conviction a denial of due process."

All I knew on December 19, 2014, six days before Christmas, was that I was royally screwed.

I packed up my golf clubs and headed home to tell Vicki what I'd learned. This wasn't the kind of news you shared by phone.

Ho ho ho.

CHAPTER TWENTY-FOUR

Incarcerated

When the appeal was denied, my mind shifted into overdrive. I was desperate to come up with a strategy to avoid prison. One option was an "appeal on the appeal." This would mean requesting a so-called *en banc* hearing. In an en banc situation, *all* the justices on the circuit, not just the three who heard your appeal, review the facts and make a ruling. Kimerer didn't want to be involved in pushing for this because he thought it was hopeless. But Minns agreed to pursue it. So we got that ball rolling.

I also suggested to Minns that we dig into the jurors' backgrounds. We'd already learned, in our initial jury research, that one of them had lied about his profession (the "convenience store clerk" who actually owned three Cricket stores), and I thought there was a chance some of the others might have "issues" that could disqualify them retroactively. I had no specific reason to think we'd find any dirt on anyone—and I didn't want to violate anyone's privacy—but I was leaving no stone unturned. The kind of jury research we needed wasn't in Minns's wheelhouse, so I called Joy Bertrand, and she quoted me a price of $28,000 to do an investigation. I said, "Fine, let's do it."

She hired an investigator but was annoyingly slow on getting started. It was January by this time, and I'd learned that I would need to turn myself in to prison in the first part of March. So time was of the essence.

On January 6, I got a surprise call from Mike Minns.

"Are you sitting down?" he asked.

I said, "Yes," then immediately stood up and started pacing the floor. "Why?"

"One of my colleagues was doing some online research," he explained, "and he stumbled on the website of an attorney who calls himself Christian Reeves. This Reeves guy is offering the *exact same services* as Chris Rusch. Christian Reeves: C. R. Do you think Chris Rusch might be operating under an alias?"

I didn't know, but I was sure as hell going to find out. I immediately went online and found this Christian Reeves guy. Though the photo on his website bore no resemblance to Rusch, I knew it was probably just a stock photo. The text described Reeves as a "recovering attorney" who offered consulting services in the same vein as Chris Rusch did. Much of the language was identical to the language Rusch had used on his site. Reeves was Rusch; I could feel it in my bones.

This might be huge. If we could show that Rusch had been operating under an alias while the trial was going on, trying to lure people into his online scams even as he was testifying that Steve and I were the ones to initiate illegal activity, we might be able to impeach his entire testimony.

I found some podcasts made by Reeves and was actually afraid to listen to them, in case I was wrong. When I finally mustered up the nerve to hit Play, my instinct was confirmed. It was Rusch's voice; I recognized it in an instant.

Reeves was Rusch.

I wanted to gather some hard evidence to prove that and also to find out how long the alias had been in play, but I knew I couldn't be directly involved, because that would taint any evidence I might find. So I went to the security team that had backed up my hard drive and hired them to do a discreet investigation.

The investigators quickly confirmed that Reeves was indeed Rusch. Better still, by using a digital archive called the Wayback

Machine, they were able to recover "snapshots" of Reeves's website going back a couple of years. Rusch had evidently started using this alias while he was between his two prison stints, *prior to the trial!* So we could now prove that while the government was paying to put Rusch up in a hotel, and while Rusch was weeping for the jury in court, he was busily trying to set up his next scam victim. This was big.

My heart started racing, and I felt a rush of lightheadedness. *Oh my god,* I thought, *if I handle this right, I'm not going to prison.* If we could put this information in front of a judge—that Rusch, during the trial, had been actively soliciting new scam victims under an alias—this might change everything.

I found out that an organization called Live and Invest Overseas was doing a seminar in Cancun. I knew that Rusch was closely associated with this group, and I had a feeling he'd be at the seminar, so I told my investigators, "Get on a plane and get down there before the seminar starts. Get a recording of him as Reeves."

The investigators went to Cancun, and sure enough, they saw Rusch there. They observed him for two days, but then they wanted $5,000 so they could attend the seminar. I said, "No way, guys. Approach him outside the event."

But they blew it. Passive-aggressive bastards. They spent several days and $30,000 of my money and came back without any photographs or recordings. Unbelievable. But by this date, it was too late to hire a new investigative team. I had them prepare their report on Rusch anyway, and it was pretty damning even without the Cancun evidence.

I hired Joy Bertrand to put together a Rule 33 motion. This is a motion you can file when you discover new evidence that you believe would have affected the outcome of your trial. A judge can respond to a 33 motion in one of three ways: deny it, order a new trial, or dismiss the verdict. By now it was late in February 2015, and I was due to turn myself in on March 13. So I told Bertrand this motion had to be put together *yesterday.* She said she understood and promised to get right on it.

But she didn't. Nope, no joy with Joy. She let time slip away. It was now only days before March 13, and I called her in a panic. "You've got to get that motion in front of a judge!" I demanded.

Bertrand proceeded to wait until March 11 and then sent an emergency order to the judge, telling him essentially, "Here's an outline of what we *plan* to file. Please give us an extension for Mr. Quiel to check in to prison." The judge, not having seen any of the actual evidence Bertrand was promising to produce, said, in effect, "[Bleep] no, Quiel needs to report."

So that was that. Up till the day before I checked into prison, I thought I was going to be able to avoid serving time, but now I knew there was no way around it.

Vicki and I got in the car and headed for El Paso, Texas. There I would surrender myself to the care and feeding of the good folks at La Tuna FCI prison. It was a six-plus-hour drive from Phoenix to El Paso, and I needed to be there first thing in the morning.

Why El Paso, Texas? Well, because the DOJ can put you wherever the hell they choose. They have total control; they can put a white-collar criminal in solitary confinement for years if they want. They answer to no one. They say they *try* to house prisoners within five hundred miles of their families. If that's true, they pushed it right to the limit for me; El Paso was about 450 miles from my home in Fountain Hills. They could have chosen to put me in the Tucson federal prison, about two hours away, but come on, what fun would that be?

I was literally in the car, on my way to El Paso, when I got an e-mail from Joy Bertrand containing the actual motion she planned to file in court. Jump for Joy. She finally filed the damn thing, but too late to keep me out of an orange jumpsuit.

On March 13, 2015—four years to the day after Vicki's dad died—I showed up at La Tuna federal prison in El Paso, Texas, at 9:00 a.m. on the dot. As I walked through the door, I made a silent promise to John Lee that although I was surrendering physically, I was not finished fighting this thing.

My check-in time was noon. So why show up early and lose my last three hours of freedom? Because I had hired a prison consultant—yes, such people exist—and he gave me some key advice about La Tuna. "Check in the minute the prison opens," he said. The way it works at La Tuna, you see, is that *all* prisoners are required to check in at the main facility, which is medium security. Then, once processed, the lower security prisoners are taken by shuttle to a satellite facility several miles away on the grounds of the Fort Bliss airfield. At that point, prisoners go to either the low-security unit or the so-called camp.

But La Tuna gets busy, and if you show up later in the day—i.e., on time—there's a good chance you'll end up spending a day, or several days, at the main facility before they finally get around to transferring you to the satellite. And you don't want to spend time at the main facility. My consultant's advice turned out to be dead-on. Many of the guys who checked in later the same day I did weren't transferred to the satellite facility till four or five days later.

La Tuna FCI looks like a four-star Mediterranean hotel on the outside. I'm not kidding; Google it. But the four-star fantasy quickly disappears when you step inside. They put me in a holding cell, stripped me down, took the street clothes I was wearing (I told them to throw them away), and issued me my prison duds. A few hours later, they marched me out to the shuttle. To get there, I had to pass within twenty yards of the door I'd walked through as a free man. Only now I was in full shackles and shuffling between chain-link fences topped by razor wire.

The transport van took me to the army airfield where my new home awaited.

At La Tuna, most white-collar guys who have no history of violence go to the camp facility, which is pretty loose and minimum-security, but I was told I'd be staying in the "low security" section, which is more restrictive. Why, I didn't know.

The low-security facility consisted of three barracks the army had erected as temporary housing. One good thing about staying at a prison on military grounds is that they don't allow sex offenders there. So at least I wouldn't be rooming with a dog rapist named Tiny. Theoretically.

I wore earplugs on the van, but the guards confiscated them before I went inside. The intimidation game. Check-in was handled military style. They ran down the list of rules with me, letting me know in no uncertain terms that I was no longer in charge of my own life. They handed me my ration of clothes then took me to the CO in charge of the barracks, who showed me to my bunk. My cell—it wasn't really a *cell*, but a large, open room containing twelve bunk beds—had a total of five occupants when I arrived. I was assigned the bunk on top of Chad, a six-foot-five, 350-pound Shrek lookalike who, I was soon to learn, created scenes from the movie *San Andreas* every time he rolled over in bed.

My cellmates were welcoming enough; that put me at ease. When you enter La Tuna, you have nothing but the clothes on your back, so my cellmates were kind enough to give me soap, a bowl, some toiletries, a toothbrush, flip-flops, all the stuff I would need until I could buy my own things at the commissary. Fortunately, the prison consultant had told me how to get money into my prison account quickly, so I didn't have to wait long for funds to arrive.

One of the first pieces of business I did at La Tuna was check in with my counselor, a guy named Franco. He was an ex-marine, a bit of a hard ass, but I got along with him okay.

Franco asked me at our first meeting, "Want to know why you're here instead of at the camp?" Yes, I did. "Because you have outstanding assault-related charges in Maricopa County."

What? Evidently, my trumped-up spousal abuse case was still on record with the feds, even though it had been dismissed at the local level. That was because *someone*—let me guess; could it have been, oh I don't know, Joy Bertrand?—had not notified the federal government of the case dismissal.

"Those charges were dismissed," I said to Franco. "I can get that cleared up right away."

"No point," he told me. "You're only going to be here ten months. By the time the paperwork gets processed, it'll be too late to make a transfer. I'm afraid you're here with us for the duration, my friend."

Joy Bertrand, the gift that kept on giving.

Franco also told me that according to my records, I owed a balance of $11,000 to the feds for court costs. In fact, I had paid that bill the day after I received it, but there was no record of such payment. I had to get a receipt sent in from the outside to prove it. The federal government is physically incapable of doing even the tiniest task correctly.

* * *

As the days unfolded, I adjusted to prison life. For the most part, I got along with my cellmates. One of them was nicknamed Cowboy, and he was exactly what you imagine when you hear that name. He'd been busted for selling coke but managed to get his thirty-year sentence cut in half by testifying against a Mexican drug lord. Well, he actually testified against an empty chair—the government couldn't find the drug lord, so they held his trial without him. The worst of my cellmates was a guy named Jeff, a ship's captain who got caught transporting coke out of Panama. Jeff was pretty much a lying scumbag, not to put too fine a point on it.

Cowboy and Jeff got along like Mentos and Coke. Which made me like Cowboy all the more.

Needless to say, when I got transferred to a smaller cell three months later, one with only four bunks in it, Jeff got transferred there too. So I spent my entire incarceration with Jeff, the lying scumbag.

Seeing prison from the inside, you come to understand why the American prison system is such a revolving door. Inmates spend most of their time sitting around, doing nothing. This kind of idleness does nothing to prepare you for managing a busy life and career in the outside world. In fact, it "de-prepares" you by making you soft and weak and unfocused. We had this kid in my cell, Greg, for example, who was thirty-one years-old and had been in for eleven years, eight of them in that very cell. *No one* made any effort to work with this kid on developing his life skills. As a result, he couldn't manage ten cents. He had no direction, no motivation, and was terrified of adult responsibility. He had a three-year-old kid resulting from a "gate pass" encounter while in prison but didn't have the slightest clue how to be a parent. I found out after I left that they called him to the CO's office one day and told him, completely out of the blue, "Pack your stuff, Greg, you're going home." I'll bet that worked out well. My guess: poor Greg's back inside already.

Most of us in the low-security unit did have prison "jobs," but they were pretty much a joke. Mine was in "Facilities"—air-conditioning, painting, light repairs, that sort of thing. I tried to keep a low profile. They put me on a crew with two other guys. These dudes saw me as their junior, but because of my experience as an electrician in the navy, I actually knew more than they did. I tried not to rub it in their faces, but one of the guys didn't take too kindly to the fact that I had a brain. We got into it, and I told the CO I couldn't work with him anymore.

"Tell you what," I proposed to the CO. "Your plumbing shack's a mess. You've got parts and supplies piled all over the place. Why don't you let me organize it?" He agreed, eager to get back to his Sudoku puzzle. The supply-organizing job could have been done in two days, but I made it last three months. By the time I was done, the supply shack looked like Home Depot. But the biggest challenge was how to fill all those hours.

The basic routine at La Tuna was to get up and be at work by seven. There was "open campus" before that, so if a CO bothered to show up at the yard, which half the time they didn't, you could get in some exercise first. On a *long* day, you were finished work by two thirty in the afternoon, then you had the rest of the day to kill. So maybe you'd wander over to the TV room, just for the air-conditioning, and watch reruns of *Two and a Half Men* (and they say we don't employ cruel and unusual punishment in US prisons) till head count at four.

There were actually four TV rooms, self-segregated by the inmates—one for local Texas people, one for African Americans, one for Mexicans, and one for people from out of the area. The same was true of the chow hall. You ate at certain tables based on race. I have to say, though, that the segregation stuff wasn't too extreme at La Tuna. Sitting in the wrong seat wouldn't typically get you killed.

In fact, one thing that surprised me was the level of respect I saw inside. Everyone said "please" and "excuse me" and in general behaved more politely than the outside population did. An honor code existed there; guys left their lockers unlocked and their belongings lying around. Still, I wouldn't describe most of the inmates as highly evolved. Maturity-wise, they were adolescents. They didn't have a lot of insight into why they were there and didn't seem interested in gaining any.

AA meetings, for example, were a farce. I had attended them in Phoenix as a form of counseling and found them helpful. So I thought maybe I could continue my AA program in prison. Ha. Meetings were supposed to be held every Monday, but they only happened about once a month. The meetings were an hour long, but half was in English and half in Spanish. The only reason anyone went to them was to get a certificate of attendance to show off at their probation hearings.

I did manage to connect with a group of guys who were doing some mock commodities trading on paper. They subscribed to the *Wall Street Journal* and shared their tips and ideas with one another. I actually learned a thing or two from these guys. Having lost my investing business, I planned to go back into stock trading when I got out.

For the most part, though, prison was a lot of gray, empty time, sitting around doing nothing. Every day we got head-counted four or five times. We went to our jobs, we went to meals, and we watched TV or read books till lights out. Then we did the same thing the next day. The highlight of my day was when I got to talk to Vicki for the ten allowable minutes.

As a rule, I got along with the COs and didn't have any major incidents. Most of the guards were decent, reasonable people; a couple of them were prime assholes. Just like you'd probably expect.

I could go into prison life in more detail, but the truth is, it was a huge bore. And maybe that was the whole point. There were no riots or prison breaks or *Shawshank Redemption* moments.

There was, however, one person I met in prison who affected my life in a truly positive way.

CHAPTER TWENTY-FIVE

The Fight Continues

I plan to continue filing motions and appeals in my case until I succeed or exhaust every option. I don't know whether I'll be successful or not, but if I am, many thanks will go to a gentleman by the name of Lindsey Springer. The funny thing is that I had to go to federal prison to meet him.

Lindsey Springer is an infamous tax protester who was a guest of La Tuna FCI at the same time I was. If you Google him—unfortunately, he shares his name with a Hollywood producer and a female porn star—you will see that he is a highly polarizing figure. Many people dismiss him as the worst kind of antigovernment nut job; others see him as a tireless fighter for the rights of citizens against an all-too-powerful IRS. My own opinion, having spent time with the man, is that he is a thoughtful, generous, caring, devoted, and committed individual.

He is also *relentless*—once Lindsey Springer sinks his teeth into a cause, he can't be stopped. It's that quality that makes him such a pain in the government's ass and explains why the feds once gave him a high-level violent offender as a cellmate and why he'll probably never walk out of prison until every minute of his fifteen-year sentence is served.

Springer is a self-described minister. Some years ago, he created a "ministry" called Bondage Breakers, which is dedicated to abolishing the IRS and supporting and educating people in their fights against it. He is in prison for, among other things, helping other ministries fight the IRS. The DOJ, however, claims that Springer was using his own ministry "in an elaborate scheme to defraud the US government of taxes" (hmm, where have I read language like that before?) and managed to convict him of fraud, tax evasion, and failure to file tax returns.

Springer is on what he considers to be a spiritual mission to help anyone and everyone who is in trouble with the IRS, both inside and outside of prison. He has taken the government to court on numerous occasions. Once, for example, the IRS raided his house and seized, among other things, $19,000 in cash. When the money was finally returned to Springer, he got only $17,000 back. He sued the government for the missing $2,000 and kept the case alive for five years before finally getting the IRS agents into a courtroom, where one of them actually claimed on the stand that he didn't know it was illegal to take money found in a home raid. (The agents were not found guilty of any violations—and yet *Lindsey* is doing time in prison.)

Springer gives his advice and guidance for free—he refuses to accept any form of payment—and often invests a tremendous amount of energy into someone's case, even if he does not like the person. I'm told he has helped a great many people get out of prison. I know he gave me a lot of encouragement, guidance, and confidence in my battle.

When I met Springer in La Tuna, I was dealing with a number of recent disappointments. The en banc appeal we'd filed had come up empty; all twelve of the judges on the Ninth Circuit ruled against us. Judge Teilborg had reviewed our Rule 33 motion and denied that as well. He was not convinced that the fact that Rusch used an alias during the trial was evidence of nefarious intent on his part or that Rusch was a "known perjurer," as Minns had claimed in the written brief he'd submitted for the motion. We tried to appeal to the Supreme Court but learned that it was refusing to hear our case, stating that its role was not to police the lower courts, but to hear cases that have wider legal ramifications.

On an unrelated note, there was trouble on my home front as well. Our oldest daughter, who was living independently, had developed a substance abuse problem and had gotten herself into some trouble. Like so many others, she began taking pain pills and got addicted. This led to use of harder substances, and while I was in prison, she had a relapse. Vicki, who was still dealing with her own PTSD, flew to Salt Lake City, where our daughter was living, brought her to a rehab facility in Seattle, and was trying single-handedly to manage her care. I was trying to help and support Vicki from inside prison but was only allowed to talk to her ten minutes a day.

I certainly didn't expect Springer to help with this latter issue, but I did talk to him about my legal situations. At that time, I was feeling pretty powerless and despondent. Not because of prison—I could handle anything La Tuna dished out—but because of all the things that were happening on the outside that I couldn't control.

Springer helped reignite my fighting spirit. He helped me acquire vital information about my case through the Freedom of Information Act (FOIA). He also taught me how to write FOIA letters and where to send them. One thing I learned from writing these FOIA letters, for example, was that most of the government people who worked on my case were not appointed legally. In fact, out of ten federal lawyers involved, a grand total of zero was correctly appointed. The Constitution, you see, calls for the nomination of US attorneys by the DOJ, after which a person may serve only 210 days before being confirmed by the Senate. During the Obama administration, the confirmation process was suspended, so no one was confirmed anymore. As of 2016, thousands of justice personnel were holding their jobs illegally. But of course, the government is allowed to break the law.

In a similar vein, I learned that the FBAR form itself—the one I was charged with failing to file and for which I still faced civil litigation by the government—is illegal *by the government's own rules*. When Springer first told me about this, I thought it was one of those goofy tax-protester arguments that you can't apply in real life. But I learned that the Paperwork Reduction Act of 1995 clearly states that the government cannot require citizens to file forms that aren't approved by the Office of Management and Budget (OMB) and issued a control number by that office. Not only did the FBAR forms not contain an OMB number, but they were specifically identified by the government as illegitimate forms. This was information I intended to use in my case going forward. How could I be legally required to file an illegal form?

I was also able to use FOIA letters to prove that the FBAR testimony given by Rusch and Bradley, which was a cornerstone of the prosecution's case against me, was false. As you know, both Chris Rusch and Cheryl Bradley testified at my trial that I filed FBAR forms in 2006 for the years 2000–2003 and therefore knew I had an obligation to file these forms in 2007 and 2008. I learned through repeated FOIA inquiries that these forms were never filed for 2000–2003. Not only did this negate a major part of the government's criminal argument, but it also proved, factually, that Chris Rusch lied at my trial and therefore *was* a known perjurer.

Springer also helped me understand that I had a right to see the criminal referral that had been made against me to get the DOJ involved, and that without a valid criminal referral, my investigation and prosecution should not have gone forward. I sent a FOIA letter to the US Attorney's office requesting a copy of its criminal referral to the DOJ. They couldn't produce it but sent me back a letter stating that grand jury proceedings are considered private. Springer helped me appeal this decision to another branch of government. After five months of waiting, I finally received a letter stating that my appeal was approved and the US Attorney would be compelled to produce the grand jury referral. We'll see what happens with that.

Lindsey Springer also encouraged me to file a habeas corpus petition for unlawful detention and referred me to an excellent attorney out of Washington state by the name of Alan Richey. He's helping with my current motions as I go forward.

Last but surely not least, Springer offered me help and support in an area where I least expected it from him. He helped me understand my daughter's substance abuse issue. The counseling he gave me in that regard allowed me, in turn, to be a better support to my daughter and to my wife, who has been helping her manage her recovery. He even sent my daughter some passages from scripture, which she, to my surprise, latched on to and was able to use effectively in her recovery. (My daughter is doing well as of this writing. She is clean and sober, has a job and an apartment, and just received a raise at work.)

So, though the government views Lindsey Springer as a dangerous criminal who needs to stay behind bars, and though much of the blogosphere regards him as a lunatic, to me he'll always be a pretty special guy.

They say success is the best revenge. What I came to see, partly through Springer's help, was that if the government was going to deprive me of my freedom and livelihood, my best "revenge" would be to use my incarceration time to become an expert in ways I could better fight the government after I got out. Once I took on that attitude, I began to view my incarceration as an educational vacation at Uncle Sam's expense. Thanks, Unc!

* * *

I finished serving my time uneventfully and was released to a halfway house after seven months. I almost didn't make it there on time. Vicki came to meet me in El Paso. Because I didn't have the proper approvals for her to pick me up, La Tuna detained me till an hour before my flight. The freeway was closed that day, and we had to drive all around creation to get to the airport, where we just barely made the plane. When we landed in Phoenix, I had fifteen minutes to make it to the halfway house on time.

The halfway house was located right across the street from the county hospital—presumably so that if any of the residents got shot, it would be a short trip to the ER. When I arrived on the scene, the house director took me aside and said, "Listen, Quiel, there's a guy here you might have some issues with."

I couldn't think of anyone from La Tuna who had a beef with me.

The guy turned out to be Steve Kerr. He had gone into the system three weeks earlier than I had and had been released three weeks sooner. I hadn't seen him in over six months.

Steve and I had a lot to talk about. After all, I was the one who introduced him to Chris Rusch. But I had also contributed a great deal toward our joint defense, which I believe helped us both get minimum sentences. And I think he recognized that. So we made whatever amends needed to be made. He ended up helping me with the process of finding a transitional job while at the halfway house.

I could have taken a job doing meaningless work for someone else, but I decided I needed to get back to my family, and I needed to get back to stock trading. That meant working from home, using my own computer system. So I fought for permission to do this. It took time to get the approval, but I ended up working from home while at the halfway house. Yes, I actually went to my home office ten hours a day, then went back to the halfway house to sleep.

After a couple of months of that absurd arrangement, I was allowed to start on home detention—house arrest—in December of 2015. That meant I lived at home and was allowed to go up to two places outside the house each day but had to do a lot of reporting in by phone. Then, on January 7, house arrest ended, and I became essentially a free man again, though I'm still on probation until January of 2017.

My life now is all about three things: enjoying my family and my freedom as never before, becoming the best independent stock trader I can be, and living up to my promise to my father-in-law, and my father, to continue to fight to clear my name. Toward that end, I am committed to exhausting every legal option available to me, regardless of expense.

For now, that entails several things. First, I will try to get my Rule 33 motion approved. After Teilborg denied it while I was in prison, we appealed it to the Ninth Circuit appellate court. There it was also denied, but we requested that it be remanded back to Teilborg for reconsideration. The Ninth Circuit refused to remand it but, based on the new evidence we now have, encouraged us to file a new motion with Judge Teilborg.

Our new Rule 33 motion contains many items the original motion did not. It includes evidence that the 2006 FBARs Rusch claimed I filed do not exist, proving Rusch to be a "known perjurer." This ought to invalidate him as a witness. It also contains sworn affidavits attesting to the fact that Rusch continues to ply his scams under an alias, and an affidavit from Swiss national Jerome Perucchi as well.

Perucchi—remember him? He was one of the original "investors" to whom Rusch introduced us in the early days of the Swiss venture. He helped Rusch do the initial corporate structuring in Switzerland and, at a key point when we needed Rusch to bring in some Swiss investment dollars, invested a million dollars of his own money in our company. Or so we thought.

That million dollars ended up being hugely significant. You see, when I followed the money trail (after getting the records from Switzerland), it became clear that the million dollars Perucchi supposedly invested actually came *from my own account*, via Chris Rusch's trust account. In other words, Perucchi invested *my own money* from the sale of my stock back into my company. So after the trial, I sued Perucchi for the $1 million, even though the money was now in an account that I technically owned. I had a hard time finding the man, and he wouldn't respond to the suit, so I sought, and was granted, a default judgment against him.

The day the default judgment was handed down, Perucchi suddenly stuck his head up out of the sand and started fighting back. He hired his own attorney and filed an affidavit with the court stating that he'd had no involvement in any investments; he only helped set up the corporations. To make a long story short, I now believe that Rusch not only falsified the notary seal on Perucchi's documents, as he admitted, but also forged all the investment documents that supposedly came from Perucchi. I believe Rusch was essentially running a Ponzi scheme over there, and Perucchi was probably more of a dupe than an active coconspirator.

I eventually settled with Perucchi, and he has signed a sworn affidavit stating that he was unaware of Rusch's actions after the initial setup work. This affidavit provides strong additional support for our contention that Rusch was, and still is, a scam artist. And the fact that the prosecutors failed to call Perucchi as a witness suggests they may have committed a Brady violation—they probably knew Perucchi could provide exculpatory testimony, but chose not to tell us about it.

As of this writing, my new attorney and I have submitted a new Rule 33 motion, containing this added evidence, to Judge Teilborg and are awaiting his response. I'm not holding my breath. My guess is that he will deny us again. As I've said before, I think Teilborg is a fair and capable jurist, but I live in the real world. And in that real world, most of these motions are denied.

If Judge Teilborg denies the motion, we will appeal it again. If the appeal fails, we will file a Rule 2255 motion, which is essentially your final shot at getting a conviction overturned in a federal case. A common reason for filing a 2255 is "ineffective assistance of counsel," which is an avenue I will probably pursue. I love Mike Minns and have no complaints about him, but he acknowledged in his own appeal brief that he erred by not mounting a defense against much of Chris Rusch's testimony, which he considered irrelevant at that time. Minns won't object if I claim ineffective counsel. A 2255 can also be filed when new evidence crops up after your conviction. When filing a 2255, you can bring in a broad range of evidence. So in ours, we will include items like the criminal referral, or lack thereof, and the illegality of the FBAR form. But there are a couple of catches to filing a 2255: (1) it can't overlap a Rule 33 motion (your Rule 33 motion has to be resolved first), and (2) you have to file it while you're still incarcerated. That doesn't leave us much time. Technically, because I am on probation, I am still incarcerated until January 2017. But here's the crazy thing: if your probation officer thinks you're not a threat, he can dismiss you early from probation. So if the government chooses to end my incarceration early—which it might do to prevent me from filing a 2255—I'll have to refuse!

In addition to these remedies that I'm seeking against the government, I am also looking for an attorney to represent me in a civil lawsuit against UBS for loss of income. As you may recall, I had a *$3 billion* offering afoot in Luxembourg, which I had to withdraw because of the criminal investigation that resulted from UBS giving up my name. I also had to close my hedge fund and basically abandon my career in hedge fund management, which were massive losses for me.

So all those options are in the works. Whether they succeed or fail is beyond my control. All I can do is keep trying and refuse to lie down and roll over.

The one thing I *can* control is my story and my right to tell it. That is why I have appeared in feature news stories on television, why I'll continue to tell my story on the Internet, and why I have written this book. The government can do whatever it wants. It can choose to single me out as guilty while letting a bunch of Swiss bankers go free, deprive me of an objective IRS audit, investigate me prejudicially, buy off my crooked lawyer so he can testify against me, interrogate my colleagues, publish my children's social security numbers online, handcuff me in front of friends, declare me guilty in the press, accept testimony against me from a blatant perjurer, and throw me in federal prison, but the one thing it can't do is stop me from telling the truth. The First Amendment is still alive and well, and though my faith in the justice system has been rocked to its core, I still believe in the fundamental power of speaking the truth. I will continue to tell my story every chance I get. I will not allow a bunch of overzealous government employees to ruin my name the same way they railroaded me into a criminal conviction and federal prison.

My name belongs to me, and I plan to protect and defend it.

I served my country in the military, as did my father, my father-in-law, and many of the men in my family. I have started and run reputable businesses that have employed hundreds of people. I have always treated clients, customers, and colleagues fairly, even when it has cost me a great deal personally to do so. I have paid more money in taxes than many people *earn* in a lifetime. I have contributed millions to charity. I have tried to be a good husband, a good father, a good friend, and a good member of my community.

No one gets to negate those things, or destroy my good name, just to advance their own career goals. No one. Not without a fight from me.

I used to believe that the justice system existed for the purpose of uncovering the truth in criminal cases. I have since learned that this isn't true. But I still believe in the power of words, and I still believe we live in a free nation. So I'll keep talking and writing and sharing my story. Words are the only weapon I have.

But I'm finding out they're a pretty damn good one.

THE DEFENSE RESTS (CONCLUSION)

So what the hell went down here? How did a businessman who did nothing wrong—who had a long history of running clean companies and who hired an attorney to *make sure* all his actions were legal and legitimate—end up losing millions and going to federal prison? Well, the easy and obvious answer is that I got involved with a guy by the name of Chris Rusch. And I let him conduct his activities with too little supervision. Though I believe he started out with good intentions, the temptation to abuse the trust I put in him proved too much for the man. He stole, he cheated, he lied, he covered up.

As I said at the beginning, I was, in a way, a victim of my own success. Had my investment business not been doing so well in those days, I would have paid much closer attention to what was going on in Switzerland and would have demanded a much higher level of accounting from Rusch. But because I was making so much income from my main business, I was willing to trust in Rusch to do what he promised he'd do, and I didn't really care *all that much* whether he succeeded or not. His venture was a gamble for me, just like all the other "gambles" I routinely made as an investor, and I figured it would either pay off…or it wouldn't.

But I do own that I put trust in Rusch and allowed him to do what he did; that part's on me. My biggest flaw, as my wife will tell you, is that I trust people too much. In the end, though, I have to say it's probably my biggest strength as well. I'm not a microman-ager. It's not in my nature to look over people's shoulders. I try to hire good people and then just let them do their jobs. That's why I'm an investor, not a COO. Most of the time my instincts serve me well. I've made tens of millions of dollars by backing the right people and letting them do what they do best. I've also built a lot of great relationships based on mutual trust—in both my business life and my personal life—and I wouldn't trade those relationships for all the stock in the S&P 500. Chris Rusch, admittedly, was one of my bad calls. I'll forever do my due diligence more carefully because of him. But I'm not going to change the fundamental way I trust in people and expect trust in return. Rusch has taken enough away from me; he's not going to take that too.

To *really* answer the question, "What the hell went down here?" we have to dig deeper than Chris Rusch. The more disturbing answer to that question is that the government abused its power. The federal government is allowed to play by its own set of rules. It has too much power, and that power goes unchecked. Blindly ambitious government employees, from the top levels of government to the lowest, are granted too much leeway to play God with human lives—bestowing freedoms and favors on some while taking those same things away from others, with little to no accountability and without sufficient checks and balances.

Am I accusing the government, outright, of corruption in my case? Hell, I'll say it: Yes, I am. Turnabout is fair play. I don't have *proof* of corruption, but neither did the government have proof against me when it chose to accuse me. The government simply looked at a few circumstantial facts and decided I *must* be a wealthy tax evader who was using a Swiss account to hide money from the IRS. Once it had committed to that story, it wasn't going to change its mind, no matter what evidence, or lack thereof, came along.

So I think I'm entitled to make a few inferences about the government, based on the facts I know. In 2009, Hillary Clinton was called in to negotiate a settlement between the IRS and the Swiss banking industry. A bunch of UBS executives were granted "deferred prosecution," and the bank coughed up the names of some of its American account holders. The number of names given was greatly reduced from the number the IRS originally asked for. Because some politically connected Americans were on the original list? Gosh, hard to say, but after the dust settled, Bill Clinton received $1.5 million in speaking fees from UBS, and the Clinton Foundation received a tenfold increase in its contributions from UBS. Those are the facts (as reported by the *Wall Street Journal*, July 30, 2015).

When that small list of names—which included mine—was turned over to the United States, the pressure was on to make those convictions stick. The government needed to get a lot of bang for its buck, so those names went straight to the DOJ, which operates under a presumption of criminality. I believe there was a mandate to get a conviction in my case, not to learn the truth. Otherwise, why would the prosecutors have worked so hard to create an illusion of stock fraud, even though they didn't charge me with that crime and had virtually no evidence to support such charges? Why would the prosecutors not ask the people who *actually worked* with Chris Rusch in Switzerland to testify, but rely instead on strangers? Why would the prosecutors resort to making a deal with an admitted felon and hinge their entire case on his testimony if they had provable facts working in their favor? And why, if they didn't make a quid pro quo deal with Rusch, did they return his passport to him shortly after the trial, so that he could resume plying his trade internationally? (FYI, it is notoriously difficult for federal defendants to get their passports back after a trial even when they're found innocent. Martha Stewart had a hard time getting *hers* back, but Chris Rusch, admitted international swindler, got his back with a handshake and a smile in sixty days.)

Do these facts *prove* corruption? I'll let you weigh the evidence and form your own judgment. In my opinion, *someone* had to pay the price for what UBS and some sneaky American account holders had been getting away with for years. So names were demanded. The DOJ people knew that heads would roll if they didn't start getting some convictions in a hurry. And Mike Quiel, hedge fund manager, fit the profile they were looking for.

Case closed.

But here's something that might surprise you. I believe I came out a winner in this thing. Really? Yes, absolutely. Now, obviously I'd have been better off if I'd never been put under investigation at all. But once that die was cast, I think I played a winning hand. My father advised me not to take a deal, and my father-in-law told me to fight the bastards. And so that was what I did and what I'm still doing. I fought. And I'm damn glad I did. If I had taken Cono Namorato's deal with the DOJ, I would have spent *three years* in prison instead of ten months. And I would have gone to prison at a time when my business was still thriving, so I would have lost out on several million dollars in income, which would have put me in the hole. Instead, I came out of this ordeal with some money in my pocket and only seven months served behind bars. Most people with my convictions serve three to five years. And that's after their case drags on for seven or eight years in court. Mine took only four. Not bad.

The best part of fighting back is that I can look myself in the mirror. And I can sleep at night, knowing I served as an example for my family that when you're unjustly accused, you stand up for yourself.

Even prison was a positive experience in a lot of ways. It transformed me from someone who always tried to fly under the radar to someone who no longer fears anyone. That fearlessness, I know, is going to serve me well for the rest of my life. It's a big part of why I'm putting this book out there.

So I made out pretty well by fighting. Does that mean I think fighting back is the right thing to do in all cases? Is that the advice I'm giving you?

Unfortunately, there's no one-size-fits-all answer. I wrote this book, in part, to help people who find themselves in the same position I did. But in truth, no two cases are exactly alike. And even if they were—even if you found yourself in circumstances virtually identical to mine—I still couldn't tell you what to do. Settle or litigate? Fight the battle or live to fight another day? One choice is not necessarily better than the other. Everyone's life situation is different.

I feel I came out a winner, yes, but I paid a hefty price. The legal fight cost me $8 million. Not everyone can afford lengthy litigation, expert witnesses, private investigators, and mock trials; in fact, most people can't. I've also spent countless hundreds of hours researching the law, reading other cases, sending out FOIA letters, and filing motions, to the point where fighting this thing has become almost an obsession for me. That's not the right course of action for everyone. For some, it might be better for their mental health to accept a settlement and walk away.

But there are a couple of things I *can* advise you on. One is this: Give up the pipe dream that innocence matters and that justice is the engine that runs our justice system. Sorry to sound like Debbie Downer, but the only one who cares about your innocence is you. No one else in the system cares, certainly no one who collects a government paycheck. Government investigators and prosecutors are busy, overworked people who are motivated to keep their jobs, advance their careers, and feed their families, like everyone else. When it comes to assigning guilt, they go for the shiniest object in the room. If you *look* guilty, you probably *are* guilty in their minds, and they're going to try to pin the rap on you.

Once the government has invested substantial time and energy in proving your guilt, it doesn't want to throw that investment away. Better to double down instead. Even if that means twisting the facts a little or ignoring some evidence here and there that might prove your innocence.

Perhaps you've seen a movie scene where a helpful citizen walks into a DA's office the day before a trial is set to begin and triumphantly slaps a piece of evidence on the table that proves the defendant innocent. Everyone cheers, "Yay, we've found the real killer!" What would *really* happen in that situation is they'd throw that good citizen in a closet and nail the door shut. Who wants to flush five months of hard prosecutorial work down the drain?

The fact is, no one in the system *profits* from your innocence, and that's where the problem lies. Police officers get promoted by making good arrests; admitting to making a bad one is bad for their careers. Investigators are rewarded for closing cases neatly and permanently. Prosecutors are promoted by gaining convictions, not letting people go. Even defense attorneys, as I pointed out earlier, are squeamish around innocent clients—defending the guilty is a much easier job.

You are the only one who gains from your innocence, so the powers that be are always aligned against you. I don't say that to be pessimistic, but to be realistic. If you are accused of a crime, mount your defense with open eyes. Know that no one is on the side of your innocence but you. Know that no one will be riding in on a white horse to save you. White horses cost money, after all, and who's going to pay for that? The justice system is not set up to deliver justice. It is set up to grind through vast numbers of criminal cases, following the path of least resistance, in a way that rewards the people who work for the system. Not you.

Here's another free piece of advice. Don't hire a lawyer just because you don't know how to do something. Do your own research. Read the laws. Download the legal forms. Create your own documents. Do your own deals. A lawyer is not necessarily your answer. If I had gone to Switzerland and set up my own investment structure there, I would have done a much better job than Chris Rusch, and I would have stayed out of legal trouble too. Most every lawyer I've ever hired, with exception of Mike Minns and the six lawyers who wrote positive letters to Judge Teilborg at my sentencings, has lied to me and in most cases has given me bad advice too.

Remember the story of my real estate venture? Chris Rusch told me I didn't have to pay taxes on those so-called phantom gains. Steve Silver, another lawyer, came along and told me Rusch was dead wrong; I *did* need to pay the taxes, and pronto. When I voiced to Silver that my shareholders were going to be upset if I suddenly forked over two-thirds of a million dollars to the government, he said, "Don't worry. You've got a five-year rollback. Pay the taxes now, and you'll get that money back." I did what Silver told me, then found out Arizona had *cancelled* its five-year rollback policy several months earlier. I was out the money.

Poor advice on top of poor advice.

At around that same time, Cono Namorato was telling me that I *had* to proffer with the DOJ and plead guilty. Thank God I didn't listen to him.

People hire lawyers to bless business deals because they think that means they'll be "covered." I'm here to tell you that's an illusion. A lawyer sells you a security blanket, but he doesn't tell you the material it's made of is flammable. It can quickly go up in smoke. As my story proves, following a lawyer's advice doesn't necessarily keep you out of legal trouble. It doesn't even necessarily stand up in court as a legal defense. Everyone on my defense team took the position that following a lawyer's advice is an absolute defense in a criminal tax proceeding. But I still went to prison.

My experiences have taught me a stark truth. That is, our system runs on power. Everyone is trying to protect the power they have and gain more of it. In the political system and justice system, power is gained by giving freedom and privilege to some while taking it away from others. That's the cold, hard fact. That's the game that's being played. And because the government makes the laws, it gets to play that game with its own special rulebook. It gets to cheat and you don't.

The moment you enter the criminal justice system, you become a chess piece in someone else's power game. Know that. Remember that. If you passively play along and just do as you're told, you *will* be played. For better or worse. But remember this too: You have power. You have the power to acquire knowledge. You have the power to think and reason. You have the power to make your own decisions, no matter what advice you're being given. That doesn't necessarily mean you must choose to fight the government, but it does mean that you must fight tooth and nail to protect *every legal right you possess*. You alone have the power to stand tall and refuse to buckle. You alone have the power to tell *your* truth.

With this book, I'm claiming my power. I hope you'll claim yours too.

ABOUT THE AUTHOR

Mike Quiel owns and manages Legend Advisory Corporation, a company he founded, and has more than twenty years of investment banking experience. He began his securities career as a stockbroker in 1987. Over the next seven years, he successfully built and sold two brokerage companies. In 1994, Mike joined Global Financial Group as a one-man branch office and began routinely outproducing multiman offices of more than twenty-five brokers. In 2001, he retired from the brokerage business to work on his own investment portfolio and to start his own consulting business. Since then he has helped secure several hundred million dollars in equity and debt financing for high-risk growth companies all around the world.

Mike lives in Scottsdale, Arizona, with Vicki, his wife of over thirty years. They are the parents of three beautiful daughters.

In 2010, Mike was falsely accused of financial and tax improprieties after his name surfaced in a deal the US government made with UBS in the wake of the 2008 bank bailout. He wrote this book to defend his innocence and to help ensure that others will not suffer similar injustice at the hands of overzealous government employees.

CPSIA information can be obtained
at www.ICGtesting.com
Printed in the USA
JSHW020554120520
5629JS00001B/87

9 781643 348759